The Cornet-Player Who Betrayed Ireland

The
Cornet-Player
Who Betrayed
Ireland

FRANK O'CONNOR

poolbeg press

First published 1981 by
Poolbeg Press Ltd.,
Knocksedan House,
Swords, Co. Dublin, Ireland.

Cover by John Dixon
Designed by Steven Hope

Printed by Cahill Printers Limited,
East Wall Road, Dublin 3.

Contents

The date appended to each story in the text is the year of first publication. *The Grip of the Geraghtys*, unpublished, is the story the author was working on when he died.

Introduction

This book has had a lengthy, hesitant, and indeed unexpected birth. When *Collection Three* was published in 1969 it was described as 'the last volume of stories by Frank O'Connor'. Having had a hand in its preparation and publication I believed it to be just that. I knew there were other stories which had never appeared in book form, but I also knew they were hard to find — incomplete rough drafts, titles referred to in letters, dog-eared and dateless tearsheets. 'Bits and pieces for thesis writers' I thought, but not material for a book.

But that (to use one of Frank O'Connor's favourite expressions) was where the ferry-boat left me. I had jumped to a conclusion on entirely insufficient evidence. I hadn't, for example, reckoned with the fascination of research; the sheer fun of tracking down a missing story, or of sifting through three or four rough drafts and suddenly seeing how they fit together. I hadn't imagined that early work could have such power, or that the 'bits and pieces' would, page by page and story by story, turn into such a golden treasure. And it might have remained a hidden treasure were it not that when discussing with David Marcus the re-publication by Poolbeg Press of early O'Connor work such as *Guests of the Nation* and *The Big Fellow*, I told him I'd discovered a number of early O'Connor stories. I should have noticed the hidden excitement in his request to read them, but I was deep in my role of researcher, getting clean copies and accurate dates. So I was a bit

startled when he called a few days later and said, quite
sternly, 'These are good stories. We must publish at least
one book of them.' I dithered. The 'last' book of stories
had already been published; how would we choose which
to include? how would we arrange them? David persisted.
'Make a list of the stories you think Frank would have
chosen,' he suggested. 'I'll do the same and then we'll
compare.' Astonishingly, our lists were almost identical.
It was this which made me agree to the book, and this
which carried us through the times when we didn't agree.

For, of course, there were those times. There's one story
I like more each time I read it, and he likes less. There is
another I flatly rejected despite his plea for inclusion. There
are a-typical stories; one so a-typical we double checked to
be sure it wasn't written by some other Frank O'Connor.
But one thing became clear the longer we worked together:
this book, unlike all the others, could not be arranged by
theme or tone or in an 'ideal ambiance' — in this book the
stories had to be arranged chronologically. Taken individu-
ally they are pure O'Connor stories, full of life and humour
and compassion. Taken as a whole, on the other hand, they
tell a story of their own: they show a writer learning his
craft — experimenting, evolving, trying one technique
after another, working ceaselessly to become the one thing
he ever wanted to be — master of his trade.

Towards the end of his life Frank O'Connor described
his idea of what a short story should be: 'It's about a
moment of change in a person's life. It's a bright light
falling on an action in such a way that the landscape of
that person's life assumes a new shape. Something happens
— the iron bar is bent — and anything that happens that
person afterwards, they never feel the same about again.'

In this collection we can watch Frank O'Connor working
his way towards those rare (he was not easily satisfied
with what he wrote) and wonderful moments when he
could sit back in his chair, smile and say: 'Mind you, that's
not a bad story.'

Harriet O'Donovan Sheehy

War

He was not used to it yet, that was it. He felt exasperated but in a quite impotent way. He did not interfere, and even had he wanted to he did not know how. Things happened, that was all.

At noon they took their first prisoners. That, too, happened curiously. Not a shot was fired. The driver ran his motor right into their sentries; obviously he had been deceived by the half-mufti in which the regular troops appeared. The Commandant whistled, and the motorists were bidden drive on to the place where he stood. As the motor car moved down the road towards him a man stood up in it, and quite casually tore to shreds some documents which he had been carrying. In the high wind the scraps of paper began to fly until they were lost among the fields around. Still he could not stop the destruction, it was all over before he understood what was happening.

He searched the prisoners carefully but he found nothing except a bomb which was in the righthand pocket of the driver's tunic.

'Do you know,' he said to the driver, 'I can have you shot as a spy?'

'You can?' said the driver in a dumbfounded fashion.

'I can. You wear our uniform.'

'It's my own uniform.'

'It's the uniform of the Irish Army.'

'And what am I?'

'You're a rebel prisoner.'

The driver's face began to change slowly. It grew pale beneath the eyes, and the mouth began to twitch, this way and that, like the mouth of a child beginning to cry. Then he began to talk in an incoherent way. A torrent of blasphemy poured from his lips, but still they retained their first look of weeping. His whole face was quite grey, like smoke.

The Commandant heard his men murmur indignantly among themselves, but he could do nothing to stop the flood of obscenity. He turned to another of the prisoners and questioned him till the hysterical driver became silent. Then he said sternly, 'Follow me,' and, taking one side of the driver, he motioned a soldier to the other.

As they walked down the road he heard a giggle behind them. Then came the crash of a rifle and a short cry, a thud, and the soldier walking in line with him rolled over and slid into the ditch at the roadside. It took the Commandant some moments to realise what had happened. The rifle of a soldier behind him had been fired, evidently with the intention of terrifying the prisoner.

He ran to the prone figure in the dyke. First he opened the tunic collar and then the tunic, looking for a wound. He heard a voice behind him murmur, 'Say an Act of Contrition,' and then go on: 'I believe in God, the Father Almighty, Creator of Heaven and earth.' He knew that was the wrong prayer but he could not correct it. The unconscious soldier opened his eyes and sat up suddenly, swearing with violence. There was nothing wrong with him, only a weakness, but still the ridiculous voice gabbled on, '— and the blessed Apostles, Peter and Paul, Peter and Paul, Peter and Paul, Peter —.'

'Come, come!' he said. 'No more of this fooling.'

· He put his three prisoners into a room off the kitchen, a tiny room that looked out upon the garden of the cottage they had occupied. He asked them if they had had food and they said no, they had been travelling since six that morning. Then he ordered the young woman of the house to prepare food for them, and she did so, bringing them cold meat and cabbage, and then some tea. He noticed that the young driver did not touch the food, but stretched his hand out eagerly for the first cup of tea. He took a mouthful and spat it out. A wry look came into his face, and then changed to a look of bitter anger. He covered his face with his hands, and the Commandant noticed that his hands were trembling violently.

About three o'clock he ordered them into the waiting lorries. The engines were running and the prisoners had taken their places when a volley rang out from a nearby field. The Commandant saw a head appear and disappear, and from the turn of the road he saw the sloping mask of a strange armoured car tilting as it rounded the corner. He ordered his men back and banged the door behind them. As he did so he heard the machine guns on the car begin their irregular chitter-chatter.

Coolly, though for a moment he felt inclined to scream with fright, he put the men into their places, leaving the prisoners where they had been. Two of them lay flat down by the wall under the tiny window. He looked round and took up a bag of meal which he put against the pane in front of a pot of paint that was standing on the sill. The window was low, and by kneeling on a second bag one could fire over the protection. He put five men to hold the room and went upstairs.

Two men were firing through the attic window at the armoured car as it raced up and down the road. It was a rudely-constructed but powerful machine, an oblong box with ends that sloped in and up, and at each side were little porches that projected about ten inches from the body. As he watched it one of his soldiers toppled over from the window and lay quite still. He could see no blood, but when he looked closer he noticed that a slight hole had been burned in the pit of the nostril. A tiny drop of blood gathered at its edge and slid across the cheek to the ear.

He knew then the man was dead. Outside on the road the deserted cars were still humming.

He went back through the kitchen to the front room and mentioned the death of the soldier to his lieutenant. One of the prisoners noticed him and understood. 'One of your fellows dead,' he shouted at the top of his voice. A tall soldier who was sitting idle by the wall looked blankly around, a Southerner, the Commandant knew him for, and deaf as a post.

'What are 'oo saying?' he shouted.

'One of your fellows dead. Dead, d'ye hear me? Dead.'

'Dead? What did he die of?'

A soldier who had been firing from the window handed his hot and empty rifle to a comrade.

'When night comes we're done,' he muttered.

The great Southerner sat stiffly up and shouted again.

'What's up? Why are ye deceiving me? What's the firing for, I say?'

'Ye're surrounded,' yelled the prisoner in a frenzy.

'Curse you, shut up!' said the soldier who was firing. But to the Commandant his voice sounded quite aloof, even genial.

'Well,' said the Southerner, 'will ye surrender so?'

At that moment there was a fierce volley of machine gun fire, and the young officer threw his Commandant to the ground. 'Cover!' he shouted. The men who were sitting up now flung themselves flat. Looking round, the Commandant saw what had happened. He had placed the bag of meal at an unsteady angle before the window and a blast of firing had swept it away and, with it, the pot of paint that had been reposing on the sill. A man's head appeared from the floor swathed in folds of thick red paint that swung from his dripping forelock. The deaf man alone had not obeyed the order to take cover. He was sitting up against a sidewall with a dazed look in his eyes, and as the Commandant rose he looked at him and shouted in a dismal voice:

'I surrender. I surrender.'

Confused, but quite without the sensation of fear, the

Commandant went to the window and replaced the bag of meal. Then he looked about him and said simply, 'It's all right.' Mechanically, as though suddenly remembering the phrase, he added: 'You can surrender when your ammunition is exhausted.'

'Say it again,' said the deaf man.

He repeated the phrase dully, and as he did so he noticed one of the men looking at him with a sneer. It occurred to him then that he was absolutely apart from these men and that they did not in the least mind what he said, and he struggled with himself to discover what had happened to him and to them which had changed their attitudes to one another. It wasn't that they were braver than he was, because he had replaced the bag of meal under fire, which none of them offered to do. It was something else that would bring him into contact with all this, but for the life of him he did not know what it was. Things were happening outside him, that was all.

He saw a man take some clips of ammunition from his sling and slip them into his pocket. Another smiled and did the same. They did not appear to mind his seeing them. The deaf man let his body slide gently to the floor and fell asleep. The Commandant heard his heavy breathing in the intervals of silence.

In the kitchen his lieutenant was standing by a window, firing from the cover of the wall, and every now and again he would sing tunelessly between set teeth:

'You called me Baby Dear a year ago.'

The Commandant walked about fearlessly, not troubling to crouch as the others did when they crossed the floor. He did not know why they did it; the windows were all barricaded. Then the lieutenant asked him about the women of the house, and that, too, struck him as being silly. Still, he opened the door of the bedroom and asked them were they all right. They were crouching in a corner, an old, old man and two women, and when a burst of firing came they turned their heads into the wall and drew up their shoulders as he had seen his sisters do when there was thunder. The elder woman was saying her rosary. He told

them they were quite safe, and smiled at them, and they
thanked him, he did not know for what. They asked him
then what time was it, and when he told them it was seven
o'clock the young woman said with a shudder that it had
been on for four hours.

'As long as that?' he said.

He suddenly thought of home, and felt a great longing
to be there and away from all this thing. It revolted him; it
was drab and stupid and unreal — unreal, that was the word.
They had found this cottage a pleasant, quiet place, and,
whatever happened, they would leave it still a pleasant,
quiet place; home would always go on here as home had
been — whatever happened. He tried to rid his mind of
the thought, but it was horribly clear to him that nothing
he could ever do would change the course of things. Even
let him not return, his sweetheart would be just the same
as she had always been, the same woman with no single
shred of difference because of anything in the world that
might happen. The thought clung to him, although he felt
that it was pushing him farther and farther from the understanding of this thing. He was thinking, and he should not
think. He tried to concentrate his mind on what was
going on around him but all he could hear was the cracking
of the rifles outside and their crashing sound within and
his lieutenant's tuneless voice singing:

'You called me Baby Dear a year ago.'

All senseless things.

'Do you know, Maurice, we'll have to surrender.'

It was his lieutenant's voice again, and he said:

'Yes, I suppose so,' and looked out over the other man's
shoulder. He could see nothing, but he heard the machine
gun fire concentrating itself outside the window. 'The cars
are running still,' he said with a smile. Then one of them
stopped. 'Fire getting very heavy,' he added. Suddenly he
heard a crash, the lieutenant's head swung away, and the
whole window became very bright. He saw a blinding,
bright, cold sky and miles of grey fields stretching away
from him. Then he felt as if something had sprung up from
the ground and hit him viciously into the mouth so that his

flesh and teeth were smashed together in the blow. He heard a shout and somebody lifted his ringing head, only to let it down again. Then it was all shouting, and he was being carried away somewhere, and somebody was forcing something into his mouth. It was liquor, but it grew salty in his mouth. He opened his eyes and spat it out and saw a great clot of blood fall on his tunic.

'Drink it,' said a friendly voice; 'you're all right.'

He heard himself talking, rapidly, incoherently, but the talk had no relation to what was going on in his mind. Fascinated, he watched the blood flow steadily down his tunic and smelt it as it fell, and the horror he could not express made him unconscious of everything except the steady drip-drip of blood from his mouth.

'Come,' said the voice, 'it's not bad. Your head is safe.'

But he could only wave his hands in a frenzy of hysteria, and blaspheme, and say petulantly, like a child:

'Let me alone! Go away and let me alone!'

(1926)

There Is A Lone House

The woman stood at the foot of the lane, her right hand resting on the gate, her left fumbling at the neck of her blouse. Her face was lined, particularly about mouth and forehead; it was a face that rarely smiled, but was soft for all that, and plump and warm. She was quite grey. From a distance, this made her seem old; close at hand it had precisely the opposite effect, and tended to emphasize sharply what youthfulness still lingered in her, so that one thought of her as having suffered terribly at some time in the past.

The man came down the road, whistling a reel, the crisp, sprinkled notes of which were like the dripping of water in a cistern. She could hear his footsteps from a long way off, keeping irregular time to the elfin music, and drew aside a whitethorn bush by the gateway to watch him from cover. Apparently satisfied by her inspection, she kicked away the stone that held the gate in place, and, as he drew level with her, stepped out into the roadway. When he saw her he stopped, bringing down his ash plant with a twirl, but she did not look up.

'Morrow, ma'am,' he cried jovially.

Then she did look up, and a helpless blush that completely

and utterly belied the apparent calculation of her previous behaviour flowed over her features, giving them a sudden, startling freshness. 'Good morrow and good luck,' she answered in a low voice.

'Is it far to Ballysheery, ma'am?'

' 'Tis seven miles.'

'Seven Irish, ma'am?'

'Seven English.'

'That's better.'

She drew her tongue across her lips to moisten them. The man was young. He was decently dressed, but flaunted a rough, devil-may-care expression. He wore no hat, and his dark hair was all a tangle. You were struck by the length of his face, darkened by hot June suns; the high-boned nose jutting out rather too far, the irregular, discoloured teeth, the thick cracked lips, the blue eyes so far apart under his narrow, bony forehead that they seemed to sink back into the temples. A craggy face with high cheekbones, all hills and hollows, it was rendered extraordinarily mobile by the unexpected shadows that caught it here and there as the pale eyes drew it restlessly about. She judged him to be about twenty-six or seven.

'You seemed to be belting it out fine enough.'

'How's that, ma'am?'

'I heard you whistling.'

'That's to encourage the feet, ma'am. . . . You'll pardon my asking, is there any place around a man would get a cup of tea, ma'am?'

'There's no one would grudge you that, surely.'

Another would have detected the almost girlish timidity of the answer, but not he. He appeared both puzzled and disappointed.

'I'll go a bit farther so,' he said stiffly.

'What hurry is on you?'

' 'Tis my feet gets cramped.'

'If you come with me you can rest them a while.'

'God increase you, ma'am,' he replied.

They went up the boreen together. The house was on top of a hill, and behind it rose the mountainside, studded with rocks. There were trees about it, and in front a long garden with a hedge of fuchsia, at one side of which ran a stream. There were four or five apple trees, and beside the kitchen garden were a few flower beds with a profusion of tall snapdragon, yellow, red and white.

She put on the kettle and turned the wheel of the bellows. The kitchen filled with blue turf smoke, and the man sat beside the door, almost invisible behind a brilliant column of dustmotes, whirling spirally in the evening sunlight. But his hands lay on his knees in a pool of light, great brown hands with knuckles like polished stones. Fascinated, she watched them, and as she laid the table she almost touched them for sheer pleasure. His wild eyes, blue as the turf smoke, took in everything about the kitchen with its deal table, chairs and dresser, all scrubbed white; its delft arranged with a sort of pedantic neatness that suggests the old maid.

'This is a fine, fancy place, ma'am,' he said.

' 'Tis a quiet place.'

' 'Tis so. The men are all away?'

'There are no men.'

'Oh!'

'Only a boy that does turns for me.'

'Oh!'

That was all he said before he turned to his meal. He was half-starved, she decided, as she watched him wolf the warm, crumbling bread. He saw her grey eyes fixed on him and laughed brightly.

'I has a great stroke, ma'am.'

'You have, God bless you. I might have boiled you another egg.'

When tea was over he sighed, stretching himself in his chair, and lit his pipe.

'Would you mind if I took off my boots, ma'am?' he asked shyly.

'Why would I? Take them off and welcome.

'My feet is crucified.'

She bent and took up the boot he removed.

'No wonder. Your boots are in need of mending.'

He laughed at her expressive politeness.

'Mending, ma'am? Did you say mending? They're long past praying for.'

'They are, that's true. I wonder . . . . There's an old pair inside these years and years. They'd be better than the ones you have if they'd fit you.'

She brought them in, good substantial boots but stiff, and a trifle large for him. Not that he was in a state to mind.

'God, but they're grand, ma'am, they're grand! One little patch now, and they'd be as good as new. Better than new, for they're a better boot than I could ever buy in a shop. Wait now! Wait!' With boyish excitement he foraged in his pockets, and from the lining of his coat produced a piece of leather. He held it up with the air of a professional conjurer. 'Watch me now. Are you watching?' The leather fitted over the slight hole and he gave a whoop of joy. She found him last and hammer; he provided tacks from a paper bag in a vest pocket, and set to mending the damage with something like a tradesman's neatness.

'Is that your trade?' she asked curiously.

'One of my trades, ma'am. Cobbler, carpenter, plumber, gardener, thatcher, painter, poet; everything under the sun and moon, and nothing for long. But a cobbler is what I do be most times.'

He walked the kitchen in his new boots with all a child's inconsequent pleasure. There was something childlike about him, she decided, and she liked it. He peered at the battered alarm clock on the smoky heights of the mantelpiece and sighed.

'I'd like to stop here always,' he said wistfully, 'but I suppose I'd better be going.'

'What hurry is on you?'

'Seven miles, ma'am. Two hours. Maybe more. And I have to be in the old doss early if I want to get a place to sleep.'

But he sat down once more and put a match to his pipe.

'Not, mind you, ma'am, that there's many could put me out of a warm corner if I'd a mind to stay in it. No indeed, but unless I had a drop in me I'd never fight for a place.

Never. I'm apt to be cross when I'm drunk, but I never hit a man sober yet only once. That was a foxy tinker out of the Ranties, and the Ranties are notorious cross men, ma'am. You see, there was a little blind man, ma'am trying to sleep, and this Ranty I'm talking about, whenever he saw the blind man dozing, he'd give his beard a tug. So I got that mad I rose up, and without saying as much as "by your leave," I hit him such a terrible blow under the chin the blood hopped out on me in the dark. Yes, ma'am hopped clean out on me. That was a frightful hard blow.' He looked at her for approval and awe, and saw her, womanlike, draw up her shoulders and shiver. His dramatic sense was satisfied.

It was quite dark when he rose to go. The moon was rising over the hills to the left, far away, and the little stream beside the house sounded very loud in the stillness.

'If there was e'er an old barn or an outhouse,' he said as if to himself.

'There's a bed inside,' she answered. He looked round at her in surprise.

'Ah, I wouldn't ask to stop within,' he exclaimed.

Suddenly her whole manner changed. All the brightness, if brightness it could be called, seemed to drop away from her, leaving her listless, cold and melancholy.

'Oh, please yourself,' she said shortly, as if banishing him from her thoughts. But still he did not go. Instead, he sat down again, and they faced one another across the fireplace, not speaking, for he too had lost his chatter. The kitchen was in darkness except for the dwindling glow of the turf inside its cocoon of grey dust, and the wan nightlight above the half door. Then he laughed, rubbing his palms between his knees.

'And still you know, I'd ask nothing better,' he added shyly.

'What's that?'

'I'd ask nothing better than to stop.'

'Go or stop as you like.'

'You see,' he went on, ignoring her gathering surprise, 'I'm an honest fellow. I am, on my oath, though maybe you wouldn't think it, with the rough talk I have, and the life I lead. You could leave me alone with a bag of sovereigns, not counting them, and I'd keep them safe for you. And I'm just the same other ways. I'm not a bit forward. They say a dumb priest loses his benefit, and I'm just like that. I'm apt to lose me benefit for want of a bit of daring.'

Then (and this time it was he who was surprised) she laughed, more with relief, he thought, than at anything he had said. She rose and closed the door, lit the lamp and hung up the heavy kettle. He leaned back in his chair with a fresh sigh of pleasure, stretching out his feet to the fire, and in that gesture she caught something of his nostalgia. He settled down gratefully to one of those unexpected benefits which are the bait with which life leads us onward.

When she rose next morning, she was surprised to find him about before her, the fire lit, and the kettle boiling. She saw how much he needed a shave, and filled out a pan of water for him. Then when he began to scrub his face with the soap, she produced a razor, strop and brush. He was enchanted with these, and praised the razor with true lyric fire.

'You can have it,' she said. 'Have them all if they're any use to you.'

'By God, aren't they though,' he exclaimed reverently.

After breakfast he lit his pipe and sat back, enjoying to the full the last moments which politeness would impose upon hospitality.

'I suppose you're anxious to be on your road?' she asked awkwardly. Immediately he reddened.

'I suppose I'm better to,' he replied. He rose and looked out. It was a grey morning and still. The green stretched no farther than the hedge; beyond that lay a silver mist, flushed here and there with rose. 'Though 'tis no anxiety is on me — no anxiety at all,' he added with a touch of bitterness.

'Don't take me up wrong,' she said hastily. 'I'm not trying to hunt you. Stop and have your dinner. You'll be welcome.'

'I chopped a bit of kindling for you,' he replied, looking shyly at her from under lowered lids. 'If there was something else I could be doing, I'd be glad enough to stop, mind you.'

There was. Plenty else to be doing. For instance, there was an outhouse that needed whitewashing, and blithely enough he set about his task, whistling. She came and watched him; went, and came again, standing silently beside him, a strange stiff figure in the bright sunlight, but he had no feeling of supervision. Because he had not finished when dinner was ready he stayed to tea, and even then displayed no hurry to be gone. He sang her some of his poems. There was one about Mallow Races, another about a girl he had been in love with as a boy, 'the most beautiful girl that was ever seen in Kerry since the first day,' so he naively told her. It began:

> I praise no princesses or queens or great
>   ladies,
>   Or figures historical noted for style,
> Or beauties of Asia or Mesopotamia,
>   But sweet Annie Bradie, the rose of
>   Dunmoyle.

A sort of confidence had established itself between them. The evening passed quickly in talk and singing — in whistling too, for he was a good whistler, and sometimes performed for dancing: to judge by his own statements he was a great favourite at wakes and weddings and she could understand that.

It was quite dark when they stopped the conversation. Again he made as if to go, and again in her shy, cold way she offered him the chance of staying. He stayed.

For days afterward there seemed to be some spell upon them both. A week passed in excuses and delays, each morning finding him about long before she appeared with some new suggestion, the garden to be weeded, potatoes to be dug, the kitchen to be whitewashed. Neither suggested anything but as it were from hour to hour, yet it did not occur to the man that for her as for him their companionship might be an unexpected benefit.

He did her messages to the village whenever Dan, the

'boy', a sullen, rather stupid, one-eyed old man was absent, and though she gave no sign that she did not like this, he was always surprised afresh by the faint excitement with which she greeted his return; had it been anyone else one might have called her excitement gaiety, but gay was hardly a word one could apply to her, and the emotion quickly died and gave place to a sullen apathy.

She knew the end must come soon, and it did. One evening he returned from an errand, and told her someone had died in the village. He was slightly shocked by her indifference. She would not go with him to the wake, but she bade himself go if he pleased. He did please. She could see there was an itch for company on him; he was made that way. As he polished his boots he confessed to her that among his other vocations he had tried being a Trappist monk, but stuck it only for a few months. It wasn't bad in summer, but it was the divil and all in winter, and the monks told him there were certain souls like himself the Lord called only for six months of the year (the irony of this completely escaped him).

He promised to be back before midnight, and went off very gay. By this time he had formed his own opinion of the woman. It was not for nothing she lived there alone, not for nothing a visitor never crossed the threshold. He knew she did not go to Mass, yet on Sunday when he came back unexpectedly for his stick, he had seen her, in the bedroom, saying her rosary. Something was wrong, but he could not guess what.

Her mood was anything but gay and the evening seemed to respond to it. It was very silent after the long drought; she could hear the thrush's beak go tip-tap among the stones like a fairy's hammer. It was making for rain. To the north-west the wind had piled up massive archways of purple cloud like a ruined cloister, and through them one's eyes passed on to vistas of feathery cloudlets, violet and gold, packed thick upon one another. A cold wind had sprung up: the trees creaked, and the birds flew by, their wings blown up in a gesture of horror. She stood for a long while looking at the sky, until it faded, chilled by the cold wind. There was something mournful and sinister about it all.

It was quite dark when she went in. She sat over the fire and waited. At half past eleven she put down the kettle and brewed herself tea. She told herself she was not expecting him, but still she waited. At half past twelve she stood at the door and listened for footsteps. The wind had risen, and her mind filled slowly with its childish sobbing and with the harsh gushing of the stream beside the house. Then it began to rain. To herself she gave him until one. At one she relented and gave him another half hour, and it was two before she quenched the light and went to bed. She had lost him, she decided.

She started when an hour or more later she heard his footsteps up the path. She needed no one to tell her he was alone and drunk: often before she had waited for the footsteps of a drunken old man. But instead of rushing to the door as she would have done long ago, she waited.

He began to moan drowsily to himself. She heard a thud followed by gusty sighing; she knew he had fallen. Everything was quiet for a while. Then there came a bang at the door which echoed through the house like a revolver shot, and something fell on the flagstones outside. Another bang and again silence. She felt no fear, only a coldness in her bowels.

Then the gravel scraped as he staggered to his feet. She glanced at the window. She could see his head outlined against it, his hands against its frame. Suddenly his voice rose in a wail that chilled her blood.

'What will the soul do at the judgment? Ah, what will the soul do? I will say to ye, "Depart from me into everlasting fire that was prepared for the divil and his angels. Depart from me, depart!" '

It was like a scream of pain, but immediately upon it came a low chuckle of malice. The woman's fists clenched beneath the clothes. 'Never again,' she said to herself aloud, 'never again!'

'Do you see me, do you?' he shouted. 'Do you see me?'

'I see you,' she whispered to herself.

'For ye, for ye, I reddened the fire,' went on the man, dropping back into his whine, 'for ye, for ye, I dug the pit. The black bitch on the hill, let ye torment her for me, ye divils. Forever, forever! Gather round, ye divils, gather round, and let me see ye roast the black bitch that killed a man . . . . Do you hear me, do you?'

'I hear you,' she whispered.

'Listen to me!

> '*When the old man was sleeping*
>   *She rose up from her bed,*
> *And crept into his lone bedroom*
>   *And cruelly struck him dead;*
> '*Twas with a hammer she done the deed,*
>   *May god it her repay,*
> *And then she . . . then she . . .*

'How does it go? I have it!

> '*And then she lifted up the body*
>   *And hid it in the hay.*'

Suddenly a stone came crashing through the window and a cold blast followed it. 'Never again,' she cried, hammering the bedframe with her fists, 'dear God, never again.' She heard the footsteps stumbling away. She knew he was running. It was like a child's malice and terror.

She rose and stuffed the window with a rag. Day was breaking. When she went back to bed she was chilled and shaken. Despairing of rest, she rose again, lit a candle and blew up the fire.

But even then some unfamiliar feeling was stirring at her heart. She felt she was losing control of herself and was being moved about like a chessman. Sighing, she slipped her feet into heavy shoes, threw an old coat about her shoulders, and went to the door. As she crossed the threshold she stumbled over something. It was a boot; another was lying some little distance away. Something seemed to harden within her. She placed the boots inside the door and closed it. But again came the faint thrill at her heart, so light it might have been a fluttering of untried wings and yet so powerful it shook her from head to foot, so that almost before she had closed the door she opened it again and went out, puzzled and trembling, into a cold noiseless rain. She called the man in an extraordinarily gentle voice as though she were afraid of being heard; then she made the circle of the farmhouse, a candle sheltered in the palm of her hand.

He was lying in the outhouse he had been whitewashing. She stood and looked down at him for a moment, her face set in a grim mask of disgust. Then she laid down the candle and lifted him, and at that moment an onlooker would have been conscious of her great physical strength. Half lifting, half guiding him, she steered the man to the door. On the doorstep he stood and said something to her, and immediately, with all her strength, she struck him across the mouth. He staggered and swore at her, but she caught him again and pushed him across the threshold. Then she went back for the candle, undressed him and put him to bed.

It was bright morning when she had done.

That day he lay on in bed, and came into the kitchen about two o'clock looking sheepish and sullen. He was wearing his own ragged boots.

'I'm going now,' he said stiffly.

'Please yourself,' she answered coolly. 'Maybe you'd be better.'

He seemed to expect something more, and because she said nothing he felt himself being put subtly in the wrong. This was not so surprising, because even she was impressed by her own nonchalance that seemed to have come suddenly to her from nowhere.

'Well?' he asked, and his look seemed to say, 'Women are the divil and all!' one could read him like a book.

'Well?'

'Have you nothing to say for yourself?'

'Have you nothing to say for yourself?' she retorted. 'I had enough of your blackguarding last night. You won't stop another hour in this house unless you behave yourself, mark me well, you won't.'

He grew very red.

'That's strange,' he answered sulkily.

'What's strange?'

'The likes of you saying that to me.'

'Take it or leave it. And if you don't like it, there's the door.'

Still he lingered. She knew now she had him at her mercy, and the nonchalance dropped from her.

'Aren't you a queer woman?' he commented, lighting his pipe. 'One'd think you wouldn't have the face to talk like that to an honest man. Have you no shame?'

'Listen to who's talking of shame;' she answered bitterly. 'A pity you didn't see yourself last night, lying in your dirt like an old cow. And you call yourself a man. How ready you were with your stones!'

'It was the shock,' he said sullenly.

'It was no shock. It was drink.'

'It was the shock I tell you. I was left an orphan with no one to tell me the badness of the world.'

'I was left an orphan too. And I don't go round crying about the badness of the world.'

'Oh, Christ, don't remind me what you were. 'Tis only myself, the poor fool, wouldn't know, and all the old chat I had about the man I drew blood from, as if I was a terrible fellow entirely. I might have known to see a handsome woman living lonely that she wouldn't be that way only no man in Ireland would look at the side of the road she walked on.'

He did not see how the simple flattery of his last words went through her, quickening her with pleasure; he noticed only the savage retort she gave him, for the sense of his own guilt was growing stronger in him at every moment. Her silence was in part the cause of that; her explanation would have been his triumph. That at least was how he had imagined it. He had not been prepared for this silence which drew him like a magnet. He could not decide to go, yet his fear of her would not allow him to remain. The day passed like that. When twilight came she looked across at him and asked:

'Are you going or stopping?'

'I'm stopping, if you please,' he answered meekly

'Well, I'm going to bed. One sleepless night is enough for me.'

And she went, leaving him alone in the kitchen. Had she delayed until darkness fell, he would have found it impossible to remain, but there was no suspicion of this in her mind. She understood only that people might hate her; that they might fear her never entered her thoughts.

An hour or so later she looked for the candle and remembered that she had left it in his room. She rose and knocked at his door. There was no answer. She knocked again. Then she pushed in the door and called him. She was alarmed. The bed was empty. She laid her hand to the candle (it was lying still where she had left it, on the dresser beside the door) but as she did so she heard his voice, husky and terrified.

'Keep away from me! Keep away from me, I tell you!'

She could discern his figure now. He was standing in a corner, his little white shirt half way up his thighs, his hand grasping something, she did not see what. It was some little while before the explanation dawned on her, and with it came a sudden feeling of desolation within her.

'What ails you?' she asked gently. 'I was only looking for the candle.'

'Don't come near me!' he cried.

She lit the candle, and as he saw her there, her face as he had never seen it before, stricken with pain, his fear died away. A moment later she was gone, and the back door slammed behind her. It was only then he realized what his insane fear had brought him to, and the obsession of his own guilt returned with a terrible clarity. He walked up and down the little room in desperation.

Half an hour later he went to her room. The candle was burning on a chair beside the bed. She lifted herself on the pillow and looked at him with strangely clear eyes.

'What is it?' she asked.

'I'm sorry,' he answered. 'I shouldn't be here at all. I'm sorry. I'm queer. I'll go in the morning and I won't trouble you any more.'

'Never mind,' she said, and held out her hand to him. He came closer and took it timidly. 'You wouldn't know.'

'God pity me,' he said. 'I was distracted. You know I was distracted. You were so good to me, and that's the way I paid you out. But I was going out of my mind. I couldn't sleep.'

'Sure you couldn't.' She drew him down to her until his head was resting on the pillow, and made him lie beside her.

'I couldn't, I couldn't,' he said into her ear. 'I wint raving mad. And I thought whin you came into the room —'

'I know, I know.'

'I did, whatever came over me.'

'I know.' He realized that she was shivering all over.

She drew back the clothes for him. He was eager to explain, to tell her about himself, his youth, the death of his father and mother, his poverty, his religious difficulties, his poetry. What was wrong with him was, he was wild; could stick at no trade, could never keep away from drink.

'You were wild yourself,' he said.

'Fifteen years ago. I'm tame now in earnest.'

'Tell me about it,' he said eagerly, 'talk to me, can't you? Tell me he was bad. Tell me he was a cruel old uncle to you. Tell me he beat you. He used to lock you up for days, usedn't he, to keep you away from boys? He must have been bad or you'd never had done what you did, and you only a girl.'

But still she said nothing. Bright day was in the room when he fell asleep, and for a long while she lay, her elbow on the pillow, her hand covering her left breast, while she looked at him. His mouth was wide open, his irregular teeth showed in a faint smile. Their shyness had created a sort of enchantment about them, and she watched over his sleep with something like ecstasy, ecstasy which disappeared when he woke, to find her, the same hard quiet woman he knew.

After that she ceased making his bed in the small room, and he slept with her. Not that it made any difference to their relations. Between them after those few hours of understanding persisted a fierce, unbroken shyness, the shyness of lonely souls. If it rasped the nerves of either, there was no open sign of it, unless a curiously irritable tenderness revealed anything of their thoughts. She was forever finding things done for her; there was no longer any question of his going, and he worked from morning until late night with an energy and intelligence that surprised her. But she knew he felt the lack of company, and one evening she went out to him as he worked in the garden.

'Why don't you go down to the village now?' she asked.

'Ah, what would I be doing there?' But it was clear that it had been on his mind at that very moment.

'You might drop in for a drink and a chat.'

'I might do that,' he agreed.

'And why don't you?'

'Me? I'd be ashamed.'

'Ashamed? Ashamed of what? There's no one will say anything to you. And if they do, what are you, after all, but a working man?'

It was clear that this excuse had not occurred to him, but it would also have been clear to anyone else that she would have thought poorly of such as gave it credit. So he got his coat and went.

It was late when he came in, and she saw he had drunk more that his share. His face was flushed and he laughed too easily. For two days past a bottle of whiskey had been standing on the dresser (what a change for her!) but if he had noticed it he had made no sign. Now he went directly to it and poured himself out a glass.

'You found it,' she said with a hint of bitterness.

'What's that?'

'You found it, I say.'

'Of course I did. Have a drop yourself.'

'No.'

'Do. Just a drop.'

'I don't want it.'

He crossed to her, stood behind her chair for a moment; then he bent over and kissed her. She had been expecting it, but on the instant she revolted.

'Don't do that again,' she said appealingly, wiping her mouth.

'You don't mind me, do you?' he sniggered, still standing behind her.

'I do. I mind it when you're drunk.'

'Well, here's health.'

'Don't drink any more of that.'

'Here's health.'

'Good health.'

'Take a drop yourself, do.'

'No, I tell you,' she answered angrily.

'By God, you must.'

He threw one arm about her neck and deliberately spilt the whiskey between her breasts. She sprang up and threw him away from her. Whatever had been in her mind was now forgotten in her loathing.

'Bad luck to you!' she cried savagely.

'I'm sorry,' he said quickly. 'I didn't mean it.' Already he was growing afraid.

'You didn't mean it,' she retorted mockingly. 'Who taught you to do it then? Was it Jimmie Dick? What sort of woman do you think I am, you fool? You sit all night in a public-house talking of me, and when you come back you try to make me out as loose and dirty as your talk.'

'Who said I was talking of you?'

'I say it.'

'Then you're wrong.'

'I'm not wrong. Don't I know you, you poor sheep? You sat there, letting them make you out a great fellow, because they thought you were like themselves and thought I was a bitch, and you never as much as opened your mouth to give them the lie. You sat there and gaped and bragged. That's what you are.'

'That's not true.'

'And then you come strutting back, stuffed with drink, and think I'll let you make love to me, so that you can have something to talk about in the public-house.'

Her eyes were bright with tears of rage. She had forgotten that something like this was what she knew would happen when she made him go to the village, so little of our imagination can we bear to see made real. He sank into a chair, and put his head between his hands in sulky dignity. She lit the candle and went off to bed.

She fell asleep and woke to hear him stirring in the kitchen. She rose and flung open the door. He was still sitting where she had seen him last.

'Aren't you going to bed at all tonight?' she asked.

'I'm sorry if I disturbed you,' he replied. The drunkenness had gone, and he did look both sorry and miserable. 'I'll go now.'

'You'd better. Do you see the time?'

'Are you still cross? I'm sorry, God knows I am.'

'Never mind.'

' 'Twas all true.'

'What was true?' She had already forgotten.

'What you said. They were talking about you, and I listened.'

'Oh, that.'

'Only you were too hard on me.'

'Maybe I was.'

She took a step forward. He wondered if she had understood what he was saying at all.

'I was fond of you all right.'

'Yes,' she said.

'You know I was.'

'Yes.'

She was like a woman in a dream. She had the same empty feeling within her, the same sense of being pushed about like a chessman, as on the first night when she carried him in. He put his arm about her and kissed her. She shivered and clung to him, life suddenly beginning to stir within her.

One day, some weeks later, he told her he was going back home on a visit; there were cousins he wished to see; something or other; she was not surprised. She had seen the restlessness on him for some time past and had no particular belief in the cousins. She set about preparing a parcel of food for him, and in this little attention there was something womanly that touched him.

'I'll be back soon,' he said, and meant it. He could be moved easily enough in this fashion, and she saw through him. It was dull being the lover of a woman like herself; he would be best married to a lively girl of eighteen or so, a girl he could go visiting with and take pride in.

'You're always welcome,' she said. 'The house is your own.'

As he went down the boreen he was saying to himself 'She'll be lost! She'll be lost!' but he would have spared his pity if he had seen how she took it.

Her mood shifted from busy to idle. At one hour she was working in the garden, singing, at another she sat in the sun, motionless and silent for a long, long time. As weeks went by and the year drifted into a rainy autumn, an astonishing change took place in her, slowly, almost imperceptibly. It seemed a physical rather than a spiritual change. Line by line her features divested themselves of strain, and her body seemed to fall into easier, more graceful curves. It would not be untrue to say she scarcely thought of the man, unless it was with some slight relief to find herself alone again. Her thoughts were all contracted within herself.

One autumn evening he came back. For days she had been expecting him; quite suddenly she had realized that he would return, that everything was not over between them, and very placidly accepted the fact.

He seemed to have grown older and maturer in his short absence; one felt it less in his words than in his manner. There was decision in it. She saw that he was rapidly growing into a deferred manhood, and was secretly proud of the change. He had a great fund of stories about his wanderings (never a word of the mythical cousins); and while she prepared his supper, she listened to him, smiling faintly, almost as if she were not listening at all. He was as hungry now as the first evening she met him, but everything was easier between them; he was glad to be there and she to have him.

'Are you pleased I came?' he asked.

'You know I'm pleased.'

'Were you thinking I wouldn't come?'

'At first I thought you wouldn't. You hadn't it in your mind to come back. But afterward I knew you would.'

'A man would want to mind what he thinks about a woman like you,' he grumbled good-humouredly. 'Are you a witch?'

'How would I be a witch?' Her smile was attractive.

'Are you?' He gripped her playfully by the arm.

'I am not and well you know it.'

'I have me strong doubts of you. Maybe you'll say now you know what happened? Will you? Did you ever hear of a man dreaming three times of a crock of gold? Well, that's what happened me. I dreamt three times of you. What sign is that?'

'A sign you were drinking too much.'

' 'Tis not. I know what sign it is.'

He drew his chair up beside her own, and put his arm about her. Then he drew her face round to his and kissed her. At that moment she could feel very clearly the change in him. His hand crept about her neck and down her breast, releasing the warm smell of her body.

'That's enough love-making,' she said. She rose quickly and shook off his arm. A strange happy smile like a newly-open flower lingered where he had kissed her. 'I'm tired. Your bed is made in there.'

'My bed?'

She nodded.

'You're only joking me. You are, you divil, you're only joking.'

His arms out, he followed her, laughing like a lad of sixteen. He caught at her, but she forced him off again. His face altered suddenly, became sullen and spiteful.

'What is it?'

'Nothing.'

' 'Tis a change for you.'

' 'Tis.'

'And for why?'

'For no why. Isn't it enough for you to know it?'

'Is it because I wint away?'

'Maybe.'

'Is it?'

'I don't know whether 'tis or no.'

'And didn't I come back as I said I would?'

'You did. When it suited you.'

'The divil is in ye all,' he said crossly.

Later he returned to the attack; he was quieter and more persuasive; there was more of the man in him, but she seemed armed at every point. He experienced an acute sense of frustration. He had felt growing in him this new, lusty manhood, and returned with the intention of dominating her, only to find she too had grown, and still outstripped him. He lay awake for a long time, thinking it out, but when he rose next morning the barrier between them seemed to have disappeared. As ever she was dutiful, unobtrusive; by day at any rate she was all he would have her to be. Even when he kissed her she responded; of his hold on her he had no doubt, but he seemed incapable of taking advantage of it.

That night when he went to bed he began to think again of it, and rage grew in him until it banished all hope of sleep. He rose and went into her room.

'How long is this going to last?' he asked thickly.

'What?'

'This. How long more are you going to keep me out?'

'Maybe always,' she said softly, as if conjuring up the prospect.

'Always?'

'Maybe.'

'Always? And what in hell do you mean by it? You lure me into it, and then throw me away like an old boot.'

'Did I lure you into it?'

'You did. Oh, you fooled me right enough at the time,

but I've been thinking about it since. 'Twas no chance brought you on the road the first day I passed.'

'Maybe I did,' she admitted. She was stirred again by the quickness of his growth. 'If I did you had nothing to complain of.'

'Haven't I now?'

'Now is different.'

'Why? Because I wint away?'

'Because you didn't think me good enough for you.'

'That's a lie. You said that before, and you know 'tis a lie.'

'Then show it.'

He sat on the bed and put his face close to hers.

'You mean, to marry you?'

'Yes.'

'You know I can't.'

'What hinders you?'

'For a start, I have no money. Neither have you.'

'There's money enough.'

'Where would it come from?'

'Never you mind where 'twould come from. 'Tis there.'

He looked at her hard.

'You planned it well,' he said at last. 'They said he was a miser . . . Oh, Christ, I can't marry you!'

'The divil send you better meat than mutton,' she retorted coarsely.

He sat on the edge of the bed, his big hand caressing her cheek and bare shoulder.

'Why don't you tell the truth?' she asked. 'You have no respect for me.'

'Why do you keep on saying that?'

'Because 'tis true.' In a different voice she added: 'Nor I hadn't for myself till you went away. Take me now or leave me. . . . Stop that, you fool!'

'Listen to me —'

'Stop that then! I'm tame now, but I'm not tame enough for that.'

Even in the darkness she could feel that she had awakened his old dread of her; she put her arms about his head, drew him down to her, and whispered in his ear.

'Now do you understand?' she said.

A few days later he got out the cart and harnessed the pony. They drove into the town three miles away. As they passed through the village people came to their doors to look after them. They left the cart a little outside the town, and, following country practice, separated to meet again on the priest's doorstep. The priest was at home, and he listened incredulously to the man's story.

'You know I'll have to write to your parish priest first,' he said severely.

'I know,' said the man. 'You'll find and see he have nothing against me.'

The priest was shaken.

'And this woman has told you everything?'

'She told me nothing. But I know.'

'About her uncle?'

'About her uncle,' repeated the man.

'And you're satisfied to marry her, knowing that?'

'I'm satisfied.'

'It's all very strange,' said the priest wearily. 'You know,' he added to the woman, 'Almighty God has been very merciful to you. I hope you are conscious of all He in His infinite mercy has done for you, who deserve it so little.'

'I am. From this out I'll go to Mass regularly.'

'I hope,' he repeated emphatically, 'you are fully conscious of it. If I thought there was any lightness in you, if I thought for an instant that you wouldn't make a good wife to this man, my conscience wouldn't allow me to marry you. Do you understand that?'

'Never fear,' she said, without lifting her eyes, 'I'll make him a good wife. And he knows it.'

The man nodded. 'I know it,' he said.

The priest was impressed by the solemn way in which she spoke. She was aware that the strength which had upheld her till now was passing from her to the young man at her side; the future would be his.

From the priest's they went to the doctor's. He saw her

slip on a ring before they entered. He sat in the room while the doctor examined her. When she had dressed again her eyes were shining. The strength was passing from her, and she was not sorry to see it pass. She laid a sovereign on the table.

'Oho,' exclaimed the doctor, 'how did you come by this?' The man started and the woman smiled.

'I earned it hard,' she answered.

The doctor took the coin to the window and examined it.

'By Jove,' he said, 'it's not often I see one of these.'

'Maybe you'll see more of them,' she said with a gay laugh. He looked at her from under his eyes and laughed too; her brightness had a strange other-world attraction.

'Maybe I will,' he replied. 'In a few months time, eh? Sorry I can't give you change in your own coin. Ah, well! Good luck, anyway. And call me in as often as you please.'

(1933)

The Miracle

The night had been fine with a light wind and scurrying clouds. Towards morning, to the accompaniment of a rising gale, rain began to fall and fell with increasing violence till it turned into a regular downpour, and wakened the light sleepers in the convent with its fierce, pebble-like volleying against their window panes.

In the cemetery behind the convent there was nothing but the rain and the darkness, or rather the double darkness that the four high walls shut in; no sound but the rain thudding dully upon the grass and the rows of wooden crosses. But yes — in one spot the downpour had a sharper sound as it toppled from stone to stone, an irregular plash and gurgle that could be heard even above the rain and wind.

When the first light struggled over the walls a silhouette rose dimly against it; it was the silhouette of a marble trumpet that filled and overflowed unceasingly onto the tiles beneath. Gradually the figure under the trumpet outlined itself, the head thrown back, the right arm lifted to support the instrument, the marble wings folded behind the marble shoulders; a tall, soldierly figure above the rows of meek black crosses. The statue of the angel stands upon a pedestal at the foot of which is a little tomb that gradually fills with the rain-water he spills from the mouth of his trumpet.

Shortly after dawn the nuns rose, and sighed as they looked out on the lenten greyness of their fields. They dressed, shivering in the icy morning air, and pattered noisily down to the chapel, their pecking voices shrill along the white corridors, their slippers flip-flapping, their beads and keys and crosses tinkling.

About two hours later a bell sounded, and the lay-sister opened the little grille in the front door. Standing in the porch she saw two curious figures; a man with a large bundle that looked like a bundle of rags in his arms, and a young woman. They were drenched, and two big pools had already formed at their feet. The man wore a long blue overcoat, and a dirty old cap, the drowned brim of which sagged over his eyes. The woman wore a black shawl drawn tight about the milky oval of her face. As the door-keeper opened to them the man raised his cap and spoke in a loud, threatening voice.

'We came to see the saint's grave, sister,' he said.

'Oh, but this isn't the day,' she replied hastily. 'Didn't you know? Wednesday or Saturday, after three: those are the visiting hours.'

'We couldn't wait,' he said. 'And we're travelling since four o'clock this morning — under that,' he added, lifting his forefinger to the spilling sky.

'I'm so sorry I can't let you in,' she said regretfully. 'You understand of course, if once we began —'

'What is it? What is it?' a jolly voice asked behind her, and Sister Clare, the bursar, came out.

'This man wants to visit the cemetery, sister. I've told him he must come back on Wednesday or Saturday.'

'That's right,' Clare added jovially, 'after three, after three!'

''Twill be no use Wednesday or Saturday,' the man replied flatly, 'no more than if you said the day of judgment.'

He half turned to go, then swung round on the two nuns and with one movement of his arm flung open his bundle.

'Look at him, will ye?' he cried with reproach in his voice.

As he tossed off the accumulation of rags they saw a bright wakeful, boy's face with two great black eyes that fixed them mournfully. It was as if those grave eyes had been turned in their direction all the while under the wrappings.

'Your son?' asked Sister Clare.

'My *only* son,' he corrected her. 'Only *child*. And he never walked since he was born eight years ago.'

'Poor little darling!' murmured Clare sympathetically. She took the child's cold cheeks in her two hands and kissed him.

'Last night,' the man's harsh voice cried over her head, 'I heard it. I heard it as plain as I hear you now. I said it to you, Birdie?'

'You did,' affirmed his wife without looking up.

'You didn't want to come?'

'You said to leave me imaginations till the weather cleared.'

'I did. I was in dread the child would catch cold.'

'And I got up and dressed him myself, dressed him and wrapped him up,' the man continued triumphantly, his eyes blazing with passion. 'With me own two hands I dressed him. Did I as much as make a cup of tea for meself?'

'You did not.'

'I didn't. And still you wouldn't believe I'd set out on me own. There you wor, sitting up in the bed, and I turned round and I was going out the door, and said to you, "Woman, woman, will you come or stay?".'

'He did, sister, he did. Them were his very words.'

'Poor creatures!' exclaimed Clare. 'And you mean to say you've had nothing to eat?'

'No, sister. He wouldn't take a bite even when the lorry stopped in Mallow.'

'I would not,' the man said emphatically. 'Would you stop if the Lord called you? What did I say to you? Did I say, "No man must delay the Lord when the Lord calls."?'

'You did.'

'Will I go and get Sister Margaret?' asked the door-keeper timidly.

'Never mind,' said Clare. 'I'll get her myself. Sit down, poor man, until I see if I can get the key of the cemetery.'

Sister Clare padded off and roused old Margaret from her devotions. Margaret was cranky. She had rheumatics and knew the sort of people that came to convents at that unearthly hour. She wished the door sister would have a bit of sense. Look at the wetting she was going to get all on account of this nonsense!

'Never mind,' said Clare, 'give me the keys and I'll go myself'.

'You'll do nothing of the kind,' said Margaret sourly. She always resented the suggestion that she was getting too old for her job.

She spent a deliberately long time searching for heavy boots 'that wouldn't cramp her feet', for shawls, for a good umbrella, and Clare was ready long before she had found them. At last they went downstairs together. Margaret did not pretend to see the 'tramps' as she called them, and stalked noisily out, opening her umbrella, clanking her keys and complaining loudly at the inconvenience to which thoughtless people always put her. Clare beckoned to the 'tramps', and they fell in, humbly and silently, behind the two nuns. The rain thumped on the umbrellas that wavered before them, seeking a path through the wind.

As she opened the cemetery gate Margaret swung round on the man and said with a snarl:

'You ought to have more sense at this hour of your life than to bring out that unfortunate child in the rain. But of course it won't matter to you if he gets double-pneumonia from it!'

'The Lord knows his own business best,' the man replied gruffly.

'Ech, you and the Lord!' growled Margaret with unintentional irreverence. 'You make me sick.'

The rain was beating about them with a perfect abandon of malevolence. Margaret lifted her skirts and hobbled at a run to the little shelter where the pilgrims were wont to sit. Covered in ivy, and hung with crutches, surgical boots, beads, crosses and scapulars, it had no furniture but a low bench placed beneath the statue of the Blessed Virgin. Margaret sat down and watched the others glumly.

'Go on!' she said scornfully.

'Kneel down and say three Our Fathers and three Hail Marys with me,' directed Clare, determined to keep up her athletic optimism under old Margaret's fire; and putting a bit of bagging on the edge of the tomb, she bravely knelt on it. Without a moment's hesitation the man knelt in a pool of water beside the grave, and his wife followed him. Clare gave out the prayers and the two 'tramps' answered them. At every response the man looked at the child in his arms as though awaiting some miraculous transformation.

'In the name of the Father and of the Son —' Clare concluded, and rose.

As she did so, the man tossed aside the heap of rags that hung about the child, stood above the tomb that was filled to the brim with water, and before she could protest had put him standing in it. The child screamed and old Margaret gave a squeal of rage.

'Aaaah, you madman, you madman!' she cried, and ran out of the shelter towards him.

'Let him alone, now, do,' he said.

He removed his arm; the child stood alone for a moment, then toppled helplessly, face forward, into the icy water. He screamed again. His father bent forward and lifted him with one arm.

'Walk!' he shouted.

'Let him out, let him out, you fool!' hissed Margaret at his elbow.

The man put out his other hand and saved the child from falling again.

'Walk!' he said, and pushed him gently forward.

The boy put out one leg timidly; he drew it back and put out the other. His father let go of him once more.

'Walk!' he said remorselessly.

And then the miracle really happened, for the child began to walk. Sobbing hysterically he tottered from one end of the tomb to the other, the water reaching to his middle.

'Do it again,' his father said commandingly. The nuns were now almost oblivious of the elements, even of the child, as they watched him perilously traverse the little bath, drenched and shivering from shoulder to heel. Margaret made the sign of the cross.

'Again,' the man rapped out. The child's strength was clearly giving way; his progress grew slower and the legs bent under his weight. But his father was satisfied.

'Praise be to you, God,' he said at last, lifting the child out of the tomb, and putting him on the ground by his side. 'Catch his hand, Birdie, and we'll walk him down.'

'Say an act of thanksgiving,' suggested Sister Clare.

'And carry him down,' added Margaret solidly.

After this the man was taken to the gardener's house where a dry suit and overcoat were provided for him; the mother and son came to the convent and had their clothes dried. They had breakfast together; the man was very loud-voiced and complacent, and ate a great deal with no suggestion of embarrassment, but his wife was very shy and only nibbled at her food.

The whole community gathered to say good-bye to them and embrace the child who had received such a signal mark of heavenly favour. The man shook hands with them all, one by one telling them very loudly that he knew when the Lord was speaking to him; he wasn't the sort of man who would raise a false alarm. By way of thanksgiving, the Mother Superior gave him a ten shilling note. This he received and pocketed, not without a certain amount of surprise, but with no undignified expressions of gratitude.

From the windows the sisters watched him go down the avenue, with his wife, the child, for their especial edification, being made to toddle between them. Then when he got tired his father bundled him up once more, and they set off at a quick pace for home.

All that day and for several days after, the community was in great glee and could talk of nothing but the miracle. Only old Margaret seemed in the least dissatisfied. At moments her nose would rise like a shining red island in a wide sea of wrinkles — a sort of involuntary grimace of distaste, which was immediately followed by a quick grab for her beads or a hasty sign of the cross. But her only expression of opinion was when she mentioned to an old crony that, thanks be to God for his infinite mercies, you couldn't expect to get used to miracles after you reached the age of seventy.

(1934)

May Night

It was a night in May, warm and dim and full of the syrupy smell of whitethorn. In a black sky a single star, blue and misty, was burning. Two tramps sat by the roadside. One was tall and thin, and in the ash-coloured twilight one might have seen that he had a long face with a drooping moustache. The other was a small man who looked fat; but that was only because he was swathed in coats, one more ragged than the next. He must have been wearing four or five in all. He had a ragged black beard that jutted out all over his face. His black hat was pasted perfectly flat over his scattered black locks that streamed about his shoulders, inside and outside the coats. Even in daylight all you could see of his person would be two beady black eyes, very bright, a stub of a nose no bigger than the butt of a cigar, and, when he moved his hands, the tips of his dirty fingers which were otherwise lost to view.

'Man,' he was saying in a high sing-song voice, 'is an animal. An animal must live. Therefore man must live. That's a syllogism; if you don't agree with it you must contradict the major or the minor or say the conclusion doesn't follow. But a man is made in the image of God and he must try and live decent. Only you, Horgan, you son of

a bitch, you're worse than an animal. An animal bites
because 'tis his nature to, but you bite because you likes
it. Horgan,' he said, spitting, 'you're neither a man nor an
animal. Why do you hang around me?'

'I don't hang around you.'

'You do. You do hang around me. No one else would
leave you do it. But I'm a weak man and I leaves you.
You're a constant source of timptation to me. When I gets
angry I hits you and then I do be sorry.'

'Where would you be only for me? Who carries you away
when you're drunk? Only for me the guards would have
you now.'

'I admit I gets drunk,' replied the fat man sternly. 'Not
like you. Nothing makes you drunk, which is another
reason I say you're not a man at all. And you leads me into
timptation. When you're with me I wants to hit you. I
wants to hit you now.'

'You try it and see what you'll get.'

'If I lose me temper I'll hit you,' said the fat man,
spitting on his stick. 'I'll hit you such a crack you won't
get over it . . . .' After a moment he sighed. 'O Lord,
behold the timptation I'm put in with this fellow. Some
day I'll do for him . . . . What did you hang that dog for?'
he cried fiercely. 'What harm was he doing you? One of
God's creatures! You savage!'

'Don't you call me a savage!'

'Savage, savage, dirty savage!' said the fat man thickly.

'By Chrisht, I'll shtrangle you!'

'Come on! Come on! Do it!' cried the fat man, springing
to his feet with extraordinary agility and brandishing his
stick. As the other began clumsily to rise there was a
sound of footsteps on the road. The fat man lowered his
stick with an oath and resumed his seat, back to back with
his companion. The tall man lit his pipe. There they sat,
looking in opposite directions and muttering the most
fiendish maledictions at one another under their breath;
the fat man in particular showed a decided ability to
manufacture curses. Some minutes later the footsteps drew
level with them, and the figure of a man emerged from the

darkness. The flame in the bowl of the tall man's pipe attracted his attention. He stopped.

'Good-night, men,' he said with a soft, country accent. 'Would ye have a light?'

'Certainly,' said the tall man in a whining and obsequious tone. 'You're welcome to a light from the pipe, the little that's in it, God help us.'

The stranger bent over him. In the light which the tramp sucked from his pipe he saw with his small, shrewd eyes the pale face of a young man. What he saw there caused him suddenly to drop his obsequiousness, and when he spoke again it was in a blustering tone.

'Where are you going to?' he asked.

'The city,' replied the young man after a barely perceptible pause.

'Looking for work?'

'Ay.' Again there was the same slight pause.

'And you'll get it I suppose.'

'What's that?'

'You'll get it, you'll get it,' repeated the tall tramp, and into his voice had crept a perceptible snarl. 'The foxy country boy. Ye'd live where honest men would starve.'

'I dunno would we.'

'Oh, don't you? Well, I know. I know men that can't get a living in their own city on account of the country johnnies.'

'Never mind him,' broke in the fat man. 'He's not from the city at all. No one knows where he comes from.'

'Don't they? Don't they now? If they don't they know damn well where you come from. With your bag under your arm!'

'Be quiet, you, Horgan! Be quiet now!'

'I will not be quiet,' hissed Horgan. 'Look at him now, young fellow! Look at him now! The man that was to be a priest. And when they were turning him out they cursed him to have the bag on his back the longest day he'd live, and he thinks when he's carrying it under his oxter that he's cheating them!'

'Ay,' said the fat man slowly in a deep voice, 'I was, I

was to be a priest. And I know curses, curses that'll bring the big, blind boils out on you so that you'll stink for ever — and you going the roads.'

'Don't you curse me!' exclaimed Horgan, not quite sure of himself.

'Ah,' said the fat man with satisfaction, shaking his head so that his long locks wagged about him, 'I'll give you a hot little *maledico vobis* that'll make you wish you never seen the light, Horgan. You mind what I say.'

'How far more have I to go?' asked the stranger.

'Fourteen mile,' replied the fat tramp.

' 'Tis a long road.'

' 'Tis so. Set down, can't you?'

'I will for a minute.'

'There's a lot looking for work.'

'There is.'

' 'Tis to England you should go,' said the fat man decisively. 'They give them money for nothing there. If I could put by a few ha'pence I'd go to England. I'd rent a little house of my own and drop the drink and go to Mass regular.'

'England!' said the young man bitterly. 'I tramped every mile of it.'

'And no work?'

'No work.'

He turned and lay on his stomach, biting a blade of grass.

'And didn't they give you the money?'

'God's curse on the ha'penny.'

'Lord, O Lord! The liars there are!' The tramp fumbled in his bag. 'A biteen of bread? ... The liars!' he added indignantly under his breath.

The young man took the crust and began to gnaw it moodily. A car whizzed by, its lights picking them out like pieces of scenery against the theatrical green of the hedges and the dead white of the hawthorn. Screwing up their eyes, the two tramps looked at their companion.

'You could have asked for a lift,' said the man with the beard.

'I'm in no hurry.'

' 'Tis hard enough to get work in the city, I hear tell.'

'I'm not going there to get work.'

'Take my advice,' said the fat man with animation, 'don't go on the roads! Don't go on the roads, young man! 'Tis a cur-dog's life.'

'I'm not going on the roads.'

'And what are you going to do?' It was the truculent voice of Horgan, breaking a sudden silence.

'What do you think?'

'Are you going to try for the army?'

'No.'

'For the guards?'

'They wouldn't take me.'

'Then what is it? Jasus, you're making a great secret of it.'

' 'Tis no secret. I'm going to say good-bye to misfortune.'

There was another silence, deeper, longer. The fat tramp caught his breath and grabbed the young man's arm.

'Don't do it!' he cried. 'No, don't do it!'

'And why not?' The young man sat bolt upright and the tramp felt a pair of wild eyes piercing him in the darkness. 'Why not, I say?'

'Because 'tis a sin, a terrible sin. Life comes from God. God is good. So life is a good thing — that's a syllogism. And if you kill yourself you'll be damned.'

'I'm damned as it is.'

'No, no, no! You don't know what it is. I know, I know, but I can't tell you. There's no one can tell you, no one! But you feel it in here' — he beat his breast frantically — 'the fire, the blackness, the loneliness, the fear. Don't do it young man, don't do it!' His voice rose to an angry impotent cry.

'Don't be a fool, Kenfick,' said Horgan; and there was the same rancour and jealousy and malice in his voice. 'He's telling lies. What's he going there for? Why can't he do it anywhere else? He's telling lies.'

'Jasus!' The stranger suddenly bent across the fat man and gripped Horgan by the throat. 'Are 'oo contradicting me, are 'oo?'

'Never mind him!' said Kenfick.

'Are 'oo contradicting me?'

'I'm not, I'm not,' screamed Horgan, frightened out of his wits and brazening it out with spleen, 'I'm asking a civil question.'

The young man's grip relaxed. He resumed his former position, lying on his stomach.

'Tell us,' said the fat man, stretching out a conciliatory hand. 'Never mind that black devil. Young man, I like you. Tell us what happened.'

'You know it all now,' replied the young man after a moment's hesitation. 'I was in England looking for work. I tramped every bit of it. I came home at the latter end. My mother said: "Go out and look for work. I can't keep you here." So I went out and I looked. I tramped Munster looking for it, begging my way. Then I came back to her. "Did you get work?" says she. "No," says I, "I didn't." "Then you must go away again," says she, "I can't keep you." I took up a bit of rope that was lying in the back room and I went out to the shed. I tied it to a rafter. Then I put a box underneath it and I tied the rope around my neck. The door opened and in she walked. "Is it hanging yourself you are?" says she. "It is," says I. "You can't do it here," says she. "Is it to be putting me to the expense of burying you?" "What'll I do then?" says I. "My feet are bleeding, and I can't tramp no more." "You can go down to the city," says she, "where the tide will wash your body away and there'll be no call for me to bury you." '

As the stranger concluded his story the fat tramp sighed angrily. He pulled his old hat farther over his eyes.

'She's no mother,' he muttered thickly. 'She's a wolf. Never mind her. Spit on her! Faugh! . . . Oh!' he cried, his voice rising to a wail, 'my mother; why didn't I mind her when I had her? And all the times she cried over me, and all the prayers she said for me, and all in the hope that one day she'd kneel for my blessing! Oh, God, what blinds us, what blinds us, O God, that we don't see our own destruction?' Bawling his lament with hoarse sobs, he began hitting the grass about him with great sweeps of his stick. 'Listen, boy,' he continued eagerly. 'Come with me. I

makes it out well; all the priests knows me; they're good to
me. Sometimes I makes one and six a day.'

'Are you going to drop me then?' asked Horgan angrily.

'I am. I'm sick of you.'

'I'll lay you out,' cried Horgan, drawing back his fist.

'Will you? Will you? Will you? Kenfick lifted his stick.
'Leave me see you now. Bah! You haven't it in you, Horgan,
You're a coward, Horgan!'

'Don't you call me a coward!'

'You are a coward!'

'I won't come between ye,' said the stranger, rising. 'I'll
go me road. I'll be no man's dog any more, waiting for the
bite to fill me. There's no use your telling me about hell
no more, mister,' he added in a husky voice. 'I was afraid
of it once, but I'm afraid of it no longer.'

'Young man, young man,' cried Kenfick, 'beware! You
don't know what you're saying. 'Tis blasphemy, young man.
Almighty God, have mercy on us all this night. Almighty
God, forgive him and save him!'

'Save!' snarled Horgan. 'Look at who talks of saving. He
saved you nicely, didn't He?'

'Yes, He did, He did. I sees what none of ye sees; I sees
the world and the people of the world, and I sees the black
angels and the white angels fighting always around them.
Don't do it, young man. Stop with me.'

'A grand life you have to offer him,' sneered Horgan.

' 'Tisn't a grand life, but 'tisn't a bad life either.'

' 'Twould be better for him be dead than tied to the
likes of you.'

'Shut up, you!'

'I will not shut up. What'll he say when he have a
month of you, dragging you along the road and you
stinking with drink, pulling you out the convent gate and
you shouting back dirty words at the nuns?'

'If I do inself, isn't it their own fault?' hissed the fat man.
'Why don't they give me the few coppers I ask for without
whinging and whining? What is it to them what I does with
them? What do they think I'm going to buy with them? A
house and shop? But women are all alike. A man have sense.

A man don't ask are you going to buy drink with it. Look at the priests! They gives me whiskey because they have sense.'

'Because they're afraid of your dirty tongue.'

'Because they have sense, they likes whiskey themselves. And they knows I'm not a bad man. They knows I'm only weak. And some day when I've a bit of money put by I'll go and live in a town and have a little house of my own, and every day of my life I'll answer the Holy Mass. And Almighty God knows it, and He's not angry with me, and some day He'll lift me up out of the gutter. I know He will, I know it well. And I know what He'll do to you, Horgan. Will I tell you?'

'Don't you say anything bad about me.'

'Ah, you're afraid! You know damn well what's coming to you and you're afraid.'

'I am not afraid.'

'Young man, young man, look at him now!' Kenfick had Horgan by the neck of the coat, shaking him back and forward. 'Look at him!' he shouted triumphantly. 'The man that was talking about death.'

And at that instant the tramps saw that the stranger was gone, vanished into the darkness of the spring night, his footsteps unheard on the thick wet grass. Horgan laughed bitterly. The fat man sat back and began to tie up his old bag. Suddenly he broke into a whine.

'O Lord!' he said, 'I should have told him. At the hour of death ... an aspiration ... My Jesus, mercy. . . . Almighty God, forgive and save him, forgive and save us all.'

For some time after he could be heard muttering ejaculations and prayers. Then Horgan lit a cigarette and he grew rigid.

'Horgan,' he said sternly, 'where did you get that fag?'

'Where do you think?' asked the other with a snarl.

'Did you steal them from that boy?'

'What do you think I was doing while the pair of ye were gassing?'

The fat man sighed bitterly. After about three minutes of silence there was the heavy thud of a stick, a scream of pain, and in an instant the two were struggling like madmen in the grass.

(1935)

The Flowering Trees

Preparations for the picnic had begun when word came of the Fiddler. On a mild Sunday afternoon in February he came and sat in what had been the garden of a big house long since deserted. With him came the Stutterer, who smoked a pipe. To Josie the other children brought the tale, but at first she paid no heed.

She had opened her account book for the year and sat over it, her rosy tongue curling pensively up her cheek. The accounts ran like this:-

Kitty Donegan	½	
Madge Mahoney	½	
Josie Mangan	1	and a appel
Peter Murphy	½	

Beneath was written at least twenty times over in great, innocent astonished letters 'Josie Mangan.' Beneath that again, 'K. Donegan lovs P. Murphy.' In the next page, 'Totell 2 pense and a appel,' altered on maturer consideration to '2½ and a appel.' Having pondered the matter still farther Josie struck out the appel and ate it.

But talk of the fiddler gradually excited her, and she grew envious of those who had found him first.

Sunday afternoon they set out, the whole gang, in ragged

formation, with all the inevitable squabbles. K. Donegan and P. Murphy headed the procession, Peter on Kitty's rusty skate. Kitty, the eldest, was a tall red-headed girl with delicate inflamed eyes and a rough face. She walked with an air of intense dignity, her red head in the air. She was in love and held her man in bonds as firm as any marriage contract with her skate, which she never for an instant allowed out of sight. To impress them all, she turned as they came to the big houses by the river's edge and let out a bawl.

'Come on aisy, can't ye? Can't ye behave yeerselves? The fiddler will be gone, Lord God, I won't come out any more with you, Josie Mangan!'

'Sure, 'tisn't my fault,' whined Josie. 'Look at Jackie.'

'Come on, Jackie, come on, love,' coaxed Kitty. 'Ah, sha, God love us! Come on now, Jackie boy, and you'll get a sweet!'

'Stop crying or you'll get a pucking,' added Josie, sniffing.

'I wants to go home!' yelled Jackie, and threw himself flat on the path. Kitty raised him and held him up by main force by the breeches.

'Almighty God, I'm cursed and damned,' declared Josie, red and tearful. Suddenly as the vision of the fiddler burst on her imagination anew, her tears changed to blind, un-reasoning fury. Her eyes blazed. She smacked Jackie's hands. She smacked his face. She pummelled his stomach till he doubled up and fell. She pinched his behind. She made faces at him. Jackie screamed. Josie caught one hand and Kitty the other, and between them they dragged him, kicking and squealing, behind them. Kitty's weight won the day. To save his arms from dislocation, Jackie had to run. By this time he had reached the stage where stupe-faction imposes itself, and the screams came only ten seconds or more after his will commanded them.

'Almighty God, grant the fiddler won't be gone!' prayed Josie.

Long before they came to the appointed place they stopped.

'Leave you go first,' said Kitty to Josie.

'No, leave you.'

'I won't. Leave Madge go.'

It was Peter who finally planned that they should disperse and approach the field from every side, like Indians. Because of her small brother, Josie was permitted to enter by the gate. The rest came across the overgrown grass fences. Like Josie, most of them pretended to be looking for flowers, though it was too early for primroses. She, with bent head, picked her way carefully as though in fear of overlooking some fugitive blossom, staying here and there between the bare trees and the shrubs. In a few minutes the old garden was alive with hushed and questing children. Suddenly there rose from somewhere a whisper that was repeated till it became a cry.

'They're not here!'

Into the clearing in the centre, where the hollow was, the children gathered with long faces. It was only too clear that the strangers were not there. Kitty Donegan pointed out the very spot where they had sat. Gloom fell on them all. Kitty sent out patrols to search the neighbouring fields. When they returned the gloom became blank and utter.

As they went homeward, squabbling and dispirited, Josie felt like tears. It was her rotten luck! Now the mysterious fiddler was gone, and would not return.

Three weeks later another miracle! A kite, a box-kite, had been seen along the river bank on Sunday, and the gang was off to investigate. 'Almighty God,' Josie prayed in her emotional way, 'grant the kite won't be gone!' Jackie was being whipped briskly along behind her. A March day of scurrying clouds, and wind and sunshine, and a May-blue sky shining and darkening behind the baby leaves. 'I'm threepence ha'penny now,' declared Josie irrelevantly. 'Ye'd better hurry up.'

'I'm threepence anyway,' said Kitty, clasping her skate under her arm.

'The summer'll be here any day now, so ye'd better hurry up,' continued Josie. 'We're a long way off sixpence yet, let alone a bob. How do ye think I can plot a picnic if ye won't even save up?'

Suddenly as they passed the field of their disappointment a strain of music rose in the air like a call.

'Sacred Heart!' cried Kitty dramatically, clutching her breast, 'they're there!'

The gang stopped, aghast, all thought of the kite banished, all stricken equally with irresolution. Finally, for want of a better plan, they agreed to do what they had done before, and soon the field was alive with bobbing heads like chickens. But for very shyness not a peg farther could they stir. A fierce dispute was going on about Kitty Donegan who was trying to bully Madge Mahoney into leading the way. It lost nothing in fierceness for being carried on in whispers. When at last Kitty threatened to go home and take the gang with her, Madge surrendered.

Slowly she left her lair, slowly she strode down the field, her hips swinging in the coyest of coy motions, her head on one side and her index finger between her lips. From their ambush the gang, some on all fours, some bent double, tensely watched her progress. She passed within a few yards of the two men, sidled by them with modestly averted eyes, went on another few yards, and then paused to admire the view of sleepy river and low hills. Apparently satisfied she drew up her frock with an old-maidish gesture and sat down, keeping her eyes all the while on the view before her. When three minutes had elapsed and nothing had occurred to her, when she had even plucked a blade of grass and sucked it nonchalantly, the better to show her indifference, Kitty went forth, birdlike, her head in the air, her lips pursed, her eyes nodding hither and thither with remote and circumspect interest. In a few minutes the whole gang was sitting with its backs to the two men.

The fiddle struck up again behind. All heads turned together. The fiddler looked up from his instrument and smiled. He was a good-looking man verging on middle-age, with a red-brown beard and blue eyes. The gang rose in mass and performed an encircling movement about him.

'Which of you can dance?' he asked, still bowing vigorously.

'She can, sir,' said Kitty Donegan treacherously, grabbing Josie by the arm. Josie grew red.

'Come on then — what's your name?'

'Josie Mangan, sir,' said the gang in chorus.

'Can you dance to that, Josie?'

'She goes to the Pipers' Club sir,' chorussed the gang.

'Ah, well, maybe that's too hard. Try a reel.' He changed the rhythm and broke into *Molly on the Shore*, and at the third bar Josie's feet began automatically to beat a response to the gay triplets. The girls stood with hands behind their backs, critically watching every step. As the music continued she took fire, the blood mounted her cheeks; she raised her head and stiffened her body till she felt it poised and motionless above her flying toes. It was impossible to make any real show of dancing in the grass where she couldn't hear as much as a heel-tap, but grass or no grass she was determined to captivate the fiddler. For the first time she found herself deliberately willing someone to admire her.

When the bell rang from the hill to call them to Benediction one star was alight, no bigger than the budding leaves among which it hung.

Each Sunday the gang went on its headlong way to the field. Sometimes their Fiddler was there, sometimes not. And always the evenings grew warmer and longer; they sat in the grass and told stories; over one night the trees seemed to shoot into leaf and bloom; and the decaying old garden came to life again. The hedges were thick with whitethorn; the fragrance was everywhere.

Sometimes the Fiddler and the Stutterer chattered while the children rambled away on their many quests. But they never knew what to make of the Stutterer. When he began to speak they looked at him in excitement, wondering what great things he was about to tell them. He would chuckle and choke and grow crimson, and wave his hands — but it never came to much that they could see.

But the Fiddler talked of everything under the sun, about Josie's father being a soldier and Josie's mother being dead, and Madge Mahoney being praised by the priest and

Peter Murphy's big brother being dead. He talked a lot about death; it seemed to fascinate him as much as the children; he harped back upon it, now lightly as though it were a great joke; then with gloomy insistence on the horrors of it, and yet again mysteriously, telling them of the Holy Souls in Purgatory or of ghosts.

He audited Josie's accounts which had assumed vast proportions and were very muddled, though this scarcely mattered because no one was likely to forget what was collected. The accounts merely defined Josie's authority which, in spite of Kitty Donegan, she was quietly but firmly extending. Sooner or later she intended to have her followers known to the world as 'Josie's Gang.' This authority was sometimes challenged, but she skilfully arranged for the Fiddler's support, and came out stronger than ever.

However, one day it came to open conflict. Kitty Donegan, with the aid of the skate and Peter Murphy, was endeavouring to split the gang. Josie lost her temper and called Kitty 'Sore-Eyes.' In spite of her age and size, Kitty was romantic and emotional. She broke down.

'You ought to be ashamed of yourself, Josie!' said the Fiddler sternly. 'It isn't her fault if her eyes are red. God made us all as we are, and when you mock anyone you're mocking the good God who created them.'

Josie, growing red, looked at him in consternation. Was this her Fiddler, holding her up to shame before her own gang? As surely as she had thought the gang hers she had looked on him as her vassal, and now he was taking the side of Kitty Donegan against her. Of the moral sense of what he said she didn't understand a word. All she knew was that her dream was shattered, herself an outcast and mere hanger-on in the new alliance between the Fiddler and Kitty. Tears flooded her eyes and she walked away. On the road she began to weep, her face buried in the grass of the wall. Jackie joined her. Only Jackie! The others, traitors and lip-servers, had gone over to the enemy.

'What is it, Josie?' he asked, beginning to cry, too.

'Never mind, Jackie!' she sobbed. 'They can have their

old gang! They can have their old fiddler! They can have their old picnic too! I'll give them back their money. And I hope to Almighty God it'll pour rain on them!'

'Oh, Josie,' he sniffed, 'won't there be no picnic?'

'And thunder,' she sobbed louder and louder. 'Thunder and forked lightning.'

'Josie,' he snivelled, 'I wants a picnic.'

'And the anger of God to strike them all dead!' hissed Josie bitterly through her tears.

She snubbed the gang. She gave them back their money. For a week she carried round a broken heart. On Sunday the pain became almost unendurable. She had sworn to avoid the field, but she couldn't. From the Cemetery Road where she was walking with Jackie she descended by a steep path to the river. There she heard the fiddle playing and everything came up once more in a flood of tears. She crept along the hedge to a spot from which she could see them, at least in part. All she did see was Madge Mahoney's dress, but it was enough.

'Stop crying, Josie!' said her brother.

'I can't,' she moaned. 'Me life is over. There's me thanks for all I done for them, all the trouble I had with the picnic and keeping the money and everything!'

Every step she took away from them seemed a step nearer her grave. She went up the road, partly from an almost unconscious intention to return when they were emerging and scorch them with a look. But when she did return they had gone; the field was deserted; a gold-brown cloudy evening had foundered in a drift of silver among the darkening leaves, and the river shone coldly beneath it.

When she reached home she found a letter awaiting her. Her heart leaped. It was from the Fiddler. In it he confessed that he was unhappy without her. He was sorry if he had hurt her; he had never meant to, and he would not have spoken like that to anyone else; it was only that a cross word sounded so nasty from a young girl of her Beautiful and Tranquil Disposition. There were other things, too, which she did not understand about the Purity of his Affection. Nor did they worry her. The great thing was that her ascendancy had been triumphantly re-established, and that Sore-Eyes Donegan had got a smack on the kisser.

On the following Sunday when she re-appeared he presented her with a lily.

'May you be always as pure as you are now!' he said.

Josie took the lily round to show the neighbours, and utilised the occasion to solicit subscriptions for the picnic. The Widow Crowley, who kept the little shop, gave a penny, but warned them against the Fiddler. And being the managing sort she was, she spread the warning, and each and all the children were instructed by their parents to avoid him.

At once the Fiddler became a secret, a conspiracy; in Josie's eyes her secret, her conspiracy; but it was Madge Mahoney, the slyboots, who had the inspiration. 'Maybe,' she said, 'if Josie Mangan asked him, he'd come on the picnic?'

The very thought made Josie crimson with delight. That would set her seal forever on the gang. Further, it would make every other gang hide its head, for never in anyone's memory had a gang taken a real fiddler with them on their picnic.

On the eve of the picnic, Josie and Kitty Donegan went into town to make the purchases. The market was crowded and the two girls pushed and shouldered their way excitedly about. Oranges fivepence a dozen, red apples fourpence ha'penny, russets threepence — they could bring themselves to buy nothing till they had handled the wares on every stall over and over again. Josie measured an orange with her fingers and then pushed her way, perspiring through the crowd, with her hand held in position to try another by.

'Almighty God,' she prayed, with closed eyes, 'grant we get sweet ones! Oh, Almighty God, I'd be disgraced forever if they were sour!'

She scarcely slept that night. Four or five times she rose and looked out at the sky.

'Almighty God,' she kept repeating in a fever, 'grant 'twill be fine! Oh, Almighty God, wouldn't it be awful if it rained?'

But it didn't rain. The morning broke cloudless and sunny and all the bells of the city were ringing joyfully. And there at the foot of the bed were the oranges and apples, russet and gold, a battered-tin kettle, rescued from an ash-bin, a teapot without a handle and two tin mugs. She sprang out of bed, dressed and ran downstairs, hot and sick with sleeplessness. Going into the kitchen she had a sudden feeling of giddiness, her head spun and she staggered. Mrs. Geney who cooked the meals for them looked round in surprise.

'What's wrong?' she asked.

'Nothing,' replied Josie sulkily.

Her father looked up from his newspaper.

'Now, mind ye,' he said sternly, 'look after yourself and Jackie. Don't sit in the sun. Don't go running under cars. Don't go too near the water. Don't eat too much of them apples or you'll be sick.'

'I'm going to go swimming,' said Jackie. Josie kicked him viciously under the table.

'You are not going to go swimming,' said his father. 'I'll flake the flaring divil out of you if I find you go swimming. And don't go sliding and tearing the seat out of your pants. And don't go near any stream or running water. And don't play hurley. Sit down quietly in the shade and enjoy yourself.'

Mrs. Geney laid a boiled egg before Josie. Then she put a rough palm under her chin.

'Look up at me,' she said.

Josie obeyed.

'I thought so.'

'What is it?' asked Mr. Mangan.

'Do you see anything?'

'N-n-o.' He looked at Josie critically through his spectacles.

'I see spots,' said Mrs. Geney.

'Lord God,' said Josie, beginning to sniff, ' 'twould be like you to see something.'

She had always disliked Mrs. Geney.

'You go back to bed till the nurse sees you, my lady.'

'I wo'not,' said Josie. 'They'll be up for me in a minute. She can see me as I am.'

'Do what you're told now!' replied Mrs. Geney.

Josie began to weep.

'Lord God, ever since you came into the house there's some misfortune down atop of me,' she moaned, climbing the stairs again. 'I wish to God I was dead and buried some place I'd be far away from you . . . Will you tell that old Crowley one to come quick, so?' she cried with a sudden change of tone. 'I'll be late for the train with you.'

She was scarcely undressed before the first of the gang was in her room. Sobbing, Josie recounted what had happened. A few minutes more and the whole mob were assembled about their fallen chief. All declared they could see no spots whatever. Josie had a mirror and kept glancing at herself in it. Then the Widow Crowley arrived, big-boned and cheerful and bossy.

'I'll give her something to make the spots come out,' she declared.

'But I'm all right, Mrs. Crowley,' cried Josie angrily.

'Of course you're all right, child.'

'But I'll be late for the train with you.'

'You can go by another.'

'What's the next?'

'Twelve,' said Kitty Donegan.

'Lord God,' said Josie, 'I'm cursed!'

'We'll wait for you, Josie,' said Kitty with sudden magnanimity.

'Will ye?'

'We will,' said the gang in resigned and melancholy tones.

'I'll come back in an hour or so and then we'll know,' said the Widow.

Camped on and about the bed, the gang discussed the many miseries caused them by the Widow. But Josie shook her head.

' 'Tisn't her at all I blame,' she declared. ' 'Tisn't her at all, but the bloody one downstairs.' She shook her fist in the direction of the door.

'Kitty,' she called in a feeble voice a moment later.

'Well?'

'Is there any spots now?'

'Naw,' replied Kitty with broad contempt.

' 'Tis all a plot of that one downstairs,' said Josie. 'Lord God, don't I know it? She's plotting this for months to spite me. No one knows what I suffered with her since me ma died. Oh, I wonder me ma's ghost don't haunt her!'

'It might yet,' said Madge Mahoney hopefully.

'That it might! That it might haunt her till she dies, raving mad! That's my prayer . . . . Madge, do you see spots?'

'Erra, no!'

' 'Tis a plot!'

'The train is gone,' said Peter Murphy with a sigh. And this reduced them all to silence. When the Widow returned Josie was vomiting and declaring frantically that she would be grand now.

Sorrowfully the gang took over the funds from her. Sorrowfully they shared out her portion of oranges and apples and sweets and buns. She lay there, sobbing, too miserable even to dispute. All day she thought of them, of the beach, of the Fiddler, her fiddler, who now, careless of her fate, was playing to them. All day she sobbed without ceasing. And at night she was lying in a long hospital ward that went up and down before her incredulous eyes like the deck of a ship. She thought hospitals at least should be kept still.

It was months before she was released. Summer was over, the days were drawing in. Of the Fiddler there was no further news; the gang had been remiss and for weeks had deserted their fortress. Maybe he had tired of waiting. Josie visited the field when the leaves were falling; she visited it three times before she realised that all was over. The Fiddler was gone.

(1936)

The Storyteller

Afric and Nance went up the mountain, two little girls in shapeless, colourless smocks of coarse frieze. With them went the lamb. Afric had found it on the mountain, and it insisted on accompanying her everywhere. It was an idiotic, astonished animal which stopped dead and bucked and scampered entirely without reason.

It was drawing on to dusk. Shadow was creeping up the mountain. First light faded from the sea, then from the rocks, then from the roadway and the fields. Soon it would dwindle from the bog; everything there would fill with rich colour and the long channels of dark bogwater would burn like mirrors between the purple walls of turf. Behind each of the channels was ranged a file of turf stacks, black sods heaped to dry and looking like great pine cones.

'And the priest came,' continued Nance, pursuing a litany.

'And what did he say?'

'He said — he said grandfather would die tonight.'

'You said 'twas the doctor said that.'

'The priest said it, too.'

'Hike, you divil!' yelled Afric. The lamb had walked straight up to the edge of a bog pool, bent down in innocent rapture and then tossed itself high into the air and off sideways like a crow.

'And mom said you were to stop talking about the boat.'

'What boat?'

'The boat you said would come for grandfather. Mom said there was no boat.'

'There is a boat. Grandfather said it. And lights.'

'Mom said there's no lights either.'

'Mom doesn't know. Grandfather knows better.'

'Mom said grandfather didn't mean it.'

'Ha!' said Afric scornfully.

' 'Tis true.'

'And I suppose he didn't mean about Shaun O'Mullarkey and the Sprid either. Or about Con of the fairies and the Demon Hurler. Or about the Gillygooley. Or the Gawley Cullawney and his mother.'

'Mom said,' continued Nance in the tone of one reciting a lesson, 'that 'twould be better for grandfather now if he hadn't so much old stories and paid heed to his prayers when he had the chance.'

'Grandfather always said his prayers. Grandfather knew more prayers than mom.'

'Mom said he told barbarous stories.'

'But if they were true?'

'Mom says they weren't true, that they were all lies and that God punishes people for telling lies and that's why grandfather is afraid to die. He's afraid of what God will do to him for telling lies.'

'Ha!' sniffed Afric again, but with less confidence. The mountain did not inspire confidence. The shadow, quickening its mighty motion, rose before them among the naked rocks. Two tiny stars came out, vibrating in the green sky. A pair of horses, head down before them, suddenly took fright and rushed away with a great snorting, their manes tossing and loose stones flying from their hooves. To the right, a cliff, a pale veil dropped sheer to the edge of a dark lake, and from its foot the land went down in terraces of gray stone to the sea's edge, a ghost-pale city without lights or sound.

It was queer. Afric thought the way Grandfather had stopped telling them stories all at once, the way he seemed to fix his eyes on the wall. Even when she had asked him about the boat he had only muttered. 'Whisht, child, whisht!' But all the same Afric knew that mom must be wrong. Grandfather had meant it all. There must be some other reason for his silence.

'Maybe death will come like a travelling man, like it came to some,' she said thoughtfully. 'A man with long, long legs and a bandage over his eyes. Maybe that's why grandfather would be afraid — a big man the size of a mountain. I'd be afraid of him myself, I'm thinking.'

It was almost dark when they reached the mountain top. There was a cold wind there, the grasses swayed and whistled, and their bare feet squelched calf-deep in the quaggy ground with its almost invisible hollows. Plunging on, they lost sight of the sea. The other side of the mountain came into view. A chain of lakes with edges like the edges of countries on the maps in school shone out of all the savage darkness, and beyond them, very far away, another inlet of the sea.

They almost failed to see the fire. It was in a deep natural hollow. It burned under a curiously shaped metal drum. On top of the drum was another metal container, narrow below and broad above like a bucket, and a jointed pipe led from this into a barrel with a tap on it. Under the tap was a mug covered by a strip of muslin. Four children were solemnly seated on the edge of the pit looking down on this queer contraption, their bare legs dangling in the firelight, their faces and heads in shadow. They were not speaking but looking with fascinated, solemn eyes at the still. Afric's father was standing before it, his hands in his trousers pockets. He was a tall, handsome man, big-shouldered, broad-chested, with a wide grey kindly face and grey eyes, but now he seemed melancholy and withdrawn.

'What way is your grandfather?' he asked.

'Mom said to tell you there was no change,' said Nance.

Nance and Afric sat within the hollow out of the wind

so that the heads and shoulders of the other children rose up on every side against the starlit sky like idols grouped in a circle. The lamb seemed to take the greatest interest in the whole proceedings, sniffed at the turf, the tub, the barrel, backed away from them, staggered to the mouth of the hollow and scampered back as though horribly shocked by something, licked the legs of the little girls and gazed with blank eyes into the fire. Its antics caused a sudden diversion among the four other children; they laughed without restraint. Then, as though they had grown self-conscious, they fell silent. Two wiped their noses in the sleeves of their little frieze jackets. Then they rose and went off silently down the mountain. After a few moments the other two did exactly the same thing. It was growing very dark.

Then their Uncle Padraic came, and, standing against the sky, leaned on a turf-cutting spade. You nearly always saw Padraic leaning on something; a wall, a turf-rick, the pillar of a gate — there always seemed to be something for Padraic to lean on. Whatever it was, his whole body fell lifelessly about it. He stood like that now against the sky, his hands resting in a crossed position on the handle, his chin resting on his hands. He was a tall gaunt, gentle man, wearing a frieze vest without sleeves over a knitted gansey and very much patched frieze trousers. He didn't say anything, but seemed to breathe out an atmosphere of tranquility. It looked as if he could go on leaning for ever without opening his mouth.

'Himself is the same way,' said their father.

Padraic spat sideways and rested his chin again upon his crossed hands.

'He is.'

They fell silent again. Their father dipped a mug in the barrel of ale and passed it up to his brother-in-law. Padraic drank and carefully emptied the mug onto the ground before returning it.

'One of ye better go for more turf,' said their father.

'I will,' said Afric. 'Keep a hold on the lamb, Nance.'

She took the bag and began to run down the mountain.

It was a high hollow starry night full of strange shadows. From behind her she heard Nance's cry of distress, and a few moments later something warm and white and woolly came between her flying feet and nearly threw her. She flung herself head foremost on the soft turf, rolling round and round downhill, while the lamb rolled idiotically on top of her, its warm nose seeking her face. There was a smell of earth and grass which made her drunk. She boxed the lamb's ears, caught it by the budding horns, pushed, shoved, wrestled and rolled with it.

'Ah, lambeen, lambeen, lambeen! You foolish lambeen! I'm going for turf and the fairies will catch you, the fairies will catch you! Look, lambeen, they're searching for you with little lanterns!'

She filled her bag with turf. The bog was now wild and dark. The channels of bogwater were shining with inky brightness; as though the bog were all a-tremble they shook, but with a suave oily motion that barely broke the reflected starlight. Below, very far below, were a few lights along the shore.

She recognized her own house on the little spit of land that pushed out into the hay. There was light only in the west window in the room where her grandfather was lying. She could imagine all the others in the kitchen in the fire-light; her mother and the baby, her mother's two sisters, old Brigid, their mother, sucking her pipe, and Padraic's children. They would be talking in low voices, and then her mother or old Brigid would go into the west room to the old man who would tell no more stories, and they would talk to him of the will of God, but still his face, pale as the little beard about his chin, would be bitter because he did not wish to die. Not wish to die and he eighty and more! And up on the mountain were she and her father, making poteen which would be drunk at the old man's wake, because he was a famous and popular man and people would come from twenty miles around on ponies and in traps to pray for his soul.

Maybe he was dying now! But Afric felt sure if he was dying there would be some sign, as there always was in the stories he told: along the road a huge man, dressed in rags, a bandage about his eyes and his hands outstretched, feeling his way to their house: all the air filled with strange lights while the spirits waited: a shining boat making its way across the dark water without a sail. Surely there would be signs like that! She looked about her furtively, suddenly trembling and all attune for the wonder. But there was nothing. Not a sound. In sudden panic she repulsed the lamb and began to run, her bag of dry sods knocking her shoulders.

It was all placid and homely up there. Padraic was sitting on an upturned tub, smoking. It was so silent you could hear the noise of the stream near-by, loud in the darkness. Her father came up from it, carrying a bucket.

'He had a long day,' he said, as though continuing a conversation.

'He had a long day,' agreed Padraic, not looking up. He spat and sucked his pipe again.

'He was a good man,' said Afric's father.

'He was. He was a good father to you.'

'He was so. 'Tis a pity he couldn't be more resigned.'

' 'Twas what they were saying.'

'He said a queer thing last night.'

'Did he now?'

'He says a man sees the world when he comes into it and goes out of it: the rest is only foolishness — that's what he said.'

' 'Tis a deep saying.'

' 'Tis deep.'

'But there's meaning in it.' Padraic went on.

'I dare say.'

'There is. He was always a deep man, a patient, long-thinking man.'

Afric was astonished. She never remembered her uncle to have spoken as much.

'Do you remember,' he continued, 'on the boat? He never liked one of us to do a thing in a hurry. 'Mother was drowned a year ago,' he'd say, 'and she'd have been round the lake since then.' That's what he'd always say.'

'He would so.'

' 'Tis a pity he didn't do more with himself — a clever man.'

' 'Tis. But he wouldn't stop in America.'

'He wouldn't sure.'

'There was nothing he cared about only the stories.'

'No, then. And he was a wonder with them.'

'He was. You wouldn't miss a day in a bog or a night in the boat with him. Often he'd keep you that way you wouldn't know you were hungry.' Afric's father spat. It was not often he made such admissions. 'And there were times we were hungry.'

'You never took after him, Con.'

'No, then. 'Twasn't in me, I suppose. But 'twasn't in our generation. I'd get great pleasure listening to him, but I could never tell a story myself.'

'The place won't be the same without him,' said Padraic rising.

'Ye'd better go home with yeer uncle,' said her father.

'I'll stop with you, Father,' said Afric.

He thought for a moment.

'Do so,' he said.

She knew then he was lonely.

When Padraic and Nance had gone, everything seemed lonelier than before, but she didn't mind because her father was with her. He wrapped his coat about her. The lamb snuggled up beside her. And now she let the mountain come alive with all its stories and its magic. Because she knew it was up here the spirits lived and planned their descents on the little cottages; at night you could often see them from the bay, moving across the mountain with their little lanterns. Sometimes the lights would be close together and you would know it was a fairy funeral. A man from the place, making poteen in the mountains at night, had come across just such a funeral, and the spirits had laid the coffin at his feet. He had opened it, and inside was a beautiful girl with long yellow hair. As he looked at her she had opened her eyes and he had brought her home with him. She had told him she was a girl from Tuam, and when inquiries were made it was found that a girl from Tuam had been buried that same day; but she wouldn't go back to her own people and remained always with the man who had saved her and married him.

Afric could see her father moving about in the smoky light, his legs seeming immense. Sometimes she saw his face when he bent to the fire. Then he sat on the upturned tub with his head between his hands. She went to sleep at last.

When she woke again the helmet of shadow had tilted. It was cold. The high hollow drum of the sky had half filled with low drifting vapours. Some one — she did not know who — was speaking to her father. Then he caught her in his arms, and the jolting and slithering of his feet in the long slopes wakened her completely. He stumbled on blindly as though he did not know she was in his arms. Even when she looked at him he did not seem to be aware of her.

There was a little crowd kneeling even at the door of the west room. The kitchen was in darkness only for the firelight, and this and the flickering of candles made the west room unusually bright and gay. The people kneeling there rose and made way for her father. He put her gently down on a stool by the fire and went in, taking off his hat. The low murmur of prayer went on again. Afric tiptoed to the room door. Yes, the west room was very bright. Her grandfather's great bearded head was lying, very pale and wasted over the bowed heads under the light of two candles. Her father was kneeling awkwardly by the bedside, covering his face with his hands. Her grandmother, old Brigid, suddenly began to keen and sway from side to side.

Afric went out. She looked up and down the lane. She was looking with a sort of fascinated terror for the big man with the bandage over his eyes. There was no sign of him. The lane was quiet only for the whispering of the bushes and a blackbird's first bewildered, drowsy fluting. There were no lights, no voices. Frightened as she was, she ran down the lane to the little cove where her father's boat was drawn up among the slimy rocks and seaweed. Over it was a grassy knoll. She ran there and threw herself on her face and hands lest anyone should spy her and take fright. The light was breaking over the water. But no boat came shining to her out of the brightness. The blackbird having tried his voice, threw it out in a sudden burst of song, and the lesser birds joined in with twitters and chuckles. In the little cove there was a ducking of water among the dried weeds, a vague pushing to and fro. She rose, her smock wet, and looked down into the cove. There was no farewell, no clatter of silver oars or rowlocks as magic took her childhood away. Nothing, nothing at all. With a strange chocking in her throat she went slowly back to the house. She thought that maybe she knew now why her grandfather had been so sad.

(1937)

Mac's Masterpiece

Two or three times a year Mac, a teacher in the monks' school, took to his bed for four or five days. That was understood. But when he gave up taking food his landlady thought it was getting serious. She told his friends she wanted to have his certified. Not another day would she keep him in the house after the abominable language he had used to her.

His friends, Boyd, Devane and Corbett, came. Mac refused to open the bedroom door. He asked to be allowed to die in peace. It was only when Boyd took a hatchet to the lock that he appeared in his nightshirt, haggard and distraught, a big, melancholy mountain of a man, dribbling, his hair in tumult.

'Almighty God!' he cried. 'Won't I even be allowed that one little comfort?'

They wrapped him in blankets and set him by the fire among his discarded toys, his dumb-bells, chest-developers, Indian clubs, sabres, shot-guns, camera, cinema, gramophone and piano, while Corbett, the bright young man from the local newspaper, heated the water for the punch. At this Mac came to himself a little and insulted Boyd. Boyd was his foil; a narrow-chested, consumptive-looking chemist with a loud voice and a yapping laugh like a fox's bark. He wore a bowler-hat at various extraordinary angles and was very disputatious.

'Bad luck to you!' growled Boyd. 'I don't believe there's anything up with you.'

'Nothing up with me!' jeered Mac. 'Devane, did you hear that? You know, Devane, that hog, unless you had a broken neck or a broken bottom, he'd say there was nothing up with you. He'd say there was nothing up with Othello or Hamlet. "Nothing up with you!" Did anybody ever hear such a barbarous locution?'

'Come on away, Corbett,' said Boyd angrily. 'We might have know the old cod was only play-acting as usual.'

'Don't rouse me now,' said Mac with quiet scorn.

'Like an old actress when she's going off, pretending her jewellery is stolen.'

'I won't be roused,' said Mac earnestly. 'What's that Lear says — "No, I'll not weep, this heart shall crack . . ." You Philistine, you Christian Brothers' brat, you low, porter-drinking sot,' he snarled with sudden violence, 'I have a soul above disputing with you . . . . Devane,' he added mournfully, 'you understand me. You have a grand Byronian soul.'

'I have nervous dyspepsia,' groaned Devane, who was organist in the parish church. He felt himself in two or three places. 'I get terrible pains here and here.'

'I see you now as I saw you twenty years ago with the fire of genius in your eyes,' Mac went on. 'And now, God help you, you go about the streets as though you were making a living by collecting lost hairpins.'

Devane refused punch. It made his stomach worse, he said.

'You're better off,' said Mac, falling serious once more. 'I say you're better off. You see your misery plain. You're only a little maggot yourself now, a measly little maggot of a man, hoping the Almighty God won't crush you too soon, but you're a consistent maggot, a maggot by night and by day. But in my dreams I'm still a king, and then comes the awakening, the horror, the gray dawn.'

He shuddered, wrapped in his blanket. Corbett rose and began to fiddle with the gramophone.

'Don't break that machine,' said Mac irritably. 'It cost a lot.'

'What you want is a wife,' said Corbett. 'All those gadgets are only substitute wives. Did you ever get an hour's real pleasure out of any of them? I bet you never play that gramophone.'

'You have a low mind, Corbett,' snarled Mac. 'You impute the basest motives to everyone.'

At that very moment Corbett placed the needle on the record. There was a startling series of cracks and then it began to give off *La Donna e Mobile*. Mac jumped up as though he had been shot.

'Oh God, not that, not that! Turn it off! There, you've done it now.'

'What?' asked Corbett innocently.

'Sunlight on the Mediterranean, moonlight on the Swiss lakes, the glowworms in the grass, young love, hope, passion.'

He began to stride up and down the room, swinging his blanket like a toga.

'The last time I heard that' — he stretched out his arm in a wild gesture — ''twas in Galway on a rainy night. Galway in the rain and the statue of O'Conaire in the Park and the long western faces like — like bullocks. There they were over the roulette-tables, counting out their coppers; they had big cloth purses. Then suddenly, the way-you-may-call-it organ began . . . Magic, by God, magic! It mounted and mounted and you knew by the shudder down your spine that 'twas all on fire; a sort of — a sort of pyramid — that's it! — a pyramid of light over your head. Turning and turning, faster and faster, the pyramid, I mean, and the lights crackling and changing; blue, red, orange. Man, I rushed back to the hotel, fearing something would spoil it on me. The last light was setting over the church tower, woodbine-coloured light and a black knot of weeping cloud.'

'Bravo, Mac!' said Boyd with his coarse laugh. He stuck

his thumbs into the armholes of his waistcoat. 'The old warrior is himself again. Haw?'

'Until the next time,' said Corbett with a sneer.

'There'll be no next time,' said Mac solemnly. 'I'm after being down to hell and coming back. I see it all now. The Celtic mist is gone. I see it all clear before me in the Latin light.'

And sure enough there was a change in Mac's behaviour. He almost gave up drink and began to talk of the necessity for solitude. Solitude, he said, was the mind's true home. Solitude filled the cistern; company emptied it. He would stay at home and read or think. He began to talk of a vast novel on the subject of the clash between idealism and materialism in the Irish soul.

But the discipline was a hard one. Though he told the maid to say he was out, he hated to hear the voices of Boyd or Corbett as they went off together down the quay. One evening as they were moving away he knocked at the window and raised the blind, looking out at them and nodding. He tried to assume a superior, amused air, but there was wistfulness in his eyes. Finally he raised the window.

'Come on out, man!' said Boyd scornfully.

'No, no, I couldn't,' replied Mac weakly.

' 'Tis a lovely night.'

'What way did ye come?'

'Down High Street. All the shawlies were out singing. Look, 'tis a gorgeous night. Stars! Millions of them!'

Softly in a wheezy tenor Boyd sang *Night of Stars and Night of Love* with declamatory gestures. Mac's resolution wavered.

'Come on in for a minute.'

They climbed over the low sill, Boyd still singing and gesturing. As usual, he had an interesting item of news for Mac. The latest scandal; piping hot; another piece of jobbery perpetrated by a religious secret society. Mac groaned.

'My God, 'tis awful,' he agreed. ''Tis, do you know what

it is, 'tis scandalous.'

'Well, isn't that what we were always looking for?' exclaimed Boyd, shaking his fist truculently. 'Government by our own? Now we have it. Government by the gunmen and the priests and the secret societies.'

' 'Tis our own fault,' said Mac gloomily.

'How so-a?'

' 'Tis our own fault. We're the intellect of the country and what good are we? None. Do we ever protest? No. All we do is live in burrows and growl at all the things we find wrong.'

'And what else can we do? A handful of us?'

'Thousands of us.'

'A handful! How long would I keep me business If I said or did what I thought was right? I make two hundred a year out of parish priests with indigestion. Man, dear, is there one man, one man in this whole town can call his soul his own?'

'You're all wrong,' said Mac crossly, his face going into a thousand wrinkles.

'Is there one man?' shouted Boyd with lifted finger.

'Bogy men!' said Mac, 'that's all that frightens ye. Bogy men! If we were in earnest all that tangle of circumstance would melt away.'

'Oh, melt away, melt away? Would it, indeed?'

'Of course it would. The human will can achieve anything. The will is the divine faculty in man.'

'This is a new theology.'

' 'Tisn't theology at all; 'tis common sense. Let me alone now; I thought all this out long ago. The only obstacles we ever see are in ourselves.'

'Ah, what nonsense are you talking? How are they in ourselves?'

'When the will is diseased, it creates obstacles where they never existed.'

'Answer me,' bawled Boyd, spitting into the fire. 'Answer my question. Answer it now and let Corbett hear you. How are the obstacles in ourselves? Can a blind man paint a picture, can he? Can a cripple run the thousand yards? Haw?'

'Boyd,' said Mac with a fastidious shudder, 'you have a very coarse mind.'

'I have a very realistic mind.'

'You have a very coarse mind; you have the mind of a Christian Brothers' boy. But if you persist in that — that unpleasant strain, I'm more ready to believe that a blind man can paint a picture than that a normal, healthy man can be crippled from birth by a tangle of irrelevant circumstances.'

'Circumstances are never irrelevant.'

'Between the conception and the achievement all circumstances are irrelevant.'

'You don't believe in matther? Isn't that what it all comes to?'

'That has nothing to do with it.'

'Do you or do you not believe in matther?' repeated Boyd, throwing his bowler viciously onto the floor.

'I believe in the human will,' snapped Mac.

'That means you don't believe in life.'

'Not as you see it.'

'Because I believe in life,' said Boyd, his lantern jaw working sideways. 'I believe that in all the life about me a divine purpose is working itself out.'

'Oh, God,' groaned Mac. 'Animal stagnation! Chewing the cud! The City Council! Wolfe Tone Street! Divine purpose, my sweet God! Don't you see, you maggot, you clodhopper, you corner boy, that life can't be directed from outside? If there is a divine purpose — I don't know whether there is or not — it can only express itself through some human agency; and how the devil can you have a human agency if you haven't the individual soul, the man representing humanity? Do you think institutions, poetry, painting, the Roman Empire, were created by maggots and clodhoppers? Do you? Do you? Do you?'

Just then there was a ring at the door and Devane came in, looking more than ever like a collector of lost hairpins.

'How are you, Devane?' asked Corbett.

'Rotten,' said Devane.

'I never saw you any other way,' growled Mac.

'I never am any other way,' replied Devane.

'You're just in time,' said Corbett.

'How so-a?'

'We're getting the will versus determinism; 'tis gorgeous. Go on, Mac. You were talking about the Roman Empire.'

Mac suddenly threw himself into a chair, covering his face with his hands.

'My God, my God,' he groaned softly between his fingers. 'I'm at it again. I'm fifty-four years of age and I'm talking about the human will. A man whose life is over talking about the will. Go away and let me write me novel. For God's sake let me do one little thing before I die.'

After that night Mac worked harder than ever. He talked a great deal about his novel. The secret of the Irish soul, he had discovered, was the conflict between the ideal and the reality.

Boyd, with whom he discussed it one night when they met accidentally, disputed this as he disputed everything.

'Idealism, my eye!' he said scornfully. 'The secret is bloody hypocrisy.'

'No, Boyd,' protested Mac. 'You have a mind utterly without refinement. Hypocrisy is a noble and enlightened vice; 'tis far beyond the capacity of the people of this country. The English have been called hypocritical. Now, nobody could ever talk about the hypocritical Gael. The English had their walled cities, their castles, their artillery, as the price of their hypocrisy; all the unfortunate gulls of Irishmen ever got out of their self-deception was a ragged cloak and a bed in a wood.'

'And is that what you're going to say in your novel?'

'I'm going to say lots of things in my novel.'

'You'd better mind yourself.'

'I'm going to tell the truth at last. I'm going to show that what's wrong with all of you people is your inability to reconcile the debauched sentimentalism of your ideals with the disorderly materialism of your lives.'

'What?' Boyd stopped dead, hands in his pockets, head forward. 'Are you calling me a sentimentalist?'

'I'm only speaking generally.'

'Are you calling me a sentimentalist?'

'I'm not referring to you at all.'

'Because I'm no sentimentalist. I'm a realist.'

'You're a disappointed idealist like all the rest, that's what you are.'

'A disappointed idealist? How do you make that out?'

'Boyd, I see ye all now quite clearly. I see ye as if I was looking at ye from eternity. I see what's wrong with ye. Ye aim too high. Ye hitch yeer wagon to too many bloody stars at the one time. Then comes the first snag and the first compromise. After that ye begin to sink, sink, sink, till ye're tied hand and foot, till ye even deny the human soul.'

'Are you back to that again? Are you denying the existence of matther again?'

'Materialist! Shabby little materialist, with your sentimental dreams. I see ye all there with yeer heads tied to yeer knees, pretending 'tis circumstance and 'tis nothing only the ropes ye spin out of yeer own guts.'

Boyd was furious. It was bad enough to have Mac dodging him, telling the maid to say he was out, forcing him to spend long, lonely evenings; but then to call him a sentimentalist, a materialist, a disappointed idealist! In fact, all Mac's friends resented the new state of things. They jeered at the tidy way he now dressed himself. They jeered at the young woman with whom he was seen taking tea at the Ambassadors'.

Elsie Deignan was a pretty young woman of thirty-two or three. She was a teacher in the nuns' school in the South Parish and had literary leanings. As a result of her experiences with the nuns, she was slightly tinged with anticlericalism. For the first time in his life Mac felt he had met a woman whose conversation he might conceivably tolerate over an extended period. He fell badly in love.

The resentment of Mac's friends grew when he was seen walking out with her. And there were strange stories in circulation about the things he was saying in his novel. They were all going into it, and in a ridiculous fashion. They were pleased when Corbett told them that Mac's employers, the monks, were getting uneasy, too. Mac knew far too much about the Order. He had often referred scornfully to the disparity between their professions and their practice; was it possible that he was revealing all this? Corbett swore he was; he also said that one chapter described the initiation of a young man into the Knights of Columbanus, skulls, cowls, blindfolding, oaths and all.

'I suppose he thinks he'll be able to retire on the proceeds of it,' said Boyd in disgust. 'The English will lap that up. I hate a man that fouls his own nest.'

'Well, don't we all?' groaned Devane, who alone of the gang was disposed to be merciful.

'That's different,' said Boyd. 'We can say things like that among ourselves, in the family, so to speak, but we don't want everyone to know about it.'

'He showed me a couple of chapters,' said Devane mournfully. 'I didn't see anything at all in it. Sentimental stuff, that's how it looked to me.'

'Ah, but you didn't see the big scenes,' said Corbett. 'And for a good reason.'

'What reason?'

'There are several nasty things about you in it.'

'He couldn't say anything about me,' said Devane.

'That's all you know.'

'By God,' said Boyd, 'he deserves all he gets. If there's anything worse than a man using his friends for copy, I don't know what it is.'

Devane, perturbed, slipped away. After a good deal of thought he went along the quays to Mac's lodgings, his head down, his umbrella hanging over his joined hands, a picture of misery. Mac was busy and cheerful. Sheets of foolscap littered the table. He had been drinking tea.

'So you're still at it,' said Devane.

'Still at it.'

'You're a brave man.'

'How so?'

'All the dovecots you're after putting a flutter.'

'What the hell are you talking about?'

'I hear the monks are very uneasy.'

'About my novel?' asked Mac with a start.

'Yes.'

'How did they get to hear of it?'

'How do I know? Corbett says they were talking to the Canon about you.'

Mac grew pale.

'Who's spreading stories about me?'

'I don't know, I tell you. What did you say about me?'

'I said nothing about you.'

'You'd better not. You'll cause trouble enough.'

'Sure, I'm not saying anything about anybody,' said Mac, his face beginning to twitch.

'Well, they think you are.'

'My God, there's a hole to work in.' Mac suddenly sat back, haggard, his hands spread wide before him. 'By God, I have a good mind to roast them all. And I didn't get to the serious part at all yet. That's only a description of his childhood.'

'I didn't see anything wrong with it — what you showed me,' said Devane, rubbing his nose.

'By God, I have,' repeated Mac passionately, 'a thorough good mind to roast them.'

'You're too old,' said Devane, and his metallic voice sounded like the spinning of a rattle. 'Why don't you have sense? I used to want to be a musician one time. I don't want anything now only to live till I get me pension. You ought to have sense,' he went on in a still crankier tone. 'Don't you know they'll all round on you, like they did on me the time I got the organ?'

' 'Tis the curse of the tribe,' declared Mac despairingly. 'They hate to see anyone separating himself from the tribe.'

'I don't know what it is,' said Devane, 'and I don't give a damn. I used to be trying to think out explanations, too, one time, but I gave it up. What's the use when you can read Jane Austen? Read Jane Austen, MacCarthy, she's grand and consoling, and there isn't a line in her that would remind you of anything at all. I like Jane Austen and Trollope, and I like Rameau and Lully and Scarlatti, and I'd like Bach too if he was satisfied with writing nice

little dance-tunes instead of bloody big elephants of Masses
that put you in mind of your last end.'

Devane left Mac very depressed. The news about the
novel had spread. People discussed it everywhere; his
enemies said they had never expected anything else from
him; his friends were uneasy and went about asking if
they shouldn't, as old friends of Mac's, advise him. They
didn't, and as a result the scandal only spread farther.

With Elsie, Mac permitted himself to rage.

'By God, I will roast them now,' he said. 'I'm going to
change the whole centre part of the book. I see now where
I went wrong. My idea was to show the struggle in a man's
soul between idealism and materialism; you know, the
Celtic streak, soaring dreams, 'the singing masons building
roofs of gold', the quest of the absolute; and then show how
'tis dragged down by the mean little everyday nature of
the Celt; the mean, vain, money-grubbing, twisty little
nature that kept him from ever doing anything in the
world only suffer and twist and whine. But now I see a
bigger theme emerging; the struggle with the primitive
world — colossal!'

'You're marvellous,' said Elsie. 'How do you think of it
all?'

'Because I'm it,' said Mac vehemently. 'I am the Celt. I
feel it in my blood. The Celts are only emerging into
civilization. I and people like me are the forerunners. We
feel the whole conflict of the nation in ourselves; the individual soul and at the same time the sense of the tribe;
the Latin pride and the primitive desire to merge ourselves
in the crowd. I can see how 'twill go. My fellow will have
to sink himself time and time again, and then at last the
trumpet call! His great moment has come. He must say
farewell to the old world and stand up, erect and defiant.'

Still, Mac found his novel heavy going. It wasn't that
ideas didn't come to him; he had too many, but always
there was the sense of a hundred malicious faces peering
over his shoulder; the Canon and Corbett; Devane, Cronin,
Boyd; the headmaster.

Then one evening the maid came to his room.

'Oh, by the way, Mr. MacCarthy, the Canon called looking for you.'

'Oh, did he?' said Mac, but his heart missed a beat.

'He said he'd call back another time.'

'Did he say what he wanted?'

'No, Mr. MacCarthy, but he seemed a bit worried.'

The pages he had written formed a blur before Mac's eyes. He could not write. Instead he put on his hat and went up to Elsie's.

' 'Tis all up,' he said.

'What?' she asked.

'Everything. Turned out on the roadside at my age to earn my living what way I can.'

'Do you mean you're sacked?'

'No, but I will be. 'Tis only a matter of days. The Canon called to see me. He never called to see me before. But I don't care. Let them throw me out. I'll starve, but I'll show them up.'

'You're exaggerating, Dan. Sure, you didn't do anything at all yet.'

'No, but they know what I can do. They're afraid of me. They see the end of their world is coming.'

'But did anything else happen? Are you guessing all this or did somebody tell you?'

'I only wish to God I did it thirty years ago,' said Mac, striding moodily about the room. 'That was the time when I was young and strong and passionate. But I'm not afraid of them. I may be a fallen giant, but I'm still a giant. They can destroy me, but I'll pull their damn' temple about their ears, the way Samson did. It's you I'm sorry for, girl. I didn't know I was bringing you into this.'

'I'm not afraid,' she said.

'Ah, I'm a broken man, a broken man. Ten years ago I could have given you something to be proud of. I had genius then.'

After leaving her he called at Dolan's for a drink. Corbett and some of the others were there and Mac felt the necessity for further information. He resolved to get it by bluff. He'd show them just what he thought of all the pother.

'I hear the church is going to strike,' he said with a cynical laugh.

'Did you hear that, too?' exclaimed Corbett.

'So you know?'

'Only that old Brother Reilly was supposed to be up complaining of you to the Canon.'

'Aha! So that's it, is it?'

'I hope to goodness it won't be anything serious,' said Corbett despondently.

'Oh, I don't care. I won't starve.'

'You're a bloody fool,' said Cronin, the fat painter who had done the Stations of the Cross for the new parish church. 'Don't you know damn' well you won't get another job?'

'I won't. I know quite well I won't.'

'And what are you going to do? I declare to God I thought you had more sense. At your age, too! You have a fine cushy job and you won't mind it.'

'Not at that price.'

'What price? What are talking about? Haven't we all to stand it and put the best face we can on it?'

'And damn' well you paid for it, Cronin!'

'How so?'

'You're — how long are you painting? — twenty-five years? And worse and worse you're getting till now you're doing Stations of the Cross in the best Bavarian style. Twenty-five years ago you looked as though you might have had the makings of a painter in you, but now what are you? A maggot like the rest of us, a measly little maggot! Oh, you can puff out your chest and eat your moustache as much as you like, but that's what you are. A maggot, a five-bob-an-hour drawing master.'

'MacCarthy,' said Boyd, 'you want your backside kicked, and you're damn' well going to get it kicked.'

'And who's going to do it, pray?' asked Mac coolly.

'You wait till you get the Canon down on you; he won't be long about it.'

'Aha,' said Mac. 'So the Canon is our new hero! The Deliverer! This, as I always guessed, is what all the old talk was worth. Ye gas and gas about liberty of conscience, but at the first whiff of powder ye run and hide under the Canon's soutane. Well, here's to the Canon! Anyway, he's a man.'

'Are you accusing me of turning me coat?' bawled Boyd.

'Quiet now, Boyd, quiet!'

'Are you?'

'Boyd, I won't even take the trouble to quarrel with you,' said Mac gravely. 'You've lost even the memory of a man. I suppose when you were twenty-five or so you did hear the clock, but you don't hear it any longer.' He sipped his pint and suddenly grew passionate. 'Or do you? Do you? Do you hear the inexorable hour when all your wasted years spring out like little toy soldiers from the clock and present arms? And does it never occur to you that one of these days they'll step out and present arms and say: "Be off now you bloody old cod! We're going back to barracks!".'

It was late when he left the pub. He was very pleased with himself. He had squelched Cronin, made Boyd ridiculous, reinstated himself with the gang, proved he was still the master of them all. As he came through the side streets he began to feel lonely. When he came to the bridge he leaned over it and watched the river flowing by beneath.

'Christ, what a fool I am! What a fool!' he groaned.

For a long time he stood on the quay outside his own lodgings, afraid to go in. The shapes of human beings began to crowd round him, malevolent and fierce, the Canon, the head, Cronin, Boyd, Devane. They all hated him, all wished him ill, would stop at nothing to destroy him.

In the early morning he went downstairs, made a bonfire of his novel, and sobbed himself to sleep.

(1938)

The Climber

When Josie and Jackie Mangan met the two little boys in Eton jackets walking up the narrow pathway past their home, they stood and gaped. The older of the two boys blushed and raised his cap, and Josie gaped more than ever for no one had ever done such a thing to her before.

'Hallo,' she said experimentally, turning and staring after them.

'Hallo,' replied the boy who had raised his cap, halting uncertainly.

'Come on away!' said his brother anxiously.

'Why don't ye come down the river,' asked Josie.

'We wouldn't be left,' said the boy.

'Who wouldn't leave ye?'

'Me mother.'

'Christmas!' said Josie. 'Who's your mother?'

'Mrs. Donoghue, the dressmaker.'

'My ould fellow is a sailor. Why wouldn't she leave ye?'

'Because it wouldn't be right.'

'Come on away!' insisted his brother, with a trace of a whine in his voice.

'We have to go now.' he said apologetically. 'Me mother will be expecting us.'

Josie thought she had never met such a nice boy. In due course he explained why he and his brother were not permitted to associate with the other children.

'We're a terrible respectable family,' he said, his voice solemn with his great responsibility. 'There are three branches of our family, the Neddy Neds and the Neddy Joes and the Neddy Thomases. The Neddy Neds are the oldest branch. My mother is a Neddy Ned. My grandfather was the best-behaved man in Bantry. When he was at his dinner the boys from the school used to be brought up to study him, he had such grand table manners. He opened the skull of an uncle of mine with the poker for eating cabbage with a knife.'

'Oh, Christmas!' cried Josie.

'My mother would be a rich woman only her father used her fortune to back a bill for a Neddy Thomas. Tim here is going to be a doctor and I'm going to be a solicitor. We're learning the violin only I have no ear. Dempsey, the gardener in the lodge, is teaching us. He only knew jigs and reels but me mother made him teach us classical music.'

'What's that?' asked Josie.

' "Maritana" is classical music. And "Alice Where Art Thou?" 'Tis much harder than ordinary music. It has signs on it and when you see the signs you know 'tis after turning into a different tune although 'tis called the same. Irish music is all the same tune and that's why me mother wouldn't leave us learn it.'

'Oh, Jay!' sighed Josie in an ecstasy of enlightenment.

'Where does your father sail?' young Donoghue asked politely.

'He don't sail anywhere now only down the river. He gave up the sea after me mother died.'

'Was he ever shipwrecked?' asked Donoghue.

'He was shipwrecked on a desert island.'

'Were there cannibals on it?'

'He didn't say. He killed a Lascar once.'

'There must have been mutiny on the boat,' Donoghue said thoughtfully. 'Whenever there's mutiny on a boat they kill the Lascars.'

'Why don't ye come down the river?' asked Josie again. 'We have a raft.'

'I'd love to,' he said, 'but me mother wouldn't leave us.'

Josie's father allowed her to do everything so long as she washed her face and didn't tell lies. The dressmaker's son had filled her with a sense of the poverty of these prohibitions. She wanted to be respectable. For hours she walked up and down outside the dressmaker's house, the door of which was always shut. She wanted Jackie to keep his hands clean; she nagged at Mrs. Geney, their father's housekeeper, to let him wear his clean suit instead of the old blue gansey.

'Couldn't you buy us a new dress even?' she said to her father.

'Isn't the one you have good enough?' Mr. Mangan bellowed.

'It is not good enough. No wonder the dressmaker says we're not good enough for her.'

'What dressmaker?' Her father pulled his beard. 'Who says we're not good enough? . . . I like her cheek,' he snorted when Josie had told her story. 'Let me tell you, young woman, that before the Donoghues were heard of the Mangans were there; and will be, please God, when they're planted. Ask her is there e'er a poet in the Donoghue family. And when she talks of money ask her did she ever hear tell of Mary Mangan of the Mountain Mangans whose fortune was spent on her wake. Ask her did she hear of Binoculars Mangan, the famous explorer that discovered the island of Pottyloo off the east-coast of India.'

For the first time Josie had a feeling of the social inadequacy, even the improbability of Binoculars Mangan and the island of Pottyloo. Very thin they seemed beside the Neddy Neds and the Neddy Thomases. More than ever she wanted to be respectable. She refused to go out with the other children; she stole Jackie's new cap from the drawer where Mrs Geney kept it, wrapped in its original tissue, and led him out by the hand.

'Now, will you keep on raising your cap,' she said. 'I don't know what sort of way you were dragged up at all, but you should always raise your cap to a lady. And if anyone raises his cap to me you ought to do the same.'

'Where are we going, Josie?' he asked.

'We're not going anywhere,' she replied firmly.

'I want to go somewhere,' he whined.

'Well, you can't. Respectable people never go anywhere. They only goes for walks.'

'I don't want to go for walks. I wants to go down the railway and look at the engines.'

'You're taking after your ould father,' Josie said morosely. ' 'Tis easy seen you're his son. A wonder he wouldn't make ould Geney keep the front door closed. You can't even sit down to a cup of tea but there's someone in on top of you, gabstering. Me father and you are lick alike. Here's Mrs. Dunphy along now. Raise your cap to her, you little caffler.'

At teatime, Mr. Mangan came in looking radiant.

'Well, I had a long chat with your little dressmaker,' he said jovially.

'How did you meet her?' Josie asked suspiciously. She felt cold and sick at the very thought of it.

'I dropped in on her, of course. Did you think I was going to let her go off with the notion that the Mangans weren't good enough for her?'

'Oh, Christmas!' said Josie. 'Now we're properly ashamed!'

'How ashamed?' cried her father angrily. 'She was delighted to meet me, of course — a very nice little woman! A charming little woman! Now she knows what a remarkable father you have. I was telling her about the time I was working in the pawn when I used to collect the loan money on the old nag. I had her splitting her sides about the hundredweight of sprats and the three-legged pot.'

'And maybe you told her how the *Avoca* went out with the drunken crew?' hissed Josie on a rising wail of anxiety.

'I did of course; and how they baptized the new pier, and the gentry had the punch made with salt water, and all the ambulances of Cork were waiting to take them home.'

'I might have known it,' said Josie between her teeth. 'I

might have known you'd disgrace me.'

She was weeping when Mr. Mangan came in to say good-night. He looked at her in astonishment.

'Here,' he said coaxingly, 'sit up now and I'll do Shylock for you.'

'You needn't mind,' she replied, turning to the wall.

For two days she was so miserable that she scarcely left the house. Even Mrs. Geney at last asked her what was wrong but Josie rejected her sympathy.

'Ah, you'll have good reason to cry before you're done,' Mrs. Geney said darkly. 'Mark my words, you'll weep salt tears over your respectability, so you will.'

Mrs. Geney's mysterious prophecy came true sooner even than she expected. That evening Mr. Mangan turned to Josie.

'You're to go down to the dressmaker's to tea tomorrow night,' he said. 'You and Jackie. And see ye wash yeer dirty faces before ye go.'

'Were you in blowing to the dressmaker again?' she asked.

'None of your impudence now, young madam,' he replied. 'You're getting too saucy. You want someone to keep you in hand.'

'Meaning that I'm not able to do it?' asked Mrs. Geney in a sudden fury that bewildered Josie.

'What's up with you?' asked Mr. Mangan. 'I never meant anything of the kind.'

'Oh, we know what you meant all right. We're not good enough for you now since you got the dressmaker.'

'What dressmaker, woman? What the blazes is after coming over you? And what's that thing on the mantelpiece?'

'Nothing,' she snapped. 'A little ornament I found in the back room, that's all.'

' 'Tis the bird from my wedding cake, and well you know it, you malicious ould hag.'

Mr. Mangan rose and stamped out of the house in a rage.

'Ah!' said Mrs. Geney gleefully. 'That put him out. Now he won't be so easy in his mind, the ould show; gladhiatoring like that at his age; he ought to be ashamed of himself and all the talk he had about your poor mother, God rest her!'

'But what's he doing, Mrs. Geney?' Josie asked.

'Doesn't the whole parish know he's in at the dressmaker's night after night? And what is he doing it for?'

'Do you mean he's going to marry the dressmaker?'

'Of course he is. And isn't that what you wanted? Didn't you want to be respectable? Now you'll be respectable whether you like it or not.'

Respectability suddenly lost half its value in Josie's eyes. She lost all desire to reform her feckless father; in fact he seemed nicer as he was. She had very little pleasure in the tea party next evening. Mrs. Donoghue was a tall, handsome woman; she shook both Josie and Jackie warmly by the hand. Josie took an almost violent dislike to handshaking. The table was laid with cups and saucers all of the same size and pattern. The two boys kept pushing plates toward Josie; pressed her to scones, cakes, and bread and butter. She wished they would let her alone and allow her to have her tea in peace.

'And now,' said the dressmaker, 'you and the boys must be good friends. I do not like them to associate with the other children; they are too rough, but you and Jackie are different. I am sure you will be able to show them some nice walks.'

Next day the two boys called for Josie and her brother. By this time she was disillusioned regarding the charms of walking. Like Jackie, she wanted to go somewhere.

'What'll we do then?' asked young Donoghue.

'I'm going down the railway,' she said ungraciously. 'I don't mind what ye do.'

'We'll come, too,' he said.

Josie led her little army along the river and through the busiest portion of town to the railway.

'Goodness!' said Donoghue, 'we were never as far as this before.'

'This is nothing,' said Josie eyeing him with contempt. 'We goes down the river on picnics and to the castle and everything.'

'I was never in a castle,' he said. 'Are there dungeons? You might find human bones in the dungeons.'

He was enchanted by the shining engines, moving slowly up and down the myriad lines of rails and crashing into long trains of wagons. Just to show him how little even this meant, Josie brought them back by the river to show him the loading and unloading of ships.

' 'Tis going to be great fun being with you,' he said with a little sigh of pleasure. 'I never did things like this before.'

'Ah, wait'll you see the raft,' said Josie.

'I know I'm going to like you. And I like your father a lot. He did Shakespeare for us one night. And he gave mother the prescription for the rheumatics that he got from the Zulu chief.'

Josie looked after him from the garden gate with a smile that was half pity, half chagrin.

'I'd like to do something to him,' she said, 'but I haven't the heart. I suppose he's nice in spite of his old one and her notions. Oh, Christmas, wasn't I a gom, thinking there was anything in being respectable. Themselves and their shaking hands and their "How-are-yous" and "thanks" and "won't-you-have-some-cakes?" If me father brings that one into the house I'll walk out of it. Look, I'm that desperate I'd do anything at this minute. I'd smoke fags or ring bells or anything.'

'Did ye see yeer father?' Mrs. Geney asked when they entered.

'No,' said Josie. 'Didn't he come in yet?'

'I don't care if he never comes in again,' cried Mrs. Geney and most alarmingly burst into tears.

'What's he after doing now?' asked Josie in panic.

'He's after shaving off his beard that he never touched since the day your mother was buried.'

His face when he came in presented a sight so horrible that Josie could not bear to look. It was round and chubby and chinless; it had lost all its majesty and romance; it looked ridiculous.

'Jackie!' Josie called to the distant cot as she got into bed.

'What is it now?' moaned Jackie.

'I'll have no mercy on him.'

'On who, Josie?'

'On the dressmaker's son. I was only going to get him to destroy his suit; and even that much I hadn't the heart to do; but now, I'll ruin him. I'll have the most terrible revenge anyone ever heard of.'

'What are you going to do?' asked Jackie.

'You'll see soon enough. They'll kill me, but I don't mind.'

Next day, when the two boys called, Josie declared they would not go either to the castle or the raft, on both of which young Donoghue seemed to have set his heart. Instead she took them up the hill and paused beside a high wall.

'We're going to climb this,' she said firmly.

'I could never climb that,' he said, looking up.

'If I can do it you ought to be able,' she sneered. 'You can stand on my shoulder.'

'But won't we be stopped?'

'Why should we be stopped? Isn't the gardener a friend of my da's?'

'Was he a sailor, too?' he asked innocently.

'He was.'

There was a great deal of difficulty in bundling the two respectable children over the wall, and it was not done without damage to their clothes. They found themselves in a wide orchard which sloped uphill. Josie led them to where a big house shone in the sun with all its width of red wall.

'Take a couple of apples,' she said.

'But will we be left?'

'Of course we will. Stuff yeer pockets well with them.'

'She helped to stuff their pockets. Next moment there was a shout and, dropping the apple which she had been trying to stuff into Donoghue's trouser pocket, Josie was off without as much as one backward glance, dragging Jackie behind her by the hand. The two boys stood stock-still, petrified by fear and bewilderment. Then they ran, too, but by this time Jackie was already over the wall and Josie following him. The two boys stood at the foot of the wall casting up glances of wild appeal, but she ignored them. She looked at the woman in riding breeches and carrying a horsewhip who was almost on top of them — the terrible Mrs. Ryder-Flynn who was reported to have the legs of a greyhound and the arms of a prizefighter. Then she loosed her hold and fell. She picked herself up, weeping though the fall had not hurt her. She was suddenly filled with remorse and pity; she felt that whoever had said revenge was sweet didn't know what he was talking about. Jackie, munching an apple, eyed her respectfully. When they got to the end of the road they saw Mrs. Ryder-Flynn emerging from her gate with a Donoghue in each hand.

Both Josie and Jackie were in bed when their father came in that evening. There was a lot of talk between himself and Mrs. Geney. First it was heated: then it dropped to a friendly mumble. Mr. Mangan came in on tiptoe. He stood at the head of Josie's bed. She pretended to be asleep.

'Ah, you fly boy!' he muttered. 'You're your father's daughter. You were too good for me. I have a good mind to murder you.'

Josie ceased to breathe.

'Sacked, dismissed, booted out without mercy. You limb of the divil. If I was another father I'd lace you within an inch of your life. Here, sit up now till I do Shylock for you.'

'Daddy!' Josie sat bolt upright in bed. 'Do Romeo.'

'I thought you said you didn't like that.'

'Never mind. Do it. can't you?'

'Aha, so that's what you were up to? All right. You're Juliet. Jackie, you can be Tybalt. Tybalt is the saucy bloke I killed. Now I'm coming into the vault with me little lantern.' He took up the candlestick and began to creep on tip-toe about the room. 'Disgraced before the world, indeed. I have a good mind to wring yeer necks, the pair of ye!'

'Is that in the play, daddy?' asked Josie.

'It is not. Shut up now. Tybalt, you little divil, will you keep quiet? How the blazes can I think you're dead if you kick like that?'

Josie sighed ecstatically. Though chinless and chubby, her father was his old feckless self again.

(1940)

Hughie

I know we should all have respected Doctor Hugh Daly more. I know we shouldn't have laughed; that he was a self-made man, a man who had risen by his own efforts; a specimen of the new Irish democracy and all the rest of it; I know all that; but to us he was just plain Hughie, and Hughie he will remain to his dying day. Mind you, you couldn't help liking him, and we always began by admitting that; we liked him, we loved him; we agreed that he deserved every credit, but it always ended by somebody saying 'Ah, Jay, do you remember when he was a curate in Jackie Roche's pub?' and from that on, we laughed and laughed.

That, by the way, was true. I mean, about his being a curate in Roche's. You would go in for a drink and find Hughie in his shirt sleeves, reading a book; a handsome, melancholy-looking man with a long thin face, dark, piercing eyes, and a shrill, monotonous, penetrating voice that was almost as inhuman as a bird's cry. He had a ravishing smile, a smile that flooded every inch of his face, but it was like winter sunlight, and when it faded his face relapsed into the most appalling melancholy.

'What's that you're reading?' you'd ask, by the way of

no harm.

'Ah, a small thing,' Hughie would say, tightening his thin little lips. 'A little philosophy book.'

'Oh, and what the blazes use is philosophy to you?' you'd ask.

'What use is philosophy to me?' he would cry, growing quite angry. 'Ah, musha, what sort of education would a man have without a bit of philosophy? Look, now, here by my hand on the shelf! What do you see?'

'What else only a bottle?' you'd say cautiously, wondering what trick he was playing on you.

'O! O! O!' Hughie would wail. 'I'm surprised at you, positively surprised at you! I wouldn't mind if 'twas only a poor working man, but a man like you, a university man! You do not, indeed, see a bottle. Far from it! What you see, my friend is only one side of a bottle. You deduce the existence of the bottle.'

He grew quite angry about it, even embittered. Once he did it to a crowd of quay-labourers, and they were sure he was ridiculing them, and smashed a couple of dozen bottles before the guards succeeded in clearing the pub. Hughie, of course, was the principal witness.

'Now, Mr. Daly,' said Phil Regan, the labourers' solicitor, in his most earnest tones, 'what damage do you say these poor men did?'

'They broke seven bottles of wine and two bottles of whiskey,' said Hughie.

'Now, are you sure of that, Mr. Daly? Remember, you're on your oath!'

'Ah, my goodness,' wailed Hughie, 'didn't I see it with my own two eyes?'

'Oh, Mr. Daly, Mr. Daly,' exclaimed Regan, 'I'm surprised at you! I am indeed! If it was a poor man like one of my clients, but an educated man like yourself! Sure doesn't the whole world know that 'twas only the side of the damage you saw? You deduced the existence of the damage.'

The whole court began to laugh; Hughie laughed as well, for he had a great gift of laughing at his own absurdities; his mind brightened and clouded as rapidly as his face; but poor Jackie Roche had no cause for laughing, and Hughie decided on a change of career.

'Ah,' he sighed, 'the people in this country have no respect for education! No respect, no respect! I'm going in for the law.'

'Why the law?' somebody asked.

'Ah, my goodness,' said Hughie, 'what a noble career! I can see myself like Daniel O'Connell rescuing poor innocent men from the gallows.'

It was Phil Regan, the solicitor, who persuaded him to go for medicine instead; of course, by persuading him that it was by far the nobler career of the two; Hughie's ideals were nothing if not exalted. That was one thing that made for Hughie's success; he took advice. Another was the way he worked; he surprised us all, because many a day the poor devil must have gone without his dinner, and but for Phil Regan's help he would scarcely have got through his course at all. They were the best of friends; the most strangely assorted pair one could imagine. Phil was a toady and diner-out who was forever making fun of the new democracy; small, rosy, plump, popeyed, with eyebrows like angle irons — his most expressive feature — and three deep lines across his forehead that emphasised them; a forelock in three little loppery ringlets, like a baby's. A civil servant's wife couldn't drop a brick but Phil was there to pick it up and hand it back to her. Hughie was tall, lank and miserable, and could never get any of the social details right. Phil chose his clothes for him; his ties, his stockings; Phil told him what knives to use, what tips to give. Every mess that Hughie was in — and he was always in some mess — he came to Phil to help him out; and then the savage streak in Phil appeared, and he began to mock Hughie till the two of them were at one another's throats.

'I despise you, Mr. Regan,' Hughie would say in a rasping voice which he took to be cold and dignified, while his neck swelled and his lean face grew purple, 'I despise you. You are nothing but a base materialist, a man without spirituality, without idealism or vision.'

'And what are you, Hughie?' Phil would ask, getting

cooler and more murderous at every word.

'I am an idealist,' Hughie would say in a trembling voice. 'A man with his eyes always on the stars. I wish to God I never met you. You've dragged me down with you, into the gutter.'

'But, Hughie,' Phil squeaked, the laughter coo-coo-cooing in his throat, his angle irons shooting up into his bulgy forehead, 'what would you do without me? Wasn't it I made you? You're not going to pretend that the Almighty God ever made a man like you? I made you, out of nothing. Even that tie you're wearing, Hughie. I chose it for you, and I showed you how to tie it. Only for me, Hughie, you'd be wearing a made-up tie.'

'There!' Hughie said in a frenzy, tearing off his tie and trampling on it, 'I trample on the tie as I trample on you and your abominable atheism. Leave me alone, please! Never let me set eyes on you again.'

Next day they would have made it up and be as thick as ever, and Phil would have another yarn about Hughie's vagaries. They couldn't exist apart — Pygmalion and Galatea: an artist and his creation.

Hughie was the oddest doctor that ever left a university. He had a bedroom manner, picked up from Phil, which was guaranteed to scare the wits out of a rugby footballer. Because he liked to air his knowledge to patients and their friends, he sat on the edge of the bed with his hands on his knees and a meditative air; thinking aloud, and enumerating every possible diagnosis with its complications. When he had bad news for relations he almost wept. 'Masses!' he would say sorrowfully, shaking his head. 'Masses!' He did that once in a house and they said when he went to the bathroom to wash his hands he called out brightly, 'Mrs. Kinsella, your cistern is out of order and I'm going to fix it for you.'

It was amazing how he got on, in spite of it all. He often talked of marriage. Phil urged him on to it. He even had the woman for him; another doctor, neither too young nor too good-looking but with a rising family behind her and an excellent practice.

'You see, Hughie,' said Phil, 'it'll be the making of you.'

'Oh, I know, I know,' Hughie said sadly. They were walking in the moonlight along the bank of the river.

'You're only at the beginning of your career, man! There's nothing you can't hope for.'

'Ah,' Hughie wailed, 'that is true; I know it; but I am a strange man, Phil. I cannot do without poetry.'

'Poetry? You have as much poetry in your constitution as a fried egg. You can have all the poetry you want on one month of Tessie Delaney's income.'

'Regan,' said Hughie seriously, with a throb of indignation in his voice, 'you are a very coarse man. I really don't know why I stand your company at all.'

'Well, I'll tell you,' hissed Phil. 'Because I'm the only one that leads the sort of life you'd like to lead; the life you would have led if only you'd been brought up in a civilised country. Damn it, man, don't you see what I'm trying to do for you? I'm trying to humanise you. What you need is mistresses; scores of mistresses, to take the Celtic chill out of your blood.'

'Ah, go away you blackguard,' said Hughie with a flattered laugh.

'But it's true for me. Oh, I know what you really did when you went to Paris with Jimmie O'Brien. You went to the Folies Bergères and you hissed! Yes, you hissed! You're a little coward.'

'Sir,' said Hughie magnificently, 'I allow nobody to call me a coward.'

'Go to hell and marry your waitress,' said Phil.

But for some reason Hughie was very slow about taking Phil's excellent advice. He did something he had never done before. He asked advice of a young girl in the house where he was lodging. She was a tall pale-gold scared-looking girl, a post office clerk, who looked like a figure out of a Rossetti picture.

' 'Tis a serious choice,' Hughie said. 'Of course, I have my career to think of. Up to this I got on well; fairly well; he added, with a melancholy air, for fear he might have committed himself too far; 'I have nothing really to complain of. But as Phil says 'tis a man's marriage decided what way he's to go when he's over forty. Many a good doctor made a mess of his life because of some good-looking nurse he got too close to in a hospital ward.'

'Indeed, yes, doctor,' said the girl, 'I suppose 'tis a danger.'

' 'Tis a terrible danger,' wailed Hughie. 'Ah, sha, don't I know it well?'

'I think your friend gave you very good advice,' she said.

'Ah yes,' sighed Hughie, 'but of a wet winter evening when I come home after a hard day's work, in and out of stuffy rooms, and I come in here and see the fire lighting, I sometimes imagine I see a little gold head in an armchair beside the fire. I'm a lonely man, Miss Foley; you mightn't think it, but I suffer the torments of the damned from melancholia, and sometimes when I wake in the morning, and hear the little birds singing outside my window I wonder to myself what are they singing for, and whether 'tis worth it all. And Doctor Delaney won't cure me of my melancholia, Miss Foley! Indeed, she won't! Far from it!'

'But how do you know that anyone else will?' she asked.

'Ah, now, wasn't I right?' Hughie said, laughing and staring at her in admiration. 'I knew when I saw you that you were a girl after my own heart. You have none of those foolish notions that girls pick up out of books. You are a sensible girl! Love is all very well; it is a pleasant illusion; indeed, yes; but it does not last and a practice does.'

He promised to speak immediately to Doctor Delaney about it, and the servant in the lodging house reported that he had a big box of chocolates in the top drawer of his dressing table. But he said no more about it to Miss Foley, and it was she who opened the subject herself to him one night when they found themselves alone in the sitting room.

'Did you speak to Doctor Delaney yet, Doctor Daly?' she asked.

'Ah, no, no,' Hughie replied with a pained look, his dark eyes piercing her and his little thin lips setting into a firmer line. 'Not yet, but I will. I will do it soon. Dear me,

I know well it is a chance I shouldn't let slip.'

'Still, I wonder,' she said with a worried look. She was a serious little soul with the face of a saint, and a shy pale smile that always trembled on the verge of tears. 'I don't know, of course, but, listening to you, I wondered whether there wasn't somebody else you preferred to the doctor.'

'Yes,' Hughie admitted tightly, 'there is.'

'And does she care for you, doctor?' she asked shyly.

'Perhaps she does,' Hughie said with a broad smile that faded in the queer way his brightest smiles always faded, into a look of blank and utter melancholia.

'Then don't you think you mightn't be doing the wisest thing after all? Haven't you money enough? What use will more money be to you if you don't love Doctor Delaney?'

'What use will money be to me?' Hughie asked in exasperation, his voice growing shriller. 'Ah, Miss Foley, a man like me that knows what poverty is like doesn't talk that way. Indeed no! And what is love that a man should give up all his chances in life for it? I knew all about it when I was your age. I was in love with a girl in Kerry; a simple girl; a labourer's daughter. It was with her that I really knew what love meant. I still have some of the letters she wrote me when I went away. Will I read one of them to you?'

'If you like, Doctor Daly,' she said with a startled air.

'Indeed, I'll do nothing of the kind,' said Hughie impatiently. 'What a thing I'd do! There! Read it for yourself. 'Tis only a simple letter, written by an uneducated girl.'

She read it, with a half-smile on her lips.

'And you never went back?' she asked.

'Ah, how could I go back?' asked Hughie angrily, his lips set, his eyes piercing hers. 'I had my career to think of. How could I think of getting married at that age, with all my studies before me? . . . Ah,' he cried, gazing at the ceiling, 'I wonder who she married after? Some farmer, I suppose, or some poor labourer like her father. And sometimes I wonder in the evenings when her husband is out at the pub, and the children are asleep, does she ever think of the old days when we used to go walking together. Ah, dear me!'

Miss Foley got up with her weak smile.

'There's your letter, Doctor Daly,' she said. 'I think men are awful, with nothing in their minds only money and advancement.'

He saw tears in her eyes but before he could reply to her, she had left the room and gone upstairs to her own bedroom. Hughie smiled, folded the Kerry girl's letter and put it back in his wallet.

Next evening when Miss Foley came in from work he was waiting for her in the hall and called her into the sitting room.

'I have some news for you,' he said with a laugh.

'Is it all settled?' she asked eagerly.

'Ah, is what settled?' he asked angrily.

'About the doctor?' she said with her timid smile. 'I thought that was what you were going to tell me.'

'Ah,' he said in a fury, 'what is all this talk about the doctor? What has the doctor to do with it?'

'But you said you wanted to marry her,' she persisted with a nervous laugh. 'You did, doctor, you did really.'

'Ah, I never thought of marrying that black devil,' said Hughie, with a thundercloud on his face. 'What a fool I'd be!'

'Then it's the other girl you're going to marry?'

'You're getting nearer it,' replied Hughie with a shy smile.

'And it's all settled?'

'It will be soon, I hope.'

'I'm so glad,' she said earnestly. 'I think you're doing the right thing. I think you'll make a good husband, and that God will bless your marriage.'

'I think so too,' said Hughie.

'But you must get it settled soon,' she said with her eager laugh. 'You mustn't put it off and off while you make up your mind. Remember she has a mind to make up too. You may be late, Doctor Daly.'

'I needn't put it off any longer,' he said angelically.

'Well, don't! Do it to-night!'

'I'm doing it now,' he said cryptically, his head bowed, 'this very minute.'

She looked at him with a puzzled frown.

'Now, Doctor Daly?'

'Ah,' he said, 'sure you must have known?'

'Do you mean me, Doctor Daly?' she asked incredulously.

'Ah, of course I do, who else?' he said shortly. He was a little put out by her evident surprise.

'But, but' her mouth laughed while her eyes were troubled, 'I couldn't possibly marry you.'

'Why not?' Hughie's voice was as shrill as an angry seabird's and he stared at her in a startled way.

'Because I'm engaged to be married to somebody else. He isn't a doctor or anything of the kind. He's only a clerk in the Post Office, but I'm very fond of him, and we're going to get married as soon as we can save enough.'

'Oh, oh, oh!' Hughie cried in an agonised voice, hitting himself on the temples with his fist. 'Isn't this terrible? And what am I going to do now?'

'I'm sure there are lots of girls who'd be proud to marry you. Maybe you might even think of that poor girl in Kerry,' she suggested timidly with sudden emotion. 'Maybe she never got married after all. She may still be waiting for you.'

'Ah,' he said cantankerously, 'what girl in Kerry? There's no girl in Kerry.'

'But, doctor, you showed me a letter from her! And I thought you were cruel; honestly, I did. I thought if you were the man I imagined you were you'd have gone back and married that poor girl; even if she wasn't as grand as some of your grand friends. She might have made you a better wife than any of them.'

'But when I tell you there's no girl in Kerry,' said Hughie indignantly. 'There never was a girl in Kerry. I wrote that letter myself because I thought it would interest you. But I see now you were a stupid sort of girl. you did not understand what was in my mind at all. I don't know now what I'm going to do. I must go and ask advice of Phil Regan.'

He did, and Phil strode around the room chuckling as he

listened to the story. Then he drove Hughie straight to the doctor's, to anticipate any possibility of its reaching her ears first. Hughie came out pale but engaged, and is now easily the most successful doctor in the county. It was said that Phil had to be restrained from accompanying them on the honeymoon. But what is quiet certain is that he and Phil are now strangers, because Mrs. Daly did not think Phil sufficiently well-mannered for the society to which she was accustomed. Phil could hardly believe his ears when first he was refused admittance. He and Hughie met a few days late in a pub.

'Here,' Phil said, 'what's all this about your wife and me?'

'Ah, marriage, marriage!' sighed Hughie cryptically.

'You're not going to pretend you're happy with that woman?'

'Indeed, I am happy,' said Hughie indignantly. 'Of course,' he continued in a wail, 'life is not a bed of roses for anyone. Dear me, no.'

'And you're going to let that jade prevent our meeting again?'

'Ah, to be sure, I'll meet you often enough,' said Hughie.

'You won't invite me to your house?'

'Ah, confound it, man!' cried Hughie hammering the counter, 'wasn't it you made me marry her? Wasn't it you with all your old blather that led me astray? It serves you right.'

And then, his sense of humour overcoming him, he chuckled, shook his head and went home exultantly.

(1941)

Last Post

Bill Cantillon and the sergeant-major went together to Sully's wake. It was a lovely summer's evening, and a gang of kids were playing at the end of the lane, but the little front room was dark only for the far corner where poor Sully was laid out in his brown habit, with the rosary beads twisted between his fingers. Jerry Foley was there already with Sully's sister and Mrs Dunn. He opened a couple of bottles of stout, while the other two said a prayer, and then they all lit their pipes and sat around the table.

'Yes,' said Bill, with another glance at the corpse, "twasn't to-day nor yesterday, Miss Sullivan. We were friends when I knew him first in the Depot, forty-three years ago.'

'Forty-three years!' exclaimed the sergeant-major. 'My, my!'

'Forty-three years,' Bill repeated complacently. 'October '98; I remember it well. That was when he joined.'

'He was a bit wild as a boy, sir,' Mrs Sullivan said apologetically, 'but, God help us, that was all! There was no harm in him.'

'If it comes to that, ma'am,' said the sergeant-major, 'we were all wild.'

'Ah, yes,' said Bill, 'but wildness like that — there's no harm in it. We were young, and high-spirited; we wanted to see a bit of the world; that was all. Life in a town like this, with people that know you, 'tis too quiet for boys of mettle.'

' 'Tis,' the sergeant-major agreed, ' 'tis a bit slow.'

' 'Twas the excitement,' Bill said, with a nod to the company, 'that's what we fancied.'

'Oh, and God help us, ye got it,' Sully's sister said quietly, rocking herself to and fro. 'Oh, my, and never to know till you heard his knock at the door; it might be two or three in the morning, and to see him standing outside with his kitbags and his rifle, after travelling for days.'

'Oh,' said Jerry, 'the kids playing outside there now will never see some of the things we saw!'

'And weren't we right?' exclaimed Bill. 'Weren't we wiser in the heel of the hunt? Now, thanks be to God, after all our rambles, we're back among our own. We have our little pensions; they may not be much, but they keep us independent. We can stroll out of a fine summer's morning and sit in the park and talk about old times. And we know what we're talking about. We saw strange countries and strange people. We're not like some of the young fellows you meet now, small or bitter or narrow.'

'Ah,' said Jerry, mournfully, 'we weren't a bad class at all. We had great spirit.

'And have still,' said the sergeant-major.

'We have,' said Jerry, 'but we're dying, and there's no one to take our place. Sully is the fourth this year. We're going fast; and one of these days the time will come for one of us; we'll be laid out the way poor Sully is laid out; the neighbours will sit round us and somebody will say: "That's the last of them gone now: the last of the old Munster Fusiliers. There isn't one left alive of the old Dirty Coats, that great regiment that carried the name of Ireland to the ends of the earth." '

And left their bones there, Jerry,' said the sergeant-major.

'Oh, God help us, they did, they did,' said Mrs. Dunn, and she burst into tears. The men looked uncomfortable.

'I'm very sorry, ma'am,' said the sergeant-major. 'Very sorry, indeed. I had no idea.'

' 'Twas her son, sir,' Sully's sister said in a quiet, little voice.

'My little boy, sir,' sobbed Mrs Dunn. 'Hardly more than a child. He was wild, too, sir, like you said, but there was no harm in him. Mr. Sullivan knew him. He was well liked in the regiment, he said.'

'We'll go out to the kitchen now and let the men have their little drink in peace,' said Miss Sullivan.

'I'm sorry, gentlemen,' Mrs Dunn said from the door. 'Ye'll excuse me. it comes over me whenever I think of old times. But, oh, Mr. Cantillon, wasn't it queer, wasn't it queer, with all the men that knew him and liked him, that he could go like that on me without tale nor tidings?'

'Who did you say that was, Bill?' whispered the sergeant-major.

'Mrs Dunn,' replied Bill. 'You must have seen her before. Every old Munster that dies, she's at his wake.'

'Dunn?' said the sergeant, with a puzzled frown. 'Dunn? What happened him? Killed?'

'No, missing.'

'Dunn? I have no recollection of the name.'

'Hourigan was the name,' Bill said softly. 'Dunn was his step-father. That was why the boy ran away from home.'

'And that's why she has it on her mind,' said Jerry. 'Every wake of every old Munster, she's at it, hoping she'll get news of him. For years after the war, as long as people were turning up anywhere over the world, she was still expecting he'd turn up. If you ask me, she's still expecting it.'

'Ah, how could she?' said Bill.

'I don't think the poor soul is right in her mind,' said Jerry softly. 'A woman like that is never right unless she can have her cry out. I think she still imagines that one night when she's sitting by the fire she'll hear his step coming up the lane and see him walk in the door to her: a man of — how old would he be now? He was only sixteen when he ran away.'

'Oh, God help us! God help us!' said the sergeant-major. 'He was young to die!'

And in the darkness they heard a man's step come up the lane, and a moment later a devil's rat-tat at the door. Mrs Dunn ran to open it.

'Broke!' exclaimed Bill with a grin.

The new arrival stumped in the hall and stood in the doorway with his cap pulled over one eye; a six-footer slumped about a crutch, and under the peak of the cap a long grey haggard face, a bedraggled grey moustache and mad, staring blue eyes. His real name was Shinnick. In France he had lost his leg and whatever bit of sense the Lord had given him to begin with. People said he was queer because he had spent so long at the front without leave. No sooner was he due for it than something occurred; he was detained for looting, leaving his post or beating up an N.C.O. They said he had earned the D.C.M. several times over and lost it again by his own foolishness — a most unfortunate man. Now he had a bed in the workhouse. He got a shilling or two for looking after the corpses. Once a month he came out and drew his pension, and after a day or two stumped back to the workhouse again — without a fluke! A most unfortunate man!

The three old soldiers looked at one another and winked. Broke was notorious for the touch. He could fly like a bird, crutch and all; head and neck strained forward like an old hen; he hadn't a spark of shame, and thought nothing of chasing a man the length of the Western Road on nothing more substantial than the smell of a pint.

'So ye're all there?' he snarled. with a grin of wolfish good-humour.

'We're all here, Joe,' Jerry said good-naturedly.

'I suppose 'twas the porter brought ye?' Broke said with a leer.

'Whisht, now, whisht,' said Bill. 'Remember the dead!'

'Ah, God, Sully, is this the way I find you?' said Broke in a wail as he threw down his crutch and manoeuvred himself on to his one good knee by the bed. 'Ah, Sully, Sully, wasn't it queer of God to take a good man like you instead of some old cripple like myself that was never no use to anybody?' He was sobbing and clawing the bedclothes with his face buried in them. Then he grabbed the dead man's hands and began kissing them passionately. 'Do you hear me, Sully boy, wherever you are to-night? Tell them who you left behind you! Tell them I'm tired of the world! I'm like the Wandering Jew, and I'm sick of pulling and hauling.   Do you hear me. I say? I made corpses and I buried corpses, and I'm handling corpses every day of the week; the smell of them is on me, Sully, and 'tis time my own turn came.'

'Here, Joe, here,' said Jerry, tapping him on the shoulder, 'sit in my chair and drink this.'

' 'Twasn't for that I came,' Broke said passionately, staring from the glass of stout to Jerry and back again.

'Sure, we know that well, old soldier,' said Jerry.

'But 'tis welcome all the same,' said Broke, swinging himself to his full height and staring down at Jerry with his queer piercing eyes. ' 'Tis my one bit of consolation. I have the pension drunk already, Jerry. As true as God I have! Jerry, could I — ? my old campaigner!'

'Ah, to be sure you could,' said Jerry.

'Wan tanner, Jerry!' hissed Broke feverishly. 'That's all I ask.'

'There's two of them for you,' said Jerry.

'May God in heaven bless you, my boy,' said Broke as the tears began to pour from his eyes. 'I'm an affliction; an old sponger, a good-for-nothing. 'Twill be a relief to ye all when I go ... Cantillon,' he snarled with an astonishing change of tone, 'put something to that like a decent man!'

'I suppose this is for the publicans?' said Bill with a scowl.

'And what do you think 'tis for, hah?' jeered Broke. 'A bed in a hospital?' With a toothless smile he whipped off his old cap and waved it before the sergeant-major's face. 'Make up the couple of bob for me, sir,' he said. ' 'Tis for the couple of drinks, I'm telling you no lies.'

Then he sat in Jerry's chair, a high-backed armchair with low arm-rests, and took a deep swig of his stout. He was restless; he glared at them all by turns; the face, like the body, lank and drawn with pain.

'Is he having a band?' he asked suddenly.

'Ah, where would he get a band, man?' snapped Bill.

'And isn't he damn well entilted to it?' said Broke.

'Begor, you couldn't get one now if you were a general,' said the sergeant-major.

'And why couldn't ye?' cried Broke. 'What's stopping ye? The man should have his due. Give him what he's entitled to, his gun-carriage and his couple of volleys . . . . Company!' he shouted. 'Reverse arms! Slow . . . . march! Strike up there, Drum Major!'

It was very queer. He raised his crutch and gave three thumps on the floor. Then, very softly, with an inane toothless smile, he began to hum the Funeral March, swaying his hand gently from side to side. The old soldiers bent their heads reverently and Bill began to beat time with the toe of his boot.

'That's a grand tune, that Chopin,' the sergeant-major said.

'I heard it one time played over a young fellow in the Sherwood Foresters,' Bill said. ' 'Twas in Aldershot, and I never forgot it.'

'Ah,' said Jerry, 'for a dead march there's nothing like the pipes. You should hear the Kilties play 'The Flowers of the Forest.' There's a sort of a —'

'There is,' said the sergeant-major. 'A sort of a wail.'

And in the dark room, by the light of the flickering candles, they began to talk of all the soldiers' funerals they had attended, in Africa, in India and at home, and the mothers began to shout from the doorsteps, 'Kittyaaa! Juliaaa!' and the children's voices died away, and there was no longer any sound but some latecomer's boots echoing off the pavements, and all the time Broke hummed away to himself, swinging his crutch like a drum major. His voice grew noisier and more raucous.

'Mind yourself or you'll do some damage with that crutch,' said the sergeant-major.

'The bloody man is drunk,' Bill said savagely.

'He isn't drunk, Bill,' Jerry said quietly. 'Watch his face!'

They stared at him. Suddenly, in the middle of a bar, he stopped dead, laid down the crutch and began to stare over the back of his chair. His face had a curious strained look. With his tongue and teeth he produced a drubbing sound — dddddrr! The old soldiers looked at one another. They heard another sound that seemed to come from very far back in Broke's throat, travel up the roof of his mouth and then expand into a wail and sudden thump — wheeeee-bump! And at the same moment Broke raised his two arms over his head and crouched down in the chair, grasping and staring wildly about him.

'Aha, Jackie,' he said in a high-pitched, unnatural voice, 'that's the postman's knock, Jackie. That's for us, boy. And that old sod of a sergeant knew 'twas coming and that's where he left us to the last.'

His right hand reached down and picked up the crutch. He raised himself and raised the crutch till it was resting on the back of the chair, and they noticed how his thumb and forefinger worked as though it were a rifle. Sully's sister and Mrs Dunn stood in the doorway and gazed at him in astonishment. Jerry raised his hand for silence.

'I'm on my last couple of rounds Jackie,' Broke hissed. 'Are you all right, little boy? You're not hurt, are you Jackie? Don't be a bit frightened little boy. This is nothing to some of the things I seen. I'll get you out of this, never fear. They can't kill me, Jackie. I'm like the Wandering Jew, boy. I have a charmed life.'

He continued to make those strange noises — wheeeee-bump, wheeeee-bump, and each time he would crouch, following the sound with his mad eyes, his arm raised above his head.

'That's close enough now, Jackie,' he said, panting. 'They have us taped this time all right. Another five minutes now! I don't mind, Jackie. Curse of God on the care I care! There's no one in the world will bother much about me only yourself. Jackie, if ever you get back to the Coal Quay, tell them the way I looked after you. Tell them the way old Joe Shinnick minded you when you had no one else on your side.'

'Oh, oh, oh!' Mrs Dunn said, but Jerry glared at her, and she clasped her hands.

'I looked after you, Jackie, didn't I? Didn't I, boy? As if you were my own. And so you were, Jackie. The first day I saw you and that tinker Lowry at you I nearly went mad. I put that cur's teeth down his throat for him anyway . . .' Broke rocked his head. His voice suddenly dropped. 'What's that, Jackie? The guns are stopped! The guns are stopped, boy! Pass us a couple of clips there, quick! Quick, do you hear? We're in for it now. There's something moving over there, beyond the wire. Do you see it? . . . Christ,' he snarled between his teeth, 'I'll give you something to take home with you.' He raised the crutch, lightning-swift, and then his voice dropped to a moan. 'Oh, God, Jackie, they're coming! Millions of them! Millions of them! And there's the moon, the way it is now over Shandon, and the old women going to early Mass.' Again his voice changed; now it was the voice of the old soldier, curt and commanding. 'Keep your head now, boy. Don't fire till I tell you. Where are you? I can't see in here. Shake hands, kid. God knows, if I could get you out of it, I would. Shake hands, can't you. What ails you? Jackie!'

His voice suddenly rang out in a cry. Sully's sister went on her knees by the door and began to give out the Rosary. Mrs Dunn was talking to herself. 'Oh, Jackie!' she was saying over and over, 'Jackie, Jackie, Jackie!' Broke was leaning over the edge of the chair as though holding up a deadweight, pressing it close to his side and staring down at it incredulously. Somehow they all said afterwards they could see it quite plainly; the shell-battered dug out with the dawn breaking and the moon paling in the sky, and Broke with the dead boy's head against his side.

'So long, Jackie,' he said in a whisper. 'So long, kid. I won't be long after you.'

Then he seemed to take something from the dead boy's body and throw it over his own shoulder. Bill nodded to the sergeant and the sergeant nodded back. They both knew it was an ammunition belt. Then Broke seemed to lay down the weight in his arms and swung himself up against the back of the chair, raising the crutch as if it were a rifle, but he no longer seemed to bother about cover. As his hands worked an imaginary bolt his whole face was distorted; the mouth drawn sideways in a grin, and he cursed and snarled over it like a madman. Something about it made the other men uncomfortable.

'That's enough, Jerry,' the sergeant-major said uneasily. 'Wake him up, now, for the love of God!'

'No,' said Jerry, though his face was very pale. 'It might bring some ease to his poor mind.'

'I'm afraid nothing will ever do that now,' said the sergeant-major. 'Quick, Jerry,' he shouted, jumping from his chair. 'mind him!'

It was over before Jerry could do anything. Suddenly Broke sprang up on his good leg; his crutch fell to the floor, and he spun clean into the middle of the room before he crashed on his face and hands. Jerry drew a deep breath. There was nothing else to be heard but the gabble of Sully's sister, 'Pray for us sinners, now and at the hour of our death.' Broke lay there quite motionless for close on a minute. He might have been dead. Then he raised his head from between his hands, and with a tremendous effort tried to lift himself slowly on hands and knees. He crashed down again, sideways. A look of astonishment came into the mad, blue eyes that was always painful to watch. His hand crept slowly down his body and clutched at his leg — the leg that wasn't there.

Then he seemed to come to himself; he swung himself nimbly up from the floor and back into his chair. 'Give the man his due,' he said in a perfectly normal voice. 'An old soldier; his gun-carriage and his couple of volleys.' But as he spoke he covered his face with his hands, and a long sigh broke through his whole body and seemed to shake him to the very heart. It was as though he had fallen asleep, but his breath came in great noisy waves that shook him as they passed over him.

'Jackie,' said Mrs Dunn in a whisper; 'My boy, my little boy!'

And from far away, over Barrackton Hill, crystal-clear and pure in the clear summer night, they heard the bugler sounding the Last Post.

(1941)

The Cornet-Player Who Betrayed Ireland

At this hour of my life I don't profess to remember what we inhabitants of Blarney Lane were patriotic about: all I remember is that we were very patriotic, that our main principles were something called 'Conciliation and Consent,' and that our great national leader, William O'Brien, once referred to us as 'The Old Guard.' Myself and other kids of the Old Guard used to parade the street with tin cans and toy trumpets, singing 'We'll hang Johnnie Redmond on a sour apple tree.' (John Redmond, I need hardly say, was the leader of the other side.)

Unfortunately, our neighbourhood was bounded to the south by a long ugly street leading uphill to the cathedral, and the lanes off it were infested with the most wretched specimens of humanity who took the Redmondite side for whatever could be got from it in the way of drink. My personal view at the time was that the Redmondite faction was maintained by a conspiracy of publicans and brewers. It always saddened me, coming through this street on my way from school, and seeing the poor misguided children, barefoot and in rags, parading with tin cans and toy trumpets and singing 'We'll hang William O'Brien on a sour apple tree.' It left me with very little hope for Ireland.

Of course, my father was a strong supporter of 'Conciliation and Consent.' The parish priest who had come to
solicit his vote for Redmond had told him he would go
straight to Hell, but my father had replied quite respectfully
that if Mr O'Brien was an agent of the devil, as Father
Murphy said, he would go gladly.

I admired my father as a rock of principle. As well as
being a house-painter (a regrettable trade which left him
for six months 'under the ivy', as we called it), he was a
musician. He had been a bandsman in the British Army,
played the cornet extremely well, and had been a member
of the Irishtown Brass and Reed Band from its foundation.
At home we had two big pictures of the band after each of
its most famous contests, in Belfast and Dublin. It was
after the Dublin contest when Irishtown emerged as the
premier brass band that there occurred an unrecorded
episode in operatic history. In those days the best band in
the city was always invited to perform in the Soldiers'
Chorus scene in Gounod's 'Faust'. Of course, they were
encored to the echo, and then, ignoring conductor and
everything else, they burst into a selection from Moore's
Irish Melodies. I am glad my father didn't live to see the
day of pipers' bands. Even fife and drum bands he looked
on as primitive.

As he had great hopes of turning me into a musician
too he frequently brought me with him to practices and
promenades. Irishtown was a very poor quarter of the city,
a channel of mean houses between breweries and builders'
yards with the terraced hillsides high above it on either
side, and nothing but the white Restoration spire of
Shandon breaking the skyline. You came to a little foot-
bridge over the narrow stream; on one side of it was a red-
brick chapel, and when we arrived there were usually some
of the bandsmen sitting on the bridge, spitting back over
their shoulders into the stream. The bandroom was over an
undertaker's shop at the other side of the street. It was a
long, dark, barn-like erection overlooking the bridge and
decorated with group photos of the band. At this hour of a
Sunday morning it was always full of groans, squeaks and

bumps.

Then at last came the moment I loved so much. Out in the sunlight, with the bridge filled with staring pedestrians, the band formed up. Dickie Ryan, the bandmaster's son, and myself took our places at either side of the big drummer, Joe Shinkwin. Joe peered over his big drum to right and left to see if all were in place and ready; he raised his right arm and gave the drum three solemn flakes: then, after the third thump the whole narrow channel of the street filled with a roaring torrent of drums and brass, the mere physical impact of which hit me in the belly. Screaming girls in shawls tore along the pavements calling out to the bandsmen, but nothing shook the soldierly solemnity of the men with their eyes almost crossed on the music before them. I've heard Toscanini conduct Beethoven, but compared with Irishtown playing 'Marching Through Georgia' on a Sunday morning it was only like Mozart in a girls' school. The mean little houses, quivering with the shock, gave it back to us: the terraced hillsides that shut out the sky gave it back to us; the interested faces of passers-by in their Sunday clothes from the pavements were like mirrors reflecting the glory of the music. When the band stopped and again you could hear the gapped sound of feet, and people running and chattering, it was like a parachute jump into commonplace.

Sometimes we boarded the paddle-steamer and set up our music stands in some little field by the sea, which all day echoed of Moore's Melodies, Rossini and Gilbert and Sullivan: sometimes we took a train into the country to play at some sports meeting. Whatever it was, I loved it, though I never got a dinner: I was fed on lemonade, biscuits and sweets, and, as my father spent most of the intervals in the pub, I was sometimes half mad with boredom.

One summer day we were playing at a féte in the grounds of Blarney Castle, and, as usual, the band departed to the pub and Dickie Ryan and myself were left behind, ostensibly to take care of the instruments. A certain hanger-on of the band, one John P., who to my knowledge was never called anything else, was lying on the grass, chewing a straw and shading his eyes from the light with the back of his hand. Dickie and I took a side drum each and began to march about with them. All at once Dickie began to sing to his own accompaniment 'We'll hang William O'Brien on a sour apple tree.' I was so astonished that I stopped drumming and listened to him. For a moment or two I thought he must be mocking the poor uneducated children of the lanes round Shandon Street. Then I suddenly realised that he meant it. Without hesitation I began to rattle my side drum even louder and shouted 'We'll hang Johnnie Redmond on a sour apple tree.' John P. at once started up and gave me an angry glare. 'Stop that now, little boy!' he said threateningly. It was quite plain that he meant me, not Dickie Ryan.

I was completely flabbergasted. It was bad enough hearing the bandmaster's son singing a traitorous song, but then to be told to shut up by a fellow who wasn't even a bandsman; merely a hanger-on who looked after the music stands and carried the big drum in return for free drinks! I realised that I was among enemies. I quietly put aside the drum and went to find my father. I knew that he could have no idea what was going on behind his back in the band.

I found him at the back of the pub, sitting on a barrel and holding forth to a couple of young bandsmen.

'Now, "Brian Boru's March" ' he was saying with one finger raised, 'that's a beautiful march. I heard the Irish Guards do that on Salisbury Plain, and they had the English fellows' eyes popping out. "Paddy," one of them says to me (they all call you Paddy) "wot's the name of the shouting march?" but somehow we don't get the same fire into it at all. Now, listen, and I'll show you how that should go!'

'Dadda,' I said in a whisper, pulling him by the sleeve, 'do you know what Dickie Ryan was singing?'

'Hold on a minute now,' he said, beaming at me affectionately. 'I just want to illustrate a little point.'

'But, dadda,' I went on determinedly, 'he was singing

"We'll hang William O'Brien from a sour apple tree." '

'Hah, hah, hah,' laughed my father, and it struck me that he hadn't fully appreciated the implications of what I had said.

'Frank,' he added, 'get a bottle of lemonade for the little fellow.'

'But dadda,' I said despairingly, 'when I sang "We'll hang Johnnie Redmond," John P. told me to shut up.'

'Now, now,' said my father with sudden testiness, 'that's not a nice song to be singing.'

This was a stunning blow. The anthem of 'Conciliation and Consent' — not a nice song to be singing!

'But, dadda,' I wailed, 'aren't we *for* William O'Brien?'

'Yes, yes, yes,' he replied, as if I were goading him, 'but everyone to his own opinion. Now drink your lemonade and run out and play like a good boy.'

I drank my lemonade all right, but I went out not to play but to brood. There was but one fit place for that. I went to the shell of the castle; climbed the stair to the tower and leaning over the battlements watching the landscape like bunting all round me I thought of the heroes who had stood here, defying the might of England. Everyone to his own opinion! What would they have thought of a statement like that? It was the first time that I realised the awful strain of weakness and the lack of strong principle in my father, and understood that the old bandroom by the bridge was in the heart of enemy country and that all round me were enemies of Ireland like Dickie Ryan and John P.

It wasn't until months after that I realised how many these were. It was Sunday morning, but when we reached the bandroom there was no one on the bridge. Upstairs the room was almost full. A big man wearing a bowler hat and a flower in his buttonhole was standing before the fireplace. He had a red face with weak, red-rimmed eyes and a dark moustache. My father, who seemed as surprised as I was, slipped quietly into a seat behind the door and lifted me on to his knee.

'Well, boys,' the big man said in a deep husky voice, 'I suppose ye have a good notion what I'm here for. Ye know that next Saturday night Mr. Redmond is arriving in the city, and I have the honour of being Chairman of the Reception Committee.'

'Well, Alderman Doyle,' said the bandmaster doubtfully, 'you know the way we feel about Mr. Redmond, most of us anyway.'

'I do, Tim, I do,' said the Alderman evenly as it gradually dawned on me that the man I was listening to was the Arch-Traitor, locally known as Scabby Doyle, the builder whose vile orations my father always read aloud to my mother with chagrined comments on Doyle's past history. 'But feeling isn't enough, Tim. Fair Lane Band will be there of course. Watergrasshill will be there. The Butter Exchange will be there. What will the backers of this band, the gentlemen who helped it through so many difficult days, say if we don't put in an appearance?'

'Well, ye see, Alderman,' said Ryan nervously, 'we have our own little difficulties.'

'I know that, Tim,' said Doyle. 'We all have our difficulties in troubled times like these, but we have to face them like men in the interests of the country. What difficulties have you?'

'Well, that's hard to describe, Alderman,' said the bandmaster.

'No, Tim,' said my father quietly, raising and putting me down from his knee, ' 'tis easy enough to describe. I'm the difficulty, and I know it.'

'Now, Mick,' protested the bandmaster, 'there's nothing personal about it. We're all old friends in this band.'

'We are, Tim,' agreed my father. 'And before ever it was heard of, you and me gave this bandroom its first coat of paint. But every man is entitled to his principles, and I don't want to stand in your light.'

'You see how it is, Mr. Doyle,' said the Bandmaster appealingly. 'We had others in the band that were of Mick Twomey's persuasion, but they left us to join O'Brienite bands. Mick didn't, nor we didn't want him to leave us.'

'Nor don't,' said a mournful voice, and I turned and saw a tall, gaunt, spectacled young man sitting on the window sill. 'I had three men,' said my father earnestly, hold up three fingers in illustration of the fact, 'three men up at the house on different occasions to get me to join other bands. I'm not boasting Tim Ryan knows who they were.'

'I do, I do,' said the bandmaster.

'And I wouldn't,' said my father passionately. 'I'm not boasting, but you can't deny it: there isn't another band in Ireland to touch ours.'

'Nor a cornet-player in Ireland to touch Mick Twomey,' chimed in the gaunt young man, rising to his feet. 'And I'm not saying that to coddle or cock him up.'

'You're not, you're not,' said the bandmaster. 'No one can deny he's a musician.'

'And listen here to me, boys,' said the gaunt young man, with a wild wave of his arm, 'don't leave us be led astray by anyone. What were we before we had the old band? Nobody. We were no better than the poor devils that sit on that bridge outside all day, spitting into the river. Whatever we do, leave us be all agreed. What backers had we when we started, only what we could collect ourselves outside the chapel gates on Sunday, and hard enough to get permission for that itself? I'm as good a party man as anyone here, but what I say is, music is above politics . . . Alderman Doyle,' he begged, 'tell Mr. Redmond whatever he'll do not to break up our little band on us.'

'Jim Ralegh,' said the Alderman, with his red-rimmed eyes growing moist, 'I'd sooner put my hand in the fire than injure this band. I know what ye are, a band of brothers . . . Mick,' he boomed at my father, 'will you desert it in its hour of trial?'

'Ah,' said my father testily, 'is it the way you want me to play against William O'Brien?'

'Play against William O'Brien,' echoed the Alderman. 'No one is asking you to play *against* anyone. As Jim Ralegh here says, music is above politics. What we're asking you to do is to play *for* something: for the band, for the sake of unity. You know what'll happen if the backers withdraw? Can't you pocket your pride and make this sacrifice in the interest of the band?'

My father stood for a few moments, hesitating. I prayed that for once he might see the true light; that he might show this group of misguided men the faith that was in him. Instead he nodded curtly, said 'Very well, I'll play,' and sat down again. The rascally Alderman said a few humbugging words in his praise which didn't take me in. I don't think they even took my father in, for all the way home he never addressed a word to me. I saw then that his conscience was at him. He knew that by supporting the band in the unprincipled step it was taking he was showing himself a traitor to Ireland and our great leader, William O'Brien.

Afterwards, whenever Irishtown played at Redmondite demonstrations, my father accompanied them, but the moment the speeches began he retreated to the edge of the crowd, rather like a pious Catholic compelled to attend a heretical religious service, and stood against the wall with his hands in his pockets, passing slighting and witty comments on the speakers to any O'Brienites he might meet. But he had lost all dignity in my eyes. Even his gibes at Scabby Doyle seemed to me false, and I longed to say to him. 'If that's what you believe, why don't you show it?' Even the seaside lost its attraction when at any moment the beautiful daughter of a decent O'Brienite family might point to me and say: 'There is the son of the cornet-player who betrayed Ireland.'

Then one Sunday we went to play at some idolatrous function in a seaside town called Bantry. While the meeting was on my father and the rest of the band retired to the pub and I with them. Even by my presence in the Square I wasn't prepared to countenance the proceedings. I was looking idly out of the window when I suddenly heard a roar of cheering and people began to scatter in all directions. I was mystified until someone outside started to shout, 'Come on, boys! The O'Brienites are trying to break up the meeting.' The bandsmen rushed for the door. I would have done the same but my father looked hastily over his shoulder and warned me to stay where I was. He was talking to a young clarinet-player of serious appearance.

'Now,' he went on, raising his voice to drown the uproar outside. 'Teddy the Lamb was the finest clarinet-player in the whole British Army.'

There was a fresh storm of cheering, and wild with excitement I saw the patriots begin to drive a deep wedge of whirling sticks through the heart of the enemy, cutting them into two fighting camps.

'Excuse me, Mick,' said the clarinet-player, going white, I'll go and see what's up.'

'Now, whatever is up,' my father said appealingly, 'you can't do anything about it.'

'I'm not going to have it said I stopped behind while my friends were fighting for their lives,' said the young fellow hotly.

'There's no one fighting for their lives at all,' said my father irascibly, grabbing him by the arm. 'You have something else to think about. Man alive, you're a musician, not a bloody infantryman.'

'I'd sooner be that than a bloody turncoat, anyway,' said the young fellow, dragging himself off and making for the door.

'Thanks, Phil,' my father called after him in a voice of a man who had to speak before he has collected his wits. 'I well deserved that from you. I well deserved that from all of ye.' He took out his pipe and put it back into his pocket again. Then he joined me at the window and for a few moments he looked unseeingly at the milling crowd outside. 'Come on,' he said shortly.

Though the couples were wrestling in the very gutters no one accosted us on our way up the street; otherwise I feel murder might have been committed. We went to the house of some cousins and had tea, and when we reached the railway station my father led me to a compartment near the engine; not the carriage reserved for the band. Though we had ten minutes to wait it wasn't until just before the whistle went that Tim Ryan, the bandmaster, spotted us through the window.

'Mick!' he shouted in astonishment. 'Where the hell were you? I had men out all over the town looking for you?

Is it anything wrong?'

'Nothing, Tim,' replied my father, leaning out of the window to him. 'I wanted to be alone, that's all.'

'But we'll see you at the other end?' bawled Tim as the train began to move.

'I don't know will you,' replied my father grimly. 'I think ye saw too much of me.'

When the band formed up outside the station we stood on the pavement and watched them. He had a tight hold of my hand. First Tim Ryan and then Jim Ralegh came rushing over to him. With an intensity of hatred I watched those enemies of Ireland again bait their traps for my father, but now I knew they would bait them in vain.

'No, no Tim,' said my father, shaking his head, 'I went too far before for the sake of the band, and I paid dear for it. None of my family was ever called a turncoat before today, Tim.'

'Ah, it is a young fool like that?' bawled Jim Ralegh with tears in his wild eyes. 'What need a man like you care about him?'

'A man have his pride, Jim,' said my father gloomily.

'He have,' cried Ralegh despairingly, 'and a fat lot any of us has to be proud of. The band was all we ever had, and if that goes the whole thing goes. For the love of the Almighty God, Mick Twomey, come back with us to the bandroom anyway.'

'No, no, no,' shouted my father angrily. 'I tell you after today I'm finished with music.'

'Music is finished with us you mean,' bawled Jim. 'The curse of God on the day we ever heard of Redmond or O'Brien! We were happy men before it . . . All right, lads,' he cried, turning away with a wild and whirling motion of his arm. 'Mick Twomey is done with us. Ye can go on without him.'

And again I heard the three solemn thumps on the big drum, and again the street was flooded with a roaring torrent of music, and though it no longer played for me, my heart rose to it and the tears came from my eyes. Still holding my hand, my father followed on the pavement. They were playing 'Brian Boru's March,' his old favourite. We followed them through the ill-lit town and as they turned down the side street to the bridge, my father stood on the kerb and looked after them as though he wished to impress every detail on his memory. It was only when the music stopped and the silence returned to the narrow channel of the street that we resumed our lonely way homeward.

(1942)

Uncle Pat

The decentest man in all Ireland is my Uncle Pat, and you'd never think it if you saw him of a morning on his way to work. He slouches along with his eyes on the ground, a scowl on his face and his lips moving; a gaunt raking galoot of a man with a pair of deep-sunk, fanatical eyes, high cheekbones and narrow temples. He looks more like your idea of a mediaeval inquisitor than a respectable Town Clerk.

He is also — may God forgive him — the laziest man in Ireland, which is saying a lot, quite a lot! I've seen him stay in bed for a week, and never get up any evening before six o'clock. About midday, Tim, his second-in-command, comes up for instructions. Tim is a stocky little fellow with a face like a fist and a pipe forever in the corner of his mouth.

'Tim,' says the Boss, with his rogue's smile, 'I was expecting you. Take a seat, boy, take a seat, that's if you can find a seat. I gave you permission to smoke, didn't I? Yes, Tim, yes, since you forgot to enquire, I'm *not* at all well.'

'Huh,' says Tim, 'I suppose you remembered the man from the Ministry was coming.'

'Tim,' says the Boss in mock alarm, 'you don't mean, you can't possibly mean 'twas today he was to come?'

'Gwan ou' that,' says Tim. 'You should be ashamed of yourself.'

'Tim,' says my uncle with a wounded air, 'is that a nice thing to suggest? You hurt me, Tim. I didn't know Mr. Hennesy was coming. An admirable man, Tim! A most distinguished member of his profession. Salute! But it's an astonishing thing, Tim, that the wind of that excellent man's arrival — salute again, Tim! Heil, Hitler! — the mere wind of it is enough to give me a bad cold in the head.'

But now and again the old conscience comes at him. That is a bad time for us. He is up at seven and has the house demented searching for the boot brushes; tramping from room to room, cursing me and Brigid and the girls. 'What sort of a house is this? Seven o'clock and no one up yet!' He refuses to speak to any of us, scarcely touches his breakfast and is at the office a full quarter of an hour before anyone is due in. And by some remarkable coincidence his bursts of zeal always happen to coincide with an all-night dance or a football match and everyone strolls in, fair and easy, around ten and finds the office as silent as the grave and Uncle Pat like an avenging angel at the head of the long table. (Usually he sits in his own office and reads detective stories.)

It is also remarkable that those fits of conscience seem to be connected by invisible strands to faint hopes in the hearts of the girls and myself that we might get him to go somewhere with us. Well, now, look what happened on the day of the races. The girls and myself went down in the car to collect him, but Uncle Pat was in one of his busy-body moods. and stood on top of the stairs, waving his arms and complaining that the whole staff had deserted him to go to the races, and left him, all alone, to do the work of a dozen. He was very sorry for himself.

'Ah, come on,' says I, 'show me what's to be done and I'll do it. You go with the girls to the races.'

'Ah, no, Willie, no,' said my Uncle — I had frightened him a bit — 'I don't mean it like that, boy. I don't begrudge you your bit of pleasure. Ye deserve it, boy, ye deserve it.'

So then I knew it was only that he was posing in the part

of St. Sebastian and I turned and left him in exasperation.

'Willie,' says he in languishing tones, just as I reached the foot of the stairs, 'tell Brigid to keep something hot for me. I don't know when I'll get through all this work.'

He was leaning over the banisters with his arms folded and a look of martyred patience on his face. Oh, he was very sorry for himself! I was still angry because he was such good company on a spree, but of course I forgot it as soon as we reached the race-course. It was a marvellous spring day with low clouds and an infinite distance of green fields stretching away to the ring of mountains on every side of us, and the misty rays of the sun-lantern picking out a bit here and there and polishing it till it shone. A heavenly day, and a little old man working a home-made marionette on an upturned box, and the trick-of-the-loop men and the three-card men, and a boozy man walking away across the field with two big pints in his hand saying to himself in a loud voice 'Now, where the divil am I bringing these?' And the girls and I gaped at the paddock, and suddenly I started and looked round and who was behind but my Uncle Pat! He raised his hat and smiled benevolently. He had another man with him, a teacher by the name of Oweney Mac.

'Well, the divil fly away with you,' says I, 'wasn't I the idiot to be breaking my heart about you!'

He frowned and beckoned me on one side.

' 'Twas Oweney Mac,' says he. 'Ye weren't out the door before he came.'

'And what about Oweney Mac?' I asked.

'Sure, my goodness,' said he in an excited whisper, 'didn't I tell you? All you have to do is to look at him. Once a year; I told you that. Once a year.'

Now that was a legend of my Uncle Pat's I could never fathom. Owney Mac was a decent, fat, hasty little man that I found it very difficult to stand. He was a most cantankerous man; he seemed to have a grievance against life, and a grievance beyond all telling, as the poet says, against Ireland. One wet day was sufficient to make Oweney Mac fume against the climate of this damned country of ours. He never by any chance happened to get on a train that was up to time, and all his experience of Irish railways had never taught him to make his appointments independent of them, so that he was always failing to keep them. 'This damned country,' he'd rage, 'that can't even run a railway.' If one of the little boys in school failed to do a message properly for him, Oweney talked for hours and hours about the difference between the fine manly intelligent little schoolboys in England and the dirty louts he had the misfortune to teach. When he fought with his wife — a decent hardworking poor woman we were all sorry for — he'd begin talking to my Uncle Pat about Irishwomen, saying that from the moment they married they never used their brains again, and that it was for the lack of intelligent conversation and because of the flaming idiots of wives they had at home that Irishmen all took to drink sooner or later. And my uncle would listen and nod with a grave face, and I kept silent with my heart full of rage. I never could understand why the Christian Brothers stood the man at all, unless for charity, and I didn't believe my Uncle Pat when he swore that Oweney Mac was a remarkably intellectual man, and that the Brothers were scared out of their wits of losing him. But the most incredible part of the story was that, according to my uncle, it was Oweney Mac's magnificent intellect and his general dissatisfaction with the people of Ireland that made him go on the booze at least once a year, and that my uncle had promised Brother O'Doherty to look after Oweney, so that nothing out of the way would happen that jewel of a man. It was all beyond me, but I knew my uncle had a devotion to Oweney Mac and wouldn't separate from him the whole week or two weeks that Oweney was working off his accumulated despair about Ireland, but whether all that was because of his vow to Brother O'Doherty, as he hinted, or because, as the girls believed, he enjoyed the excuse for going on a beano himself, I should find it hard to say. Anyway, there the old rascal was with his rogue's smile and all at once he laid his hand on my arm and closed his eyes and sniffed.

'What do I smell, Willie?' he says in a faraway voice. 'I smell the crushed grass.' He opened his eyes and winked at me. 'Come on, boy,' he said cheerfully. 'We'll put all our troubles aside. We have the spring clouds and the young trees; we have the smell of the crushed grass.'

'We have,' I said, for I was still a bit out of humour with him, 'and the shade of the whiskey tent.'

He grabbed me by the arm and guffawed.

'God bless you, Willie,' he said. 'You always spoke the true word. I said it. You have the soul of a poet. 'Tis all in that, isn't it — the smell of the crushed grass and the shade of the whiskey tent. Go away, you ruffian!'

'You ought to be ashamed of yourself,' said I.

'And, oh, Willie,' he said, as though suddenly recollecting something and speaking in an anxious and confidential tone, 'tell Brigid to keep something hot for me. I don't know when I'll be able to get home.'

But I notice the ring in his voice was somehow different. It may have been for Brother O'Doherty's sake he was looking after Oweney Mac, but I didn't altogether like the eagerness with which he responded to the call of duty.

It wasn't until next morning that I learned what happened them after that, for, so far as myself and the girls were concerned, the earth might as well have opened and swallowed them. It wasn't easy either to make sense of my uncle's story which was that they had had to abandon two publichouses owing to the absence of a piano, and that they had to go all the way to Georgestown before they found one. Why a piano? you'll ask. Well, it seems, according to my uncle's version of it, whenever Oweney Mac's loathing and disgust of Ireland reaches its climax, he becomes absolutely possessed by a passion for music. Italian music, preferably; music with sunlight and laughter in it, as he says himself in his most exasperated tone of voice; and in proof of that I may mention how I found him two days later stretched in bed, with a dozen full bottles of beer at one side and a dozen empties at the other while he sat bolt upright with his hands clasped and his eyes shut, listening to the gramophone bawling out *Di Provenza*. And

while I gazed at him, in stupefaction, I must say, because I'm
a normal sort of chap without any particular intellect to
make me unhappy, Oweney began to mutter to himself. 'A
child of the sun, a child of the sun, and here I am, in exile
among the Eskimos of the frozen North.' But if Italian
music wasn't to be had, Oweney got on quite nicely with
any other sort, and my uncle had the greatest difficulty in
detaching him from the piper outside one publichouse. 'Ah,
listen, man, listen,' he was saying irritably to the piper,
'what sort of music is that? Nnnnannnannnaa! Look up at
the sun, man! Listen to the birds singing. They're not doing
any of your old Nnnnannna. Be cheerful, for God's sake!
We'll be dead long enough.'

At last they found a publichouse in Georgestown with a
piano in the parlour and Oweney began to sing and play.
When he finished one drink he bawled for another, almost
without ceasing his music, and as my poor Uncle wouldn't
know *God Save the King* from *The Soldiers' Song* he amused
himself by looking at a mysterious quart bottle of medicine
which happened to be standing on top of the piano, until,
as he said himself, it put a sort of spell on him. As Oweney
Mac thumped the keys the bottle danced like a *prima
ballerina* in a Russian ballet, and by watching it my uncle
was able for the first time in his life to pierce to the very
soul of music. When Oweney played *La Donna e Mobile* the
old medicine bottle became transformed into the very
incarnation of feminine light-mindedness, and when he
played *Di Provenza* it seemed to suffer from all the nostalgia
of the south and advanced by imperceptible anguished
trips towards the edge of the piano as though it were about
to plunge over the abyss. There were tears in my uncle's
eyes; so he says at any rate; but even the emotions of the
medicine bottle tired him in the absence of intellectual
conversation, and after a while he rose quietly and went
downstairs to the kitchen to have a little chat with the
publican's wife. He wanted to explain to her about his
life-long attachment to Oweney Mac, and Oweney Mac's
genius which nobody really appreciated only himself, and
how Oweney Mac's highly-strung temperament broke down

once a year owing to the misunderstanding and neglect of
an unenlightened population, but I doubt if the publican's
wife understood much he told her, because when once my
uncle took a glass he began to grow emotional, and when
he grew emotional he passed from incoherence to complete
silence during which he illustrated everything with gestures
and expressions. It was really remarkable how one tolerated
him in this condition; one hung upon every tragic wave of
the arms as though some wonderful meaning were at any
moment going to transpire.

However, the publican's wife got called away, and my
uncle went upstairs to Oweney's rendering of *Your Tiny
Hand is Frozen* and when he opened the door his eyes
strayed affectionately back to the position in which he
had last seen his old friend, the bottle-ballerina. But to his
horror it wasn't there. It stood beside the piano stool,
quite empty. Oweney, in my uncle's absence, had become
thirsty and drank it all. Uncle Pat called for help and
insisted on laying Oweney Mac out on the sofa. Then the
publican and the publican's wife came, and assured him
that there was nothing really dangerous in the bottle.
only some sort of cough mixture, whereupon Oweney
began to get sick, and to give him air my uncle conducted
him to the corner of the publichouse where he put him
leaning up against the wall. It was race day and of course
the town was crowded with cars returning. 'How are you
feeling now, Oweney?' asked my uncle. 'This damned
country!' gasped Oweney. 'I'll make them pay. I'll show
them up. There isn't a country in the world where they'd
give a man beer like that.' 'That wasn't beer,' said my uncle,
'but don't worry, boy. Don't move. You'll be as right as
rain in a few minutes.' And then he began to think again of
the publican's wife, and being fond of company, without
minding much what sort of company, and there being no
great fun in standing at a street corner with a man in poor
Oweney's condition, he thought he might as well go back
to the kitchen and reassure her.

It was precisely as he retired that a civic guard came up
to Oweney Mac and pointed to a car by the publichouse.

'I'm sorry, sir,' says he, 'but I wonder if you'd mind shifting your car to the other side of the road. 'Tis almost impossible for anyone to get past it.'

Oweney looked at the motor car and then he looked at the young policeman, and it seemed to him that there wasn't in the wide world another country where such a thing could happen: a policeman asking a man to drive a car that wasn't his, and nothing could have convinced him that the guard was not doing it for spite.

'Drive it yourself,' he snapped.

'I requested you to remove the car to the other side of the road,' said the guard, flushing.

'And I told you to do it yourself,' replied Oweney.

'You mean you refuse?' says the guard.

'I do refuse, I most certainly refuse,' replied Oweney Mac, and he added a few words on the subject of policemen and this young policeman in particular guaranteed to produce hot feelings. The end of it was that Oweney Mac was hauled off to the barrack and pushed into a cell to think better of it.

Then, ten minutes or so later, out comes my Uncle Pat, only to find his comrade missing. Naturally, he was scared. He went from publichouse to publichouse, enquiring, but discovered nothing — which is hardly to be wondered at, considering that his own family often found him impossible to understand when he tried to translate his meaning into signs. After that he went to the police barrack. He began by throwing his arms about the sergeant and endeavouring to explain his vow to Brother O'Doherty and the loss of his companion. Perhaps, after their experience with Oweney Mac, the guards were a bit hasty.

'Is it the man in the cells you're looking for?' asked the sergeant.

'Cells?' shouted my uncle. 'Did you say cells? Oweney Mac in the cells? For what, in God's name?'

'For refusing to remove his motor when requested,' says the sergeant.

With one wide sweep of his arm and a look of rage and disgust my Uncle Pat consigned the sergeant to perdition.

'Don't tell me,' says the sergeant ironically, 'that you're looking for a fight too?'

'Fight?' exclaimed my uncle. 'The Attorney General.'

'Splendid,' says the sergeant, 'I'll have him sent for at once. Stop in there with your pal till he arrives.'

You could scarcely believe it; the two most respectable men in our town in the cells like any common drunks. My uncle was half demented. The like had never happened to him before. Oweney Mac was sitting on a bench with his head between his hands, and my uncle drew himself up with clenched fists and took in a long breath that was intended to convey to Oweney Mac what he thought of it. Then the first bout of rage came on him and he thundered like a lunatic on the door demanding a solicitor, the Attorney General and the Chief of Police. That relieved his mind a little and he turned on Oweney Mac again.

'Motor car?' he asked. 'What motor car?'

'There was no motor car at all, man,' says Oweney Mac irritably. 'How could there be a motor car? I'll prove there was no motor car. Inside a week I'll have that policeman and the damned saucy sergeant and the Chief of Police, I'll have them walking the roads. Every man of them! Two thousand pounds damages I'm demanding.'

'But did you, did you explain there was no motor?' asked my uncle.

'Of course I didn't explain,' shouted Oweney Mac. ' 'Tis their business to prove it.'

'Wait till I tell them,' says my uncle.

'Do nothing of the kind,' says Oweney in a rage, grabbing my uncle and flinging him on the bench. 'Then they'd let us out and we'd have no case at all. We must stay here till they bring us before the magistrate till we show the whole wide world the sort of misfortunate country this is.'

Whereupon the two old idiots went fast asleep, swearing vengeance on every policeman in Ireland. It was four next morning when I got on their track, through the local police who knew my uncle well and would have done anything for him. I adduce it as an example of the plain common sense of fellows like me that before I set out I equipped myself with two bottles of beer from home. In some way I felt they might prove useful.

When I reached the barrack in Georgestown I found them still sleeping and the sergeant a little bit nervous about what they might do when he waked them. It was then I thought of the two bottles of beer. I planked them on the table before him. The sergeant looked at me and I looked at him. Then he winked and took down his keys. I will say that whatever his faults of temper he was an understanding sort of man. He woke the two old rascals, and whatever their fury was like when they were arrested it was nothing to what they showed at being wakened at half past four of a cold spring morning. My uncle grabbed his hat and rushed out of the cell without as much as replying to the sergeant's enquiries. He halted in his rush when he perceived me. Then he perceived the two bottles. So did Oweney Mac who followed him with a very swollen countenance.

'I'm sorry,' the sergeant said mildly, 'about the hour because I'm afraid ye won't be able to get refreshments for some time to come, but if I could oblige ye in any way —.'

I noticed the smile that began to dawn at the corner of my uncle's mouth. I think he preferred a good joke to anything on earth. Oweney Mac flew into a passion and seized him by the arm.

'Don't do it, Clancy,' he shouted. 'We'll make these fellows pay for many a bottle before we're finished with them.'

'Ah, yes, Oweney,' said my uncle, 'but 'twouldn't be the same at all. You ruffian,' he said to the sergeant, 'you should be ashamed of yourself.'

The sergeant winked at me and I winked at the sergeant. My uncle has added a new story to his repertory. 'Did I ever tell you,' it begins, 'how I drank a bottle of beer that cost two thousand pounds?'

(Unpublished. Broadcast, but date unknown, probably early 1940's.)

The Adventuress

My brother and sisters didn't really like Brenda at all but I did. She was a couple of years older than I was and I was devoted to her. She had a long, grave, bony face and a power of concealing her real feelings about everything, even about me. I knew she liked me but she wasn't exactly what you'd call demonstrative about it. In fact there were times you might even say she was vindictive.

That was part of her toughness. She was tough to the point of foolhardiness. She would do anything a boy would do and a lot of things that few boys would do. It was never safe to dare her to anything. Someone had only to say 'Brenda, you wouldn't go up and knock at that door' and if the fancy took her Brenda would do it and when the door was opened concoct some preposterous yarn about being up from the country for the day and having lost her way which sometimes even took in the people she called on. When someone once asked if she could ride a bicycle she replied that she could and almost proved her case by falling under a milk-van. She did the same thing with horses and when at last she managed to break her collar-bone she took it with the stoicism of a Red Indian. She would chance her arm at anything and as a result she

139

became not only daring but skilful. She developed into a really stylish horsewoman.

Of course to the others she was just a liar, a chancer and a notice-box and in return she proved a devil to them. But to me who was always prepared to concede how wonderful she was, she was the soul of generosity.

'Go on,' she would say sharply, handing me a bag of sweets or a fistful of coppers. 'Take the blooming lot. I don't want them.' I suspect now that all she really wanted was admiration, for she would give the shift off her back to anyone she liked. Like all natural aristocrats she found the rest of the world so far beneath her own standards that all were equal in her eyes and she associated with the most horrid children whose allegiance she bought with sweets or cigarettes — pinched off my brother Colum most of the time.

She got away with a lot because she was my father's favourite and knew it. The old man was tall, gaunt and temperamental. He might pass you for weeks without noticing your existence except when you happened to be doing something wrong. We were all in a conspiracy against him — even Mother, who rationalised it on the plea that we mustn't worry poor Dad. When eventually there were things to worry about (like Colum taking to the bottle or Brenda heaving herself at the commercial traveller's head) the suspicion of all the things we were concealing from him in order not to worry him, finally nearly drove the old man to an early grave.

The rest of us went in fear and trembling of him, but Brenda could cheek him to his face and get away with it and to give her her due she never allowed any of us to criticise him in front of her. Oedipus complex or something I suppose that was.

One year she took it into her head that we should give him a Christmas box as we gave Mother one.

'Why would we give him a Christmas box?' asked Colum suspiciously. 'He never does anything for us.'

'Well,' said Brenda, 'how can we expect him to be any different when we make distinctions between Mother and him? Anyway, only for him we wouldn't be here at all.'

'I don't see that that's any good reason for giving him a Christmas box,' said Colum who was at the age when he was rather inclined to look on it as a grievance. 'What would you give him?'

'We could give him a fountain pen,' said Brenda who had it all pat. 'The one he had he lost three years ago.'

'We could,' said Colum ironically. 'Or a new car.'

'You needn't be so blooming mean,' snapped Brenda. 'Rooney's have grand pens for ten and a tanner. What is it, only too bob a man?'

There was some friction between Brenda and Maeve as to which of them should be Treasurer and Colum supported Maeve only because he knew she was a fanciful sort of girl who would get out of a Grand National Appeal in imitation print and then bother her head no further about it; but Brenda realised that this was sabotage and made short work of it. The idea was hers and she was going to be president, Treasurer and Secretary — and God help anyone that got in the way.

Two bob a man was reasonable enough, even allowing for another present for Mother. Coming on to Christmas we all got anything up to ten bob a man from relatives up from the country for the Christmas shopping and Brenda watched us with an eye like a hawk so that before Christmas Eve came at all she had collected the subscriptions. I was allowed to go into town with her to make the purchase and seeing that I was her faithful vassal she blew three and six of her own money on an air-gun for me. That was the sort Brenda was.

We went into Rooney's which was a combined book and stationery shop and I was amazed at her self-possession.

'I want to have a look at a few fountain pens,' she said to a gawky-looking assistant called Coakley who lived up our road. He gaped at us across the counter. I could see he liked Brenda.

'Certainly, Miss,' he said and I nearly burst with reflected glory to hear her called 'Miss'. She took it calmly enough as though she had never been called anything else. 'What sort of pen would you like?'

'Show us a few,' she said with a queenly toss of the head.

'If you want something really first-class,' said Coakley, producing a couple of trays of pens from the glass-case, 'there's the best on the market. Of course, we have the cheaper ones as well but they're not the same at all.'

'How much is this one?' asked Brenda, looking at the one he had pointed out to us.

'Thirty bob,' said Coakley. 'That's a Walker. 'Tis a lot of money of course but 'tis worth it.'

'They all look much alike to me,' said Brenda, taking up one of the cheaper ones.

'Aha!' said Coakley with a guffaw. 'They're only got up like that to take in the mugs.

Then he threw himself across the counter, took a fountain pen from his own breast pocket and removed the cap. 'See that pen?' he said. 'Guess how long I have that!'

'I couldn't' said Brenda.

'Fifteen years!' said Coakley. 'Fifteen blooming years. I had it through the war, in gaol and everything. I did every blessed thing to that pen only stop a bullet with it. That's a Walker for you! There isn't another pen in the market you could say the same about.' He looked at it fondly, screwed back the cap and returned it to his pocket. You could see he was very fond of that pen.

'Give it to us for a quid!' said Brenda.

'A quid?' he exclaimed, taken aback by her coolness. 'You might as well ask me to give it to you for a present.'

'Don't be so blooming mean,' said Brenda sharply. 'What's ten bob one way or another to ye?'

'Tell me,' said Coakley, raising his hand to his mouth and speaking in a husky whisper. 'Do you know Mr. Rooney?'

'No,' said Brenda. 'Why?'

'You ought to go and ask him that,' guffawed Coakley behind his hand. 'Cripes!' he exploded. 'I'd love to see his face.'

'Anyway,' said Brenda, seeing that this line was a complete washout, 'you can split the difference. I'd give you thirty bob but I'm after blowing three and six on an air-gun for the kid. I'll give you twenty-five bob.'

'And will you give me two pound ten a week after I'm sacked?' asked Coakley indignantly.

Even then I thought Brenda would take the dearer pen even if it meant throwing in my air-gun to make up the price. I could see how it hurt her pride to offer my father anything that wasn't of the very best.

'All right so,' she said, seeing no other way out. 'I'll take the one for ten and a tanner. It looks good enough anyway.'

'Ah, 'tis all right,' said Coakley, relenting and trying to put things in the best light. 'As a matter of fact, 'tis quite a decent little pen at the price. We're selling dozens of them.'

But Brenda wasn't consoled at all. The very way he said 'a decent little pen' in that patronising tone reduced it to mediocrity and pettiness in her eyes while the fact that others beside herself were buying it put the finishing touch to it. She stood on the wet pavement when we emerged with a brooding look in her eyes.

'I was a fool to go near Coakley,' she said at last.

'Why, Brenda?' I asked.

'He never took his eyes off us the whole time. Only for that I'd have fecked one of the decent pens.'

'But you wouldn't do that, Brenda?' I said aghast.

'Why wouldn't I?' she retorted roughly. 'Haven't they plenty of them? If I had the thirty bob I'd have bought it,' she added. 'But that gang is so mean they wouldn't even thank me for it. They think I'm going to offer Daddy a cheap old pen as if that was all we thought of him.'

'What are you going to do?' I asked.

'I'll do something,' she replied darkly.

That was one of the joys of being with Brenda. When I came to an obstacle I howled till someone showed me how to get round it, but Brenda saw three separate ways round it before she came to it at all. Coakley had given us a nice box for the pen. The price was pencilled on the box and when we got home Brenda rubbed it out and replaced it with a neat '30s'. She smiled at my look of awe.

'But won't he know, Brenda?' I asked.

'How would he know?' replied Brenda with a shrug. 'They

all look exactly alike.'

That was the sort of thing which made life with her a continuous excitement. She didn't give the matter another thought, but I kept looking forward to Christmas morning, half in dread my father would find her out, half in expectation that Brenda would get away with it again.

In our house we didn't go in much for Christmas trees. At breakfast on Christmas morning Maeve gave mother a brooch and Brenda gave Daddy the little box containing the pen.

'Hallo!' he said in surprise. 'What's this?' Then he opened it and saw.

'Oh, that's very nice,' he said with real enthusiasm. 'That's the very thing I was wanting this long time. Which of ye thought of that?'

'Brenda did,' I said promptly, seeing that the others would be cut in pieces before they gave her the credit.

'That was very nice and thoughtful of you, Brenda,' said my father, making, for him, a remarkably gracious speech. 'Very nice and thoughtful and I'm sure I'm grateful to ye all. How much did you pay for it?'

(That was more like Daddy!)

'I think the price is on the box,' said Brenda nonchalantly.

'Thirty bob!' said my father, impressed in spite of himself and I looked at the faces of Colum, Maeve and Brigid and saw that they were impressed too, in a different way. They were wondering what tricks Brenda was up to now. 'Where did you get it?' he went on.

'Rooney's' replied Brenda.

'Rooney's?' repeated my father suspiciously as he unscrewed the cap and examined the nib. 'Ah, they saw you coming! Sure, Rooney's have Walker pens for thirty bob!'

'I know,' said Brenda hastily. 'We looked at them too but we didn't think much of them. The assistant didn't think much of them either. Isn't that right, Michael?'

'That's right,' I said loyally. 'Them were the best.'

'*They* were the best, dear' said Mother.

'Ah,' said my father, growing more suspicious than ever.

'That assistant was only taking you out for a walk. Which of them was it? Coakley?'

'No,' said Brenda quickly before I could reply. 'A fellow I never saw there before.'

'Hah!' said my father darkly. 'I'd be surprised if Coakley did a thing like that. That's terrible blackguarding,' he added hotly to Mother. 'Willie Rooney trying to get rid of his trash on people that don't know better. I have a good mind to go in and tell him so. Jerry Taylor in the yard has a Walker pen that he bought ages ago and 'tis still good for a lifetime.

'Ah, why would you worry yourself about it?' said Mother comfortably. She probably suspected that there was mischief behind, and in her usual way wanted to keep it from Father.

'Oh,' said my father querulously, 'I'd like to show Willie Rooney he can't treat me like that. I'll tell you what you'll do, Brenda,' he said, putting the pen back in the box and returning it to her. 'Put that away carefully till Thursday and then take it back to Rooney's. Have nothing to say to any of the other assistants but go straight to Coakley and tell him I sent you. Say you want a Walker in exchange for that and no palaver about it. He'll see you're not codded again.'

I will say for Brenda that her face never changed. She had a wonderful way of concealing her emotions. But the fury among the family afterwards was something terrible.

'Ah,' said Maeve indignantly, 'you're always the same, out for nothing only swank and grandeur.'

'I wouldn't mind the swank and grandeur only for the lies,' said Colum. 'One of these days you'll be getting yourself into serious trouble. I suppose you didn't know you could be had up for that. Changing the prices on boxes is the same thing as forgery. You could get the gaol for that.'

'All right,' said Brenda contemptuously. 'Let them give me the gaol. Now, I want to know what I'm to do to make up the extra quid.'

'Make it up youself,' snapped Maeve. ' 'Twas your notion

and you can pay for it.'

'I can't,' said Brenda with a shrug. 'I haven't it.'

'Then you can go and find it,' said Colum.

'I'll find it all right,' said Brenda, her eyes beginning to flash. 'Either ye give me the extra four bob a man or I'll go in and tell my old fellow that 'twas ye persuaded me to change the price.'

'Go on, you dirty cheat!' said Maeve.

'Oh, leave her do it,' said Colum. 'Leave her do it and see will he believe her.'

'Maybe you think I wouldn't?' asked Brenda with cold ferocity.

Colum had gone too far and he knew it. It was always in the highest degree unsafe to challenge Brenda to do anything, because there was nothing you could positively say Brenda would not do if the fancy took her, and if the fancy did take her there was nothing you could positively say my father wouldn't be prepared to believe. I knew she was doing wrong but still I couldn't help admiring her. She looked grand standing there with the light of battle in her eyes.

'Come on!' she snapped. 'Four bob I want and I'm jolly well going to get it. It's no use pretending ye haven't got it because I know ye have.'

There was a moment's pause. I could see they were afraid.

'Give it to her,' said Colum contemptuously. 'And don't talk to her again, any of ye. She's beneath ye.'

He took out some money, threw two two-shilling pieces on the table and walked out. After a moment Maeve and Bridget did the same in silence. Then I put my hand in my pocket and took out what money I had. It wasn't much.

'Are you going to walk out on me too?' Brenda asked with a mocking smile.

'You know I wouldn't do that,' I said in confusion.

'That's all right so,' she said with a shrug. 'Keep your old money. I had it all the time and I'd have paid it too if only that gang had the decency to stick by me when I was caught.' Her smile grew bitterer and for a second or two I thought she might cry. I had never seen her cry. 'The trouble about our family, Michael' she went on, 'is that they all have small minds. You're the only one that hasn't. But you're only a baby, and I suppose you'll grow up just like the rest.'

I thought it was very cruel of her to say that and I after standing up for her and all. But Brenda was like that.

(1948)

The Landlady

Three of our chaps were lodging together at the end of the town in the house of a widow called Kent. They lived like rajahs, and in England during the war that was something to congratulate yourself on. I envied them; and I was far from being the worst off of the Irish crowd. After a fortnight in a dosshouse I managed to get lodgings in the house of an old coachman who had married the lady's maid in the Big House. They left when the owner got divorced. 'Of course, we couldn't stay after that,' said the old lady to me. I fancy she had a grievance against him for not staying married because herself and the old man never stopped talking about him. 'Of course, he wasn't English,' she said.

The other lodger was a poor devil of a Czech with a doll in the W.A.A.F.'s and about three sentences of English. I don't know what fun she got out of him, but English girls were great on foreigners. Every time there was a raid on he dressed and tramped up and down the room, and I declare to my God, I think he used to carry a suitcase. 'You can see he's not English,' said the landlady with a great air of resignation. (After that I never walked round myself except in my bare feet, but even then I don't think she

148

looked on me as a proper Englishman.)

At last the Czech's doll got fed up with hearing the same three sentences the whole time, and when the old dame told me I saw by the look in her eye that something good was coming. 'Of course,' said I, 'he's not English, is he?' and she looked at me with a new respect. 'No, he isn't, is he?' she said, and after that she gave me tea after my dinner. It was extraordinary how far you could get with that one phrase. The fellows in the factory loved it.

Myself and the other three Irish lads used to meet every night in a pub under the Castle and compare notes on our landladies. It was a nice old pub with harness badges all over the walls. They were always talking about how their landlady went on the tiles; up to Oxford or down to Brighton with a chap called Clements in the chemist's shop. She was blonde and pretty and as bold as brass. She had a little girl of five but that was no inconvenience to her. She explained it all to the lads too, just in case they mightn't understand; how she didn't believe in marriage and all she wanted was a good time, and even if Clements asked her to marry him, she didn't know whether she would or not.

'Oh, the woman is a cow,' Kenefick used to say. 'A nice-looking cow, but a cow just the same.'

Kenefick was a bit of a card. He was an insignificant little man with a battered old hat, tin specs and a small moustache. At the same time, like all small men he had a great opinion of himself. Normally he'd have to crane his neck to look at you, but when he wanted to be serious, he stuck his hands in his trousers pockets, put out his chest, buried his chin in it and looked at the floor yards away as though he was looking down at you. In a queer way I always had great regard for Kenefick. In his own way he was a clever chap and as honest as they make them. I had a sneaking suspicion that he was connected with some political organization, but it was just as well his landlady didn't know that because she had a holy horror of one of the Irish chaps being found with bombs in her house. She was sure we all carried them.

Even about a little thing like that Kenefick and Mac couldn't agree. MacNamara thought that Kenefick was frightfully disillusioned. Mac was tall and thin and good-looking, with a slight cast in one eye, and though he came from some God-forsaken little place in West Cork, he put on an English accent and English airs, saying 'Old chap' and 'Old man' at every hand's turn. He was always trying to introduce himself into groups of G.I.'s and Tommies to explain to them that they mustn't confuse the Irish lower-classes who worked in the factories with educated Irishmen like himself. That got on Kenefick's nerves, and he took occasion to make it clear that his mother was a washer-woman and his father a builder's labourer out of a job. 'Mac,' he said one night, 'is getting so grand he pronounces "Mass" as "church". '

And, of course, when they talked about their landlady Mac felt it was up to him as a man of the world to defend her.

'But, my goodness, Stevie,' he said, sticking his thumbs in the armholes of his vest, 'isn't it the girl's own business? Damn it, old man, we'd all do the same if we got a chance.'

'Well,' said Kenefick glumly, 'what's stopping you?'

'Ah, but look here,' said Mac, refusing to be put down by what he called Kenefick's 'narrow-mindedness,' 'you're not pretending a little thing like that makes any difference?'

'I'm not pretending anything at all, Mac,' snarled Kene-fick. 'I'm stating it as a fact. Merciful God,' he said with a sweep of his arm to indicate all the W.A.A.F.'s and A.T.S. in the pub, 'do you think girls like that are going back to scrub floors and bring up kids on ten bob a week?'

'But why should they?' asked Mac.

'No reason at all, Mac,' said Kenefick, 'only your old one did it.'

'Ah, but look here, Stevie, look here,' said Mac, pretending to be cut to the heart by Kenefick's old-fashioned ideas, 'you must admit that in marriage there are hard cases.'

'Hard cases?' said Kenefick with the eyes popping behind the tin specs. 'There's nothing else only hard cases. That's what I'm trying to knock into your thick head. There's no such thing as a happy marriage any more than there's such a thing as a happy family. All you can do is to make the best of what you have.'

'Still, Stevie,' said Long, beginning to stutter, 'there's marriages you can make nothing out of.'

Longie was the third of the gang, a country boy, supposed to be from somewhere in Limerick or Clare, though he never told us precisely where. Like all country boys he never told you anything precisely, not knowing what use you might make of it.

'I'm not denying that either, Tim,' said Kenefick.

'But what are you going to do about them, man?' shouted Mac, as if he expected Kenefick to hand him a solution then and there.

'I'm not going to do anything at all about them,' said Kenefick. 'What do you think I am, a clinic or what?'

'But look here,' said Mac triumphantly, feeling that at last he had Kenefick in a corner, 'just suppose you're going with a doll.'

'There's no need to suppose anything,' said Kenefick, looking at the floor. 'I am.'

'I'm not referring to anyone in particular,' said Mac.

'What she doesn't know won't harm her,' said Kenefick.

'Well,' said Mac, full of concern for all poor suffering humanity, 'supposing — God between us and all harm! — you found out there was madness in her family?'

'That's for me to make sure of, Mac,' said Kenefick, looking at him sternly over the specs.

'You'd be sure of a lot if you were sure of that, Stevie,' said Long, shaking his head and looking away in the distance.

'You'd be sure of nothing if you married a doll that might walk out on you in the morning,' said Kenefick.

They got great value out of that landlady.

But then, all of a sudden, things took a nasty turn. Celia Kent and the chemist had some sort of row, and she stopped going away for week-ends with him. Kenefick, being a cold-blooded, realistic chap, couldn't refrain from pointing out to Mac that that was the way affairs like that always ended up, but by this time Mac was in such a state of illumination that even this didn't worry him. He said the fellow might have his own reasons.

But it stopped being a joke when Celia Kent said she was closing up the house and taking a job in a factory. As I say, looking for digs in wartime was no joke. The town we were in was packed like a cattle-truck, and the only alternative was the place where I was, but the factory was about three miles away. That was a terrible joint. Every night, wet or fine, it was a pleasure to me to jump on my bike and get away from it.

Kenefick offered to increase the rent, but Mrs Kent said it wouldn't be worth her while. For all her old gab she was cut up about whatever the fellow in the chemist's had done to her. That night when the three Irish lads came into the pub by the Castle they were nearly scratching one another's eyes out. I can't say I felt much sympathy for them. They never showed any for me.

'Well,' I said, 'maybe the next landlady ye get, ye won't be so critical.'

'But what the hell are we to do, lads?' said Mac, giving me a fishy look with his squint eye. 'This is getting frightfully serious.'

'There's nothing we can do, there's nothing we can do,' said Kenefick, jingling the coins in his trousers pockets and looking at the floor. You could see the man was hurt at the very suggestion that there was anything he hadn't thought of. ' 'Tisn't money she wants — ye saw that.'

'What does she want?' asked Mac.

'She wants a man,' said Kenefick glumly — and he didn't put it as nicely as that either. Kenefick believed in calling a spade a spade.

'Ye might kidnap Clements and make him marry her,' said I, but the three of them looked at me the way you'd look at a man who made a joke in a wakehouse.

'Well,' said Mac, half in joke and half in earnest, 'what's wrong with one of ourselves?'

'Couldn't be done, Mac,' said Kenefick, still studying

the floor. 'We haven't the knack of that sort of thing.'

'Who was talking about that sort of thing?' asked Mac. 'What's wrong with the girl anyway?'

Kenefick raised his eyes slowly from the floor and took a good look at Mac to see if he was in his right mind.

'Are you suggesting one of us ought to marry her?' he said.

'No,' said Mac, having it put up to him like that. 'I only wanted to know what was wrong with her.'

Kenefick put back his head and laughed till the tears came to his eyes.

'Holy God!' he said. 'How is it none of us thought of that before?'

The very notion of it seemed to put them into good humour again.

'Well,' I said, 'Mac always had a great liking for this country.'

'Here, boys,' said Mac, beginning to giggle, 'do you think she would have me? I'm not a bad-looking chap, sure I'm not.'

'Damn fine-looking chap, Mac,' said Kenefick. 'Besides, she can always get rid of you.'

At that Mac let on to be deeply offended.

'What way is that to encourage a man?' he said indignantly. 'I'm only suggesting it for the good of the crowd.'

'But what matter, Mac?' said Kenefick. 'As you say yourself — a little thing like that!'

At the same time I was surprised. I saw that for all his larking Mac was more in earnest than he let on to be. He went off for a round of drinks and started blackguarding with the barmaid. I don't know what there is about a squint that women like, but Mac could be popular enough when the fancy took him.

'Here, lads,' he said, coming back with the drinks, 'we're forgetting the spokesman of the party. Stevie is the right man for this job, a fine, educated chap and all.'

'Anything to oblige, Mac,' said Kenefick, taking it in good part, 'but certain interested parties mightn't understand.'

'Good God!' said Mac, letting on to be staggered. 'Has anyone in this place any sense of responsibility? You wouldn't mind doing a little thing like that for the sake of a friend, Jerry?' he said to me.

'I'd be delighted, Mac,' said I. 'Ye wouldn't have a spare bed?'

'What about Longie?' said Kenefick, sprawling against the counter and pulling the old hat down over his eyes. 'We all know he's from Limerick, and no one ever went back there that could avoid it.'

We were all entering nicely into the spirit of the thing when he said that. Longie didn't laugh.

'I think he'd be a lucky man that would get her, Stevie,' he said with a stammer.

'Think so, Tim?' asked Kenefick, getting serious too.

'We talk as if the woman ought to be honoured,' Longie said, raising his eyebrows into his hair. 'She's beyond us.' Then he shook his head as if he didn't know what was coming over the world and looked at his drink. 'Beyond us,' he said.

That was one of the longest connected statements we ever got out of Longie, so it cast a sort of gloom over the proceedings.

'You might be right, Tim,' said Kenefick.

'Would you marry her, Longie?' said Mac excitedly.

'I wouldn't have the chance, Mac.'

'But would you? Would you if you had?' repeated Mac.

'To tell you the truth, Mac,' said Longie in a low voice, 'I'd consider myself honoured.' The he raised his brows, looked sadly at me as if I was the one who was responsible for all the levity, shook his head once or twice and repeated 'Honoured.'

'I'll make you a fair offer so,' said Mac. 'We'll toss for it.'

This time there was no larking about it. I could hardly credit it but Mac was in earnest. He wanted to marry that girl and settle down in that nice little house of hers, and be a respectable English husband, only he was afraid that the rest of us might think he was a fool. What he really wanted from Longie was encouragement. Longie looked at him and gave a hearty laugh.

'Winning or losing wouldn't improve the chance of a fellow like me, Mac,' he said.

'All right, all right,' snapped Mac, getting impatient with his obtuseness. 'If one of us doesn't succeed the other can have a shot. But are you game?'

Longie gave a sort of lost look at him, at me, and then at Kenefick, as if he was asking himself what you could do with such a foolish man. Then he laughed again.

'I'm game,' he said.

'Come outside so and we'll toss,' said Mac. 'There's no time like the present.'

Kenefick leaned back against the counter with his arms stretched out, his legs wide and one of them cocked up against it — trying to make himself look twice the size. He looked at them like a judge, over the specs and under the brim of the old hat.

'Are ye in yeer right minds?' he asked.

'Never felt better, old man,' said Mac, tossing his head and rubbing his hands.

'Ye're not forgetting, by any chance, that the woman has a family already?' said Kenefick, looking from one to the other.

'Oh, as you're so fond of saying yourself,' said Mac with a laugh, '— a little thing like that!'

'Oh, just as ye like,' said Kenefick, and he finished his drink and went out into the yard after them. It was easy to see he was puzzled. The moonlight was coming in the back passage and a W.A.A.F. and her fellow were sitting there, holding hands. It looked grand out in the yard with the moonlight shining on the old tower of the church.

Kenefick took out a coin, looking very grave. That was where the man's height came in: he couldn't help taking advantage of any occasion that made him feel six feet two.

'Well, lads,' he said, 'what's it to be?'

'Harps,' said Mac.

Kenefick flicked the coin in the air and then stepped aside. He took out an old torch and flashed it on.

'Well, Mac,' he said, 'you seem to be out of this anyway.

Our turn now, Tim!'

'You have nothing to do with this, Stevie,' said Longie after a moment, raising his big paw.

'Who said I had nothing to do with it?' Kenefick asked as if he was looking for a fight.

I tumbled at once to what he meant. He was leader of that gang, and he wasn't going to have them getting out of hand and doing cracked things on their own. It's extraordinary the way vanity takes small men.

'You have other responsibilities,' said Longie, and you could see he was troubled about it.

'Time enough to meet trouble when you come to it,' said Kenefick. Then he looked at me, threw back his head and brayed. 'Holy God!' he said. 'Look at Reilly's face! He thinks we're mad.'

'I know what my landlady would say about ye if she saw ye now,' I said.

'Well, call, man!' said Kenefick.

'Heads, Stevie,' said Longie.

Kenefick tossed again, and it came up harps.

'Well,' he said, turning on his heel, 'that settles it.'

'Yes,' said I, 'and if the girl saw ye 'twould settle ye as well.'

We had another drink, and then went home together up the Main Street, past the Castle and the old church. I was walking with Kenefick. I could see the man still didn't know what to make of it, or how serious the others were, or whether they were serious at all. I don't think he even quite knew what to make of himself, and that probably bothered him most.

'Well,' I said, 'I saw some queer things in my time, but I never before saw three man tossing for a doll. What the devil ailed Mac?'

'Ah,' said Kenefick, 'fellows like him are kept down too much at home. The Yanks are the same. Some of them take it out in drink and more in women. I suppose 'tis only natural.'

'It looked more like hysterics to me,' said I.

He gave a lonesome sort of laugh out of him at that.

'There might be something in that too,' he said.

But he was right about one thing. From the time Longie and the Kent woman started knocking round together, there was no more talk about breaking up the happy home. The thing was a mystery to me for the man had no conversation, but after the Czech and his W.A.A.F. I said it couldn't last.

'Sure, of course it won't last, man,' said Mac with a superior smile.

'I don't know,' said Kenefick. 'I wouldn't be too sure of that. Longie is an interesting fellow. He has a mind of his own.'

'What mind?' said Mac. 'Is it a half idiot of a country boy?'

Kenefick said nothing to that, but when Mac went out the back, he threw back his head and bawled.

'Holy God, Jerry,' he said. 'He's jealous.'

Mind you, I didn't believe him, but he was right. Celia Kent was the sort of woman that when she likes a man always wants to give him things, and from the time she started going out with Longie, she was giving him pullovers and scarves and slippers, and all sorts of things poor Longie didn't want and didn't know what to do with, but it drove Mac wild. He said he was paying as much as Longie and he was entitled to the same treatment. One night when Longie got two rashers of bacon instead of one, he didn't talk until supper was over, then he took his hat and went over to Belmore on the bus and arranged to share with a couple of other fellows there. The same night Kenefick came belting up to my place and I gave notice. I didn't mind how many rashers Longie got so long as I got something to eat.

I was there for the wedding in the Town Hall. I was there too a couple of months after when two bobbies called at the factory and marched Longie off. It seems all the time he had a wife and a house full of kids at home in Clare. Neither Kenefick nor myself heard of it till after, and he called for me to go to the barrack with him. To give the man his due he was very upset.

'Oh, I might have guessed it, I might have guessed it,' he

said, as if it was a miracle to him that he didn't forsee it all. 'And, merciful God,' he said, throwing out his arms like windmills and rolling his eyes to Heaven, 'can't you imagine what the wife and kids are like?'

I could; only too well. A poor devil of a country boy, married at eighteen, and knowing no more of life than a city kid, what chance has he?

When we got to the barrack Long was after being released, and Kenefick said we should cycle back home and tell the Kent girl. It was a spring day with high clouds and a high wind, and there was Kenefick, bent over the handlebars, shouting about Long.

'What the hell did he want to marry her at all for?' he said. 'Couldn't he tell the girl the truth and go and live with her like anyone else?'

'Ah,' said I, 'he had too much respect for her.'

'Respect?' said Kenefick. 'What sort of respect is that? Couldn't he leave her to Mac?'

'Maybe he liked the girl himself,' said I.

'He took a damn queer way of showing it,' said Kenefick.

When Celia heard us she came running out, rubbing her hands in her white coat. Kenefick put on a solemn air, drawing his shoulders up round his scraggy neck, till all he wanted was the black tie.

'Anything wrong, Stevie?' she said in holy terror.

'I'm afraid so, Celia,' he said, clearing his throat. 'Longie's after being arrested.'

'Arrested?' she said, getting pale. 'What was it? Something political?'

'Worse than that,' said Kenefick, who didn't see her point of view about bombs at all. 'It seems he's married already.'

'Tim?' she said. 'Tim married? But why didn't he tell me?'

'Why didn't he tell *me*?' said Kenefick, with his eyes beginning to pop, implying that this was the sort of thing that always happened when people wouldn't ask his advice. 'I could have told him he wouldn't get away with it.'

'What will they do to him?' she asked.

'God knows,' said Kenefick glumly. 'He's released now

of course. He might get six months.'

'Released?' she said. 'But where is he?'

'Walking mad, I suppose,' said Kenefick with a toss of his head. Then he gave her a sharp look. 'You know, of course, that none of us had any idea more than yourself.'

'Oh,' she said with a shrug, 'I don't mind. There's no harm done. I was a fool to take it seriously, that's all. If he'd trusted me I should have behaved just the same.'

'Jerry is probably right,' said Kenefick. 'He says Longie thought too much of you.'

'Do you think so really?' she said to me, but all the same she flushed up. It was the same as the presents. Any little compliment, no matter how silly it was, gave her pleasure. 'Well, it sounds just dotty to me, but if you say so I suppose I'd better go and look for him.'

When we got out in the road, Kenefick lifted the front wheel of his bike and brought it down with a wallop on the road.

'And to think I might be married to that girl!' he said.

It sounded very queer coming from Kenefick, after all he said about her.

'Well,' I said, 'you could still, if it came to that.'

'That one would go into the river after someone she liked,' said Kenefick.

She wouldn't, and I was very surprised to hear a level-headed fellow like Kenefick suggesting it, but it showed me the way the wind was blowing. That evening when neither Longie nor Celia put in an appearance, I almost began to believe the man was right about that too. We made our own supper, went up to the pub, and then dossed down. It was late when the other pair came in. They had an argument about whether or not Longie was going to have his supper, and, judging by the noises, she won. Then she brought us up cups of tea. Kenefick was lying with a book on his knee and one arm under his head, and he looked at her over the specs.

'So you found him?' he muttered.

'Yes,' she whispered. 'In Belmore, looking for lodgings! Of all the dotty bastards! Just fancy! He said his luck was out. "It's not your luck," I said. "It's just that you're dotty." ' Then she laughed, swaying on her heels with her hands behind her back. 'Of all the silly things to do to someone you say you like! That fellow's barmy! Just barmy! He says he wants to come back, and now I suppose I shall have to keep going somehow till he comes out of gaol. Fancy me with a bloke in gaol! That old cat, Mrs Drake, won't half be hopping.'

Then they came up to bed, and for hours they continued talking. She seemed to be speaking pretty sharp to him. I suppose girls like that can nag, just like others. Then the sirens began, and the wailing drifted away across the country, like a bloody big banshee, wringing her hands.

'I was the one that should have married her,' says Kenefick all of a sudden out of the darkness.

I knew what he meant all right. I felt a little bit that way myself. He was the most independent of them. It was just as if some row he was having inside himself was settled, and he wasn't a foreigner any more. Of course, Mac wouldn't have agreed with that at all, but then Mac would never be anything only a foreigner. As my old landlady said 'You could see he wasn't English.'

(1949)

Baptismal

The first serious job I got in the Active Service Unit was as
secretary, bodyguard, and messenger boy to Peter Daly, the
Brigade Commandant. It was a terrific thrill for me. I was
only just turned eighteen. The two of us lived in one room
of a big deserted house outside the city, and I came home
only once a week to change my underclothes. The family
asked no questions and the neighbours treated me as
something like a national hero.

Not that Daly was anyone's idea of a Big Shot. He was a
handsome, tall, broadly-built, easy-going fellow who wore
big specs over his blue eyes, and he had the most disarming
manners. Whenever he got into one of his famous scrapes he
always tried to get out of it by charm. When charm failed
he fell back upon the other thing, but only when it did fail.
He was always most apologetic about these adventures of
his, and when he talked of them it was only to blame his
own foolishness and sympathize with whatever poor
unfortunate might have got hurt on the enemy side. Even
about spies he always managed somehow to say the good
word. He would describe how one of them behaved when
he found himself trapped and then add reflectively, 'Cripes,
Mick, 'twas a blooming shame to bump him off. Sure, he

didn't know what he was doing half the time. I blame Jack Kenefick a lot for that, blackening him to Headquarters.' To a romantic young fellow of eighteen his conversation was a series of anti-climaxes. Why he picked me out at all I don't know, but I think it must have been my studiousness. He rather regarded himself as a spoiled scholar.

'Ah, I shouldn't be in this thing at all, Mick,' he confided in me with a smile. 'I ought to have been a teacher like my old fellow, but the bad drop came out in me. Too bloody wild — that was the trouble with me. Sure, I broke the old man's heart.'

'You might go back to it after,' I suggested.

'Ah, I'm too old, man,' he said regretfully. 'I'm too old. But I'll tell you what I'd like to do if I ever got the chance. I'd like to take up the fiddle properly. Cripes, man, I'm very fond of the fiddle! Do you know, I think if I had the training I might make a bloody good fiddler. Would you believe that?'

I was ready to believe anything about him then; a fellow who had got away half a dozen times from military and police, how could he fail to be a champion fiddler? Now, I'm not so very sure.

We had been knocking round together for a couple of weeks when one day, just before lunch, as we were on the way to one of our meeting places, Daly decided to go up the quays for the sake of quietness. It was a spring day; one of those late March days which are like mid-summer except for the faint cloud of green on the trees. There was hardly a ripple to break the painted hillside reflected in the river. There was hardly a soul except for three little girls playing hop-scotch. Suddenly his lower lip came up like a shutter. 'Look out now!' he said, almost without moving his lips. There was no need for me to look out. We were half-way up, too far to do anything but continue on our way while an armoured car cruised slowly down at our side of the street. There was an officer in a steel helmet watching from the turret, and he had a revolver strapped to his wrist. The officer looked closely at us and Daly looked coolly back at him.

For one moment it seemed as if we might get past, but then the officer bent his head and said something to the driver. Almost at the same moment Daly's gun came from under his coat and fired twice. I fired too for the sake of effect, but the whole thing was over before my finger found the trigger. The armoured car swung suddenly out of control and mounted the pavement within a few feet of us.

'Run for it now!' shouted Daly, doubling up, and as we reached the shelter of a side street the machine gun on the armoured car started to tear the bricks off the corner.

Daly didn't halt until we had traversed two or three back streets and were approaching the main east to west thoroughfare. He was grinning broadly and his eyes had a sparkle in them. I wasn't in the least sparkling. I was an exceedingly harrassed young man. Everything had gone too fast for me.

'Think we got that officer?' I panted, trying to make my voice sound matter-of-fact.

'If we didn't we gave him a good fright,' said Daly, stopping to straighten his tie in a shop window.

'What'll we do now?' I asked, panic suddenly catching up with me.

'We'll look at the ducks,' he replied with a chuckle, and, taking me by the arm, he led me up the long, tree-shaded avenue towards the park. It was pretty full; we had to share a bench with a couple of old bobbies discussing horses and jockeys, and I had the mortification of listening to Daly talking about ducks to a couple of barefooted kids.

'I'll give you a penny now if you'll point out the drake to me,' he said.

'That wan, mister,' said one.

' 'Tis not,' said the other. 'There he is mister!'

'Ye're both wrong,' said Daly. 'How old are ye?'

'Nine, mister.'

'And where do ye go to school?'

'Sullivan's Quay, mister.'

'And you mean to tell me in Sullivan's Quay school they don't teach fellows of nine to know a drake from a duck? What sort of old school is that?'

Then he gave them both pennies. He seemed to like kids. Later in the afternoon, when we felt the holds-up would have eased off a bit, we went back down the way we had come to an ice-cream shop where we had tea. Having missed my lunch, I was ravenous. As we came out a newsboy was skeltering past and I bought a paper. There it was, in the *Late News*, a few insignificant lines.

> Shortly after one o'clock today an armoured car was ambushed close to the North Gate Bridge by a party of me armed with revolvers, sub-machine guns and bombs. In the subsequent engagement, Martha Darcy (8) 42 Coleman's Lane was injured, and, on admission to the hospital was found to be dead. Several of the attackers are believed to have been wounded.

I laughed with mortification at the last sentence, but Daly's face clouded.

'I didn't see any kids, did you, Mick?' he asked anxiously.

'As a matter of fact, I did,' I said. 'There were three of them playing pickie.'

'I wish to God I'd seen them,' he said gloomily.

'Why?' I said. 'It wouldn't have made any difference.'

'Maybe not,' he said, 'but I might have taken some precaution.'

We went on down a side street. It was all very well for him, but it seemed rather uncalled-for to spoil sport over my baptism of fire. Of course, I was sorry for the kid too, but there was nothing we could do about that now.

'Like a drink?' I asked, seeing him so low.

'Do you know, I think I would,' he replied thoughtfully, and we went into the first pub we came to and sat in the snug, which was empty.

'Stout?' I asked.

'No, whiskey,' he replied. 'I need it.'

'Oh, it's a bit of a shock all right,' I agreed, 'but you can't let things like that prey on you. You need all the nerve you have.'

'I know that, Mick,' he said in a depressed tone, 'but I was always very fond of kids.'

'Oh, so was I,' I agreed, 'but still, accidents happen.'

'That doesn't make it any easier for the fellows that

cause them though,' he said with a half smile.

'I don't honestly see how you can say we caused it,' I argued. 'After all, it isn't as if we used the machine gun.'

'Ah, I know all that,' he said with a trace of impatience, 'but, merciful God, Mick, death isn't a matter of argument. A kid of eight, playing pickie on the pavement — what does it matter who fired the shot? A lot you'd care if she was yours! The kid is dead, and that's all about it.'

'I grant you that,' I expostulated, 'but after all, kids get killed every day. They get killed because a commercial traveller with a thirst wants to get in before closing time, or because some slum landlord wants to squeeze the last ha'-penny out of their fathers and mothers, and it doesn't matter to anybody. Our job does matter. It matters to the kids themselves more than it does to us.'

'Oh, that's the right way to look at it,' he agreed with a nod. 'I know you're right. It's only that I'm a bit of a fool about kids.'

For a few moments his face changed again; the lower jaw hardened as though he were trying to speak without moving his lips and a hard look came in his eyes. 'But I'm telling you, Mick Mahoney, if the kid was mine, I'd never stop till I got some of the fellows that were responsible, and I wouldn't mind much which side they were on.'

I felt rather like an offended David singing before Saul. I thought Daly really let his taste for anti-climax go a bit too far. He seemed to read what was in my mind for he suddenly gave an attractive grin and went to the counter.

'I suppose you think I'm a bit dotty?' he said over his shoulder, half in amusement, half in mockery.

'I didn't think you were so very dotty this morning.'

'You'll go back and tell the squad that Peter Daly is nothing but an old softy?' he went on.

'I'll say he's a very lucky man.'

'Cripes, do you know, 'tis true for you, Mick,' he exclaimed with sudden boyish ingenuousness. 'If they managed to get us today 'tisn't other people's troubles we'd be fretting about now. We ought to be down on our bended knees. We'll have another drink and then we'll knock off for the day. Do you know what I feel like doing? Going to the blooming Opera House! 'Tis years since I saw a show.'

We finished our drinks and set off down the same side streets towards the river. Daly was in better fettle; he was even laughing at himself.

' 'Pon my soul, Mick,' he said, 'but we're a comical mob. A lot of blooming amateurs that'll never be anything else. And it all comes of not having a little garden of your own. It does, I declare to my God!'

Then as we passed the corner of a street leading to the river a group of old women at the opposite wall bawled at us.

'Don't go in there, boys! There's English soldiers in there.'

Daly paused and then crossed the road to them.

'What's that you said, ma'am?' he asked with his head cocked.

'Soldiers, sir,' gabbled one. 'They're mad drunk. They smashed the head of one poor man up the road.'

'How many of them are there?' asked Daly, and again his jaw was set.

'Four of them, sir.'

'Have they guns?'

'No, sir, only bottles and belts.'

'That's all right so,' he said and his face cleared. 'We'll see have they any empties. Come on, Mick,' he said to me, 'and give that gun of yours a rest. We did enough of harm today.'

'Oh, just as you like,' I said, well-pleased that it wasn't going to mean anything more serious.

He went ahead of me, pushed in the swing door, and stood with his back to it, erect and resolute.

'What's going on here?' he shouted.

There was a lot going on. It was an old-fashioned pub with a pedimented mahogany display stand and an arcade of mirrors. The mirrors were in smithereens and the display bottles were smashed or overturned and dripping on to the floor. They were obviously being used as cock-shots. Four

Tommies in solitary grandeur were sitting at a table in the middle of the glass-covered floor with a couple of bottles of whiskey before them.

'Here's the bloody I.R.A. boys!' yelled one, a little runt of a man, and with extraordinary swiftness and accuracy he sent a bottle flying at Daly's head. Daly ducked; the bottle smashed against the wall, and then in three or four great strides he was across the room and throttling the little man at the other side of the table. Two of the Tommies bolted; no doubt they thought the whole I.R.A. was after them. The fourth was pluckier; he flung himself on Daly and I flung myself on him. He was pretty beefy, and I haven't the build for all-in wrestling, but, on the other hand, he was half-canned and I wasn't. We wrestled while I waited for a chance to trip him and I noticed Daly and the smaller Tommy rolling across the floor. Daly was the more powerful, but the Tommy fought with tremendous agility. Suddenly there was a loud bang, and the smaller Tommy sprang up and bolted. I started to pull my own gun, but the big fellow wouldn't oblige me by waiting. I followed him to the door and saw the two of them disappearing down the street. I raised my gun but I hadn't the heart to fire. With a certain feeling of complacency I returned, sticking my gun back in my holster, and then I noticed Daly still prostrate on the floor.

'What is it, Peter?' I asked.

'I'm shot,' he replied in a dull voice, his lower jaw stiff.

'Shot?' I echoed incredulously. 'Where are you shot?'

'In the chest. He had a gun all the time. I'm done for.'

I saw the tiny hole the bullet had made in his vest and tried to repress the panic that rose in me.

'You're not done for as long as you can still talk about it,' I said with assumed cheerfulness. 'The hospital is only at the end of the street. Can you make it?'

'I'll try,' he said between his teeth.

I put my arm under his shoulders and he raised himself firmly enough.

'It can't be very bad when you can do that,' I said, but he didn't reply.

'What is it at all, sir?' one of the old women asked as I helped him out.

'Ye were wrong about the guns,' I said bitterly. 'One of ye run ahead to the hospital and tell them there's a wounded man down the road.'

When we reached the side door of the hospital two of the women were already there, talking in the hall to a young doctor in a white coat.

'Ye can't stop here, lads,' he said. 'The place is full of soldiers.'

'This man is badly wounded,' I informed him. 'You'll have to do something for him. He can't go any further.'

'Where is he hit?' he asked, helping Daly to a bench.

'The left side.'

'All right. Leave him here and I'll do what I can for him. But for Christ's sake clear out you, and take whatever stuff ye have with you. Those fellows upstairs are mad.'

'What ails them?'

'One of their fellows was killed by the bridge this morning and they're out for blood. Come back when they're gone and ask for me. MacCarthy is my name.'

'So long, Peter,' I said to Daly who was lying back on the bench with somebody's coat under his head. 'I'll see you later on.' But his eyes were closed and he didn't answer me.

I went out again into the warm summer-like evening. Before the hospital I saw four or five armoured lorries with sentries posted. I dumped the guns in a little paper shop nearby and went back again to the park. It had turned cold; the park had emptied and I had the bench all to myself. Suddenly I found myself shaking all over. I wasn't really afraid for Daly. A man with a bullet in his heart doesn't walk a couple of hundred yards as he had done. And still I was scared. I was as bad about him as he had been about the kid. Those weeks of constant association had brought him closer to me than people I had lived with all my life, and death had become real to me through him. I almost wished I had never met him.

I returned when the park was closing. The avenue was

quiet, and the young trees made an early dusk. The lorries had gone so I went to the main hall and asked for MacCarthy. He came down the stairs three at a time with his white coat flying. He didn't know me.

'How's the patient?' I asked lightly.

'Oh, your pal! I'm sorry but he's dead.'

'Dead?' and I must have gone white for he steadied me with his hand.

'Come up to my room and have a drink. Who was he, by the way?'

'Peter Daly, the Brigade Commandant.'

'Good God!' he exclaimed from the nationalist half of his mind. 'The poor devil was dead before you were out the door,' he added professionally.

'Would you like a look at him?'

'I suppose I might as well,' I said hopelessly. Between weariness and strain I was on the point of tears.

Rattling on about the way the English soldiers had gone on in the hospital, he led the way across a yard to a shed like a garage with a big door that opened on a side street and a small window high up which let in little light. He switched on a solitary light with an office shade. Under it three figures were laid out, and the nearest was Daly's. He looked very peaceful and somehow different, as if only the fighter had died in him and left the fiddler he had wanted to be.

But what really froze the blood in me was the grouping of those figures on the slab, for one was a little girl of eight with a high bumpy brow and brown, bobbed hair and the other was the fair-haired officer whose face I had last seen looking down at me from the turret of the armoured car. In spite of the bandages you could see that the back of his head was gone. It all came intolerably close to me; I was walking up the quay beside Daly, and the officer was watching us from the armoured car and the little girl was playing hop-scotch a hundred yards away under the trees in their first leaf. Everything was living and shining at one moment and at the next it was black out. It was like being in at the end of the world. I said nothing to the doctor; I didn't think he'd understand.

Later in his room while we were drinking, looking down on the dark river and the slumland streets beginning to light up in the dusk I tried to explain to him. It was like a weight on my chest, but as I expected, he didn't really know what I was talking about. He thought I was tight. You have to be through a thing like that to understand it, and even then what you feel isn't understanding. I suppose there really isn't anything to understand.

(1951)

What Girls Are For

For years I couldn't see what God intended girls for at all. They struck me as the most useless articles and a real nightmare in the home. The way they went on about their old frocks and their silly dolls disgusted me. There was my sister, Biddy, for instance. She was more than a year younger than I was. Nothing worried her. She maundered round the house like a half-idiot, humming to herself, having forgotten whatever it was she was looking for.

You couldn't send her on a message because she forgot what it was the moment she was outside the door, and a quarter of an hour afterwards you found her playing down the avenue with the money in the pocket of her pinafore and the hair hanging down over her right eye. Then she would brush back the hair as if it was the cobweb on her brain and say: 'Oh, I forgot.'

Sometimes I thought that she wasn't half the fool she let on to be. Because, of course, I came in for most of the errands. I had to pay for having a head on me. As if I hadn't responsibilities enough as Chief Gang Leader!

She couldn't even understand why I should be Chief Gang Leader. According to her, there was no necessity for it, and no honour in having the job. To her the avenue where she played hopscotch with the Daly kids was only just an avenue like any other, but to me, the bend in it was no man's land, a place I had to approach carefully, and the corner by the gas lamp the frontier of our gang territory and the scene of endless desperate battles with the Tram Terrace kids, who were kept out of the avenue at all only by dread of our Corner Patrol.

While I worried myself sick about how I was to keep up the Corner Patrol, she went home and reported that I was playing with the Hendrick children. Of course, I wasn't playing with them; I didn't even like them. But what could you do with mothers and fathers that kept their sons in at night to do homework instead of letting them out on patrol? If the patrol broke down, little chance the Dalys or Biddy would have had of playing hopscotch in the avenue. The Tram Terrace kids — a ferocious gang! — would have seen to that.

I broke her of the spying by getting the whole gang to torture her one night. She went screeching to father — she had a special screech for father's benefit that he could hear from the end of the avenue — and I got a good hiding, but after that she left the gang alone. As I told her: 'A torture is worse than a good hiding any day.'

She had no idea — nobody who hasn't been in the position himself could have any idea — of the worry and expense of being Chief Gang Leader. We got a penny a week — twopence if we were lucky — and any Chief Gang Leader will tell you that you can't run a gang on that.

You had to arm chaps that had no guns — and the ones you couldn't over-awe by exceptional strength or daring, you had to give things to. I often thought if only I had a shilling a week instead of a penny I could have bought over sufficient forces to clear not only the avenue but the whole road, and make our territory impregnable from the sea-front to Tram Terrace.

That was really why I used to make what I called Viking raids and Biddy called stealing. It wasn't stealing really; it was all for the gang funds. She had endless places she used to hid her money in, but sometimes I found it even then, and she went screeching to father. 'He took my penny — boo-hoo-hoo!'

It was disgusting. Though she knew better than to tell mother when I made Viking raids on the housekeeping money, she used to be always at me in a low, blood-curdling voice, following me round like an old witch. 'You'll be caught yet, Willie Jackson. The police will be up to you. You took three shillings out of mummy's purse. God sees you.' Sometimes she drove me so wild that I went mad and twisted her arm or pulled her hair or made smithereens of her old dolls, and then she went off, screeching again, and I got clouted. I got more cloutings through her than through anything else. I hated her.

It was while I was worrying about the gang that we had a baby. Frankie was small and fat and nearly always in good humour, and whenever he saw Biddy or me he laughed himself sick. He always thought when you covered him up that he was losing his toes and would start looking to see what had happened to them.

'Toes, Frankie!' I'd say, and first he'd look at his hands and give them a chew to see that they were the real article, and then he'd begin working his arms and legs, cross-eyed with excitement till he had the last stitch of clothes off him and could see his toes again.

I was allowed to lift him when he had wind, but Biddy wasn't, because she was still too small. Yet, in spite of that, she was the one he liked best. It was a bit of a disappointment to me. He knew her very step on the path, and he'd try to lift himself, and then make a queer coughing little noise that he used only to draw our attention. It was different from the way he coughed when he was hungry, because then he was usually cross, but this other cough was all a joke. Biddy came up then and coughed back, and they went at it till he was exhausted. After that he shook his head at her, and that was a signal for her to waggle her pigtails at him. When she shook her head they danced from shoulder to shoulder. Frankie goggled, trying to follow them, till he ended up with his two eyes looking different ways.

But when he grew a little older, it became a nuisance. He wouldn't even take a bottle except from her, and when she wasn't around and we couldn't get her, he kicked up a terrible row. In the end, if Biddy wanted to do anything or go anywhere, she had to take off her shoes and whisper, and even then he could sometimes recognize the whisper and you'd hear him in the bedroom, beginning to cough ....

Then he got a bad cold — it was looking for his toes when there was nobody around that brought it on — and, one night, Biddy woke me and whispered fiercely into my ear.

'Willie,' she said, 'our Frankie is ill. I hope he's not going to die.'

'How do you know he's ill?' I asked.

'That's not a right scream at all,' she said. 'Listen to it!'

I listened and, sure enough, it frightened me. I got up and went to the door of mother's room.

'Is Frankie ill, Mummy?' I asked.

'I think he's got a bit of a cold,' said mother lightly. 'Run back to bed now or you'll be getting another. Frankie will be better in the morning.'

He wasn't better in the morning. He was all hot and choking and his face was very red. Miss Regan, the health visitor, was called in, and she thought it better to send for the doctor. Biddy and I stayed for a while with him in the big bedroom, but he wouldn't play with us at all. Biddy tossed her pigtails and just once he smiled and made a little motion of his head, but all at once he began to wail, and you could almost hear him telling you that he was too sick to play. When mother tried to give him a drink he screamed and pushed it away, and it was from Biddy he took it at last. We had to go to school, and I went in misery, wondering if he'd be dead before I got back. Life without that baby seemed impossible.

The doctor came in the afternoon, and I knew from the way he spoke to mother that Frankie was very bad.

I didn't know what to do with myself. It was terrible watching him trying to get his breath, coughing and choking and terrified out of his wits, and not to be able to do anything for him. Mother went into town to get the medicine the doctor ordered.

I went out to play, but every five or ten minutes I went mooching back with a sense of guilt on me until at last Miss Regan shouted at me not to be all the time opening the bedroom door. Then I went to the front door and started to cry all to myself. The road was almost empty and there was no one to watch my tears. I realized then the hollowness of being Chief Gang Leader.

Miss Regan came out to see if my mother was coming and saw me crying. 'What are you crying for?' she asked brusquely.

'Frankie's going to die,' I said and I was so babyish with grief that I turned and put my head in her skirt and my arms about her legs.

'God is good, child,' she said, patting me on the head, but that did not comfort me. I never yet heard anyone say that God was good unless they meant that He'd need to be. And when she went in again I made the sacrifice of my life and promised Him that if only Frankie didn't die I'd give up the Viking raids and hand over the position of Chief Gang Leader to Ernie Thompson.

I felt a fellow couldn't do more. If God didn't pay attention to that, He'd never pay attention to anyone.

Then my mother came in from town with a bottle and a jar with a spout. I heard her and Miss Regan discussing the way you should use it. They put medicine and boiling water in the jar and put the spout to Frankie's lips, but the moment they did, it started him coughing, and he went black in the face, screaming and waving his arms.

'Let me try him,' said Miss Regan quietly, and she took Frankie herself, but he only got worse. Biddy was sitting, watching them and saying nothing.

'You're only chocking him, Miss Regan,' she said all at once. 'If you'd give him to me, I'll have a try,' said Biddy.

'Silly girl! What could you do more than the rest of us?' replied Miss Regan.

'She's very good with him all the same,' said my mother. 'He'll do things for her he wouldn't do for me.'

'I suppose it'll do no harm, anyway,' said Miss Regan.

She put Frankie on Biddy's knee, and Biddy took the spout of the jar in her own mouth and began coughing like mad.

Frankie gave her a look. The poor kid seemed to think he was missing something special.

'Frankie try now!' she said, and she put the spout of the jar in his mouth again, but again he choked and began to wail.

'It's no good,' said my mother distractedly. 'The poor child would be safer in bed.'

'Let her alone now, ma'am,' said Miss Regan, watching Biddy with a smile, and I saw that she really thought Biddy was being quite clever with him.

Biddy didn't wait for any orders. The moment Frankie began to cry, she put the jar back in her own mouth and coughed again, and Frankie turned round and looked up at her. He couldn't make out for the life of him what fun she got out of it, but he felt that there must be something in it for him. Next time he coughed, Biddy coughed louder, and this time he didn't cry. It was extraordinary the way she got him quietly sucking away at the jar.

' 'Pon my soul,' said Miss Regan with amusement, 'you'd think he knew what she was saying. Do you know, Mrs. Jackson, if I were you I'd light a fire in her room and leave him along with her tonight.

'And supposing he got a bad turn?'

'You'd hear him just the same,' said Miss Regan. 'I think he might rest easier with her around.'

That night our room felt grand with the big, roaring fire that father stoked down and the candle lighted by Biddy's bed. But it wasn't so grand when I tried to get to sleep. Frankie was getting worse all the time. Every five or ten minutes he had his fits of choking and screaming, and several times they were so bad that either father or mother came in to see how he was. I was a very heavy sleeper and it took a lot to wake me, but that did it, and somehow, when I woke, I was too sleepy to be sorry for him or for anyone, only myself, and I wished that God would make up His mind quickly about whether He wanted me to be Chief Gang Leader or not.

Biddy didn't seem to mind so much; she wasn't such a heavy sleeper, and she seemed to hear every sound. It was nearly morning when I woke and saw her sitting by the fire in her nightdress with Frankie on her lap, turning his head to see where the candlelight was coming from. She was giving him his inhalation; although mother had told her to knock on the wall, she had boiled the kettle herself.

Then father came in with a dressing-gown wrapped round him, and he just stood and nodded at her two or three times.

'Shall I get you the boiling water for his inhaler?' he asked in a meek little voice that didn't sound like daddy's at all.

'I got it myself, Daddy,' she said, and, to my astonishment, he only nodded again.

'Good girl!' he said. 'I'll put him back in the cradle for you now.'

'No, Daddy,' she said, 'I'll bring him into my own bed. He won't get so frightened there.'

'You might be right,' said my father thoughtfully. 'I'll put a bottle in for you.'

And away with her across the room with Frankie in her arms and father not saying a word to her. The girl was breaking every rule and, instead of being ticked off, she had everyone waiting on her hand and foot, and only dying to get more orders from her.

Even the next day when the doctor came she had to be in the room with him for fear Frankie would get frightened, and I noticed that he gave his instruction first to her and then to mother. As he went out, he said to mother: 'That's a smart little girl of yours, but I wouldn't let her tire herself too much.'

Mother put her to bed, but once she went, Frankie kicked up a row again. Whenever mother or Miss Regan went near him he only screeched. The child was mad with rage, and they were afraid to cross him for fear of putting him into convulsions.

Biddy heard him even in her sleep, and while Miss Regan and mother were both singing songs to him, trying to keep him quiet, the door opened and in came Biddy with her hair over her eyes and her lids glued together with sleep.

You could see she didn't know where she was, but she couldn't keep away from the child. I was full of pride in her then and really sorry about smashing up her old dolls. I suppose it was on them really that she practised it.

That night was the worst of all. Whatever the doctor had told her, Biddy made up her mind not to take her eyes off Frankie, she just sat up in bed with her hands round her knees or lay back, trying to look at a couple of comics my father had bought her. He was in a couple of times to stoke the fire and see if there was anything she wanted, and then I fell off asleep. Suddenly she woke me. Again it was coming on to morning, for the dawn was just peeping in the window.

'Willie!' she whispered, 'Willie, wake up! Frankie's better.'

'All right,' I groaned. 'Let me alone.' I was still half asleep.

'But listen, can't you? Listen!' And then she gave a small cough, and I heard an answering cough from the cradle.

At that, I got up at once. Biddy was sitting by the cradle, just looking at the baby. She had a peculiar soft look on her face. I thought maybe she was still half asleep like I was. Then she wagged her head and began to toss her hair from side to side.

Frankie smiled and tossed his own head three or four times. You could see the kid was better. The first thought in my mind was: I'm not Chief Gang Leader any more, and just for the moment I felt a bit sorry for myself, but then I realized that I wasn't really sorry at all, and the thought went to my head.

'I'm going to tell mummy,' I shouted and made for the door.

'No, no!' Biddy said, starting to whine. 'You mean, dirty thing. I should tell her.'

But she spoke too late, for I had dashed into the big bedroom, and at my first words my father leaped out of bed and came thumping after me.

'What's up, Biddy?' he asked.

'That mean thing,' Biddy said, pointing at me with one hand, while she rubbed her eyes with the other. 'He went in and told you, and he wouldn't let me tell you, and it was I made Frankie better, and he never did anything at all. Boo-hoo-hoo!'

'I did do anything at all,' I shouted, wild with the injustice of it. 'I promised God to give up the gang if he made Frankie better.'

'You little puppy!' my father said angrily. 'Couldn't you let the child come in herself?'

'I only wanted to tell you quick,' I said, and threw myself on the other bed and began to cry, too.

'Of all the families!' said my mother, raising her hands to heaven. 'Aren't you ever done squabbling? And none of you caring whether the child is better or not.'

But it was all just like old times, and I saw that, Chief Gang Leader or no Chief Gang Leader, I would still be persecuted by that girl for the rest of my days. That, I suppose, is mainly what girls are for.

(1951)

Adventure

1

When adventure came to me first, it came in a form I was not expecting. I was living in Cork; I was turned twenty, and I felt my life was at an end. I knew it could only be renewed by some impossible female, preferably foreign and experienced in love, though not so experienced as not to be converted overnight to the ideal of absolute fidelity, which was all I felt strong enough for. I was sure there must be such women in the world. Meanwhile I neglected no opportunity of searching for them in quarters where you might have expected them to appear, like the Operatic Society, but the only woman I got to know there was a nice little girl called Doris Beirne who sang in the chorus and lived not far away from me in Gardiner's Hill, a quarter of unexceptionable respectability.

If I had been trying to elude adventure instead of seeking it. I should have seen the hand of Divine Providence in that. Even for Cork Protestants the Beirnes were astonishingly placid. The old man, who didn't seem to have an enemy in the world, was musical, and his wife's sister,

Miss Adams, who kept house for him, though anything but musical and playing Doris's accompaniments in the style of a retired drum major, was equally inoffensive. Doris herself was so sweet and earnest that she either waded or jumped the jokes you made to her, as if they were part of an obstacle race.

She was being courted in a family manner by a young shopkeeper called Tom Diamond. Tom was a good fellow, a cricketer, and fond of his glass. Miss Adams, who admired him enormously, explained to me that he had inherited an excellent business bled white by his family, and that it might be years before he could settle down. Obviously, she hoped Doris could wait. He and I saw a good deal of one another at the house but never became friends. At first I thought this was due to jealousy on his part, but it wasn't. Miss Adams' notions of his circumstances were all second-hand, and the family knew little more of him than I did, and that, according to my standards of the time, was not enough to base a friendship on.

Very different was my response to Martin Holmes. Holmes was English; a businessman, loud-voiced and blustering like one who had begun on the road, but very different from other commercials I had met. He was a powerfully built man, rather fat, fond of his food, and all curves like a prima donna. It was an experience to walk behind him down the road, for he seemed to move downwards as well as forward; he cocked his head right and left, and with each step a wiggle seemed to start at the nape of his neck and travel down all his curves to his ankles. It gave him a slight suggestion of levitation, as though he wore pneumatic shoes. I think now I liked him for his own sake, but I find it hard to be sure because I liked him so much for the incidental excitements he brought with him, gaiety, recklessness, unrest. He gave you an impression of extroverted infallibility, of knowing the answers to everything. He drove unerringly at reckless speeds, taking chances that made you jump, When he entertained it was in lavish style, and he talked of things that nobody in Cork even mentioned, that I sometimes thought were known only to myself.

Holmes had the gift of intimacy, the gift of calling you by your Christain name at the first meeting and, when he got to know you, of treating you as father confessor and pouring out on you his past humilations and weaknesses. He had done about everything, and that was informative: a man could do these things and yet remain attractive and sensitive. He was obviously not easy in his mind about them, and that was equally satisfactory: whether or not you wanted to be on the right side, you were. You could advise and admonish. You could help. You could even make it easier for him by confessing your own troubles, and that was a great relief.

In spite of all these attractions, Doris's aunt didn't really like him. Perhaps she hadn't so much to confess. She was a lively, gossipy little woman with a snub nose, so that the reading glasses never came really in front of her eyes, and she usually talked with her head down. She was lively, even jolly, but she thought dinner in the Imperial extravagant and anything stronger than lemonade sinful. Holmes laid himself out to capture her; he brought her presents; he pretended it was really on her account that he came to the house, and reserved for her the deep, charmer's voice which he assumed to difficult women customers.

'Miss Adams,' he would say, putting his arm fondly about her shoulder, 'don't you realize what a holiday it is for me to get you out? Don't you realize what a favour you are doing me?'

'Favour?' she exclaimed. 'Spending your money? I would do you a greater favour by frying a couple of rashers for you.'

He knew it was all no good. In spite of his bounce and brag he was far from complacent, and with feminine curves had a sort of feminine sensibility. Actually he sized it up far better than I.

'You know, Dick,' he said one night when he was driving me home, 'Doris's aunt hates the sight of me.'

He spoke without resentment, even with amusement, as though he thought it was one up for the old lady.

'I wouldn't say she hated you,' I said doubtfully. 'What makes you think that, Martin?'

'She doesn't trust me with Doris,' he said. 'She thinks the world of Diamond. You can't blame her, of course.'

I could, and did. Diamond was a very nice, quiet fellow, if it was nice, quiet fellows you wanted, but Holmes, whatever his faults, was an exceptional man. Doris knew that. So did Diamond, though he didn't let it appear. He came weekly to the house, just as before, and even when Doris was out with Holmes stayed on, chattering to her father and aunt, sucking his pipe and apparently not in the least disturbed. Holmes appeared to be quite touched by Diamond's devotion, and went out of his way to do little bits of business for him when he went to England.

'You know, Dick,' Holmes said to me one night when we were having a drink at his hotel, 'if I ever behaved badly to Doris, Tom would stick a knife in me.'

'A knife?' I said incredulously. 'Tom Diamond? You're a blooming romantic, man! Diamond wouldn't stick a knife in anybody.'

'Not even somebody who'd injured Doris?'

'Not even somebody who'd murdered his grandmother.'

'I wouldn't be too sure,' Holmes said thoughtfully. 'He thinks Doris is marvellous, and the funny part of it is, he's right.'

That astonished me equally, because you don't usually think the girl up the road is marvellous, especially in a provincial town where the least adventurous has to keep half his mind free for fantasy, and where you could easily grow up next door to a future international celebrity without seeing him as anything but a joke. To understand what Holmes meant, I had to imagine myself a stranger from Mars and try to look at familiar things with strange eyes, but even then I had to justify Holmes more by reason than faith.

Looked at like that, Doris was unusual all right; unusual, not for any particular quality, but for an accumulation of apparently unimportant details: the way she remembered little things her father and aunt liked, the way she deferred to other people's wishes, the way she called at the hospital to inquire for a neighbour and remembered to ask about another's son who was in the Civic Guards in Dublin. I had known other girls who did these things, but what in them were little spots of colour applied hap-hazard, in Doris formed a design. They came to her not from outside and from the copying of good models, but from an interior core of spirituality which might equally well express itself in other ways.

Of course, Holmes, coming from outside, could see that design as I couldn't, but there was more than that in it. As I have said, the man had a feminine sensibility, and could relate some trifling action of Doris's to a wider conception of her character. I was grateful to him for that, because I still have a large, muddled masculine myopia which makes it possible for me to see generalizations but remain all the time blind to the minute tensions of which ordinary daily life is made up.

At the same time I retained a slight suspicion of Holmes, though this didn't argue any particular perspicacity in me and was merely the normal attitude of the provincial in rebellion, who while flouting the conventions of provincial life retains a lot of the astuteness on which they are based. That, at first, meant nothing: just that I felt ungenerously that in this life one gets nothing for nothing, and if Holmes was kind to me it was because in some way he found, or hoped to find, me useful. But I soon had other reasons for suspicion.

2

One particular evening is very vivid in my mind. In the usual Cork way it built itself up out of nothing. I went for a boring walk up the tree-shaded Western Road, where the crowds coming towards me threw long straight shadows along the pavement, and the girls who passed me out had their faces lit with the setting sun. I ran into Diamond, who having failed to keep an appointment with some of his cricketing and boozing pals, was also at a loose end. We strolled on together. As usual I found him pleasant enough, though as unforthcoming as at Beirne's. It was all non-committal; amusing anecdotes of matches and sprees and praise of his friends. Not a note of malice. At an age when intimacy implies malice, it remained like a barrier between us. I got more and more depressed.

Suddenly a car halted, and we were hailed. Holmes and Doris were inside, and we crossed the road.

'Hop in,' Holmes said commandingly, throwing open the back door for us.

'We're going for a walk,' protested Diamond.

'You're coming for a drink,' said Holmes, looking straight out in front of him. 'Hop in.'

'You know, I think you've had enough, Martin,' Doris said with a gentle smile.

'Nonsense, dear, I haven't begun,' he replied in a lordly way.

I was delighted, I won't say I was actually bored stiff with Tom Diamond's conversation, but at least I felt I should have real conversation — fireworks!

'Don't do that, Martin!' Doris said sharply as, within a minute of starting up, Holmes cut out a car which was sleepwalking up the middle of the road.

'Silly beggar!' Holmes said with a contemptuous backward glance and put on speed.

It wasn't a pleasant spin. He was showing off like mad at the wheel. His talk was all of what his eye caught — a new-model car wrongly designed, a newly built house badly planned: he sang; he passed every blasted thing on the road by inches, and then threw back some withering comment at the driver. After a complete circle in the middle of a busy highway, taken at full speed, he stopped the car dead in front of a pub near the river. He ordered double whiskeys for himself and me, beer for Tom Diamond, who seemed to have taken a sudden aversion to anything stronger, and sherry for Doris. Then he had a long and knowing talk with the publican about distilleries and their managements. He was very queer, frighteningly queer. I still couldn't make up my mind whether or not he was drunk. I've seen drunks in every stage from fuddlesomeness to fight, but I've never really seen anyone else like that. For a real drunk he was far too quick on the draw, far too observant of every shade in our quickly changing attitudes to him, far too alert in the way he pounced on them. He was more like a lunatic. He shouted; he let his voice grow shrill; he told indecent stories with an atrocious laugh which would have taken all the fun out of them even if they had been funny.

Doris grew white. She didn't protest, but once she said in the pained tone of a kid, 'Oh, dear, Martin!' I knew that what was hurting her was not what Holmes said, for she had already accepted him, and Doris was the sort who accepts people entire; nor even that I was listening, for she knew I liked him and would make excuses. It was Tom Diamond's presence that really cut her to the heart, because he represented her family, her upbringing, her childhood. Diamond sank into a deeper and deeper gloom, and between them they performed a dumb duet of misery that almost made me scream.

I wanted Diamond to put a stop to it, but he didn't, and even then I think I half understood that he couldn't. At last Holmes got up to go to the lavatory and told us as much in an infantile way. He didn't even appear to be drunk then; he was too alert, too agile. In a fury I dashed after him and caught him outside the door.

'Do you realize what you're doing?' I asked savagely.

I was astonished at his response. He suddenly smiled, a frank, boyish, good-natured smile, and took my two hands in his.

'Do you think I'm drunk, Dick?' he asked in a quiet voice.

'Do you expect me to believe you're hurting that girl deliberately?' I asked.

'You're a good pal, Dick,' he said emotionally. 'A very good pal. You're not afraid to speak your mind to people you like. You do like me, don't you?'

'I also like Doris, if you want to know,' I said.

'I don't, Dick. I knew it, and she knew it. She trusts

you as she trusts nobody else. Don't mind me, Dick, I swear I'm not really drunk. Just playing the fool. Sometimes, I have to do it.'

At that moment I could have sworn Holmes was as sober as I was. But when he returned to the room he went on worse than ever. This time I forced him out to the car, where he immediately showed his real condition by falling asleep in the back. Doris drove, I sat beside her, and she and Diamond chattered lightly and amiably all the way home. I couldn't talk. I could think of nothing but the stupefied man whose head was lolling over on to Diamond's back. I was bewildered by his apparent sobriety of a short while before. Not until long afterwards did I realize that he hadn't been sober; it had been an improvisation such as he would have put up if a cop had stopped us on the way back, the last reserve of a man whose whole life was an act.

Diamond surprised me. When we parted after leaving the others, he suddenly held out his hand, a thing he never did.

'Thanks, Dick,' he said. 'I don't know what we'd have done without you.'

I was startled and moved by the sudden intimacy of his tone.

'Have you ever seen anything like it?' I asked in bewilderment.

'Never,' he replied with a slight shake of his head. 'I'll take care that I never run the risk of it again either.'

His quietness and gravity were almost over-whelming. I knew that he meant it. I had a sudden flash of perception into the mind of that apparently good-natured and superficial young man, and realized that even if he was not the sort who went about sticking knives into people, his judgements could be equally final and annihilating. It really was an extrordinary evening. I went home and didn't sleep. To see unexpected depths in one person is upsetting enough; to see them in two people at the same time makes you doubt if you are really as wise as you imagine yourself to be at the age of twenty.

3

Next morning Holmes called at my office, quite himself again and with no trace of a hangover. The typist was with me, and he diverted himself by studying the joinery in my stationery cabinet.

'Shocking!' he said. 'You must let me get you a proper one sometime.' Then he sat in the chair at the other side of my desk. 'I called to apologize,' he went on in a deep voice with a slight trace of parson's unction in it. 'I don't quite know what for, but Doris said I should. Was I awful?'

'Pretty bad.'

'I don't remember,' he said gravely, shaking his head. 'I've promised Doris to give up spirits for good. We got engaged this morning. Sometimes things get too much for you. I can't live without that girl, Dick.'

First he put his face in his hands, then leaned on the desk, his head buried in his arms, and sobbed. I was dreadfully embarrassed. Intimacy is all very well, but only when you know how to take it, and this was well beyond my experience. I got up and put my hand awkwardly on his shoulder.

'Did you come for congratulations or sympathy?' I asked with a lightness I didn't feel.

'That's what I'd like to know myself,' he replied, straightening himself and wiping the tears from his face. 'Shall I make a success of it?'

'If you don't, Doris will,' I said.

'That's just what I'm afraid of,' he said gravely. 'I don't want her to make all the sacrifices. I've lived a hard life, but I know the decent thing when I see it.'

We went out for coffee, and, brightening up, he told me again about his life and its empty temptations. They didn't sound so empty as he told them, but I could see that he coveted the permanence and seriousness of Doris. I could almost sympathize with him. That morning I felt closer to him than I had ever felt before.

But Diamond kept his word. He ceased altogether to go to the Beirnes', and Miss Adams, who had been told of the engagement, attributed it to that. I let her. Holmes now stayed at the house whenever he was in Ireland, and Doris and he went off together on his rounds. They rented a house some miles from the city, an old house with a big garden. Holmes intended to make his home in Ireland, and visit England only on business.

In odd ways he continued to disturb me, though I shan't pretend it was altogether unpleasant. He told me, for instance, that Doris and he were lovers, and I am afraid the impropriety of this was lost in the wonder of knowing that such things could be, a subject on which I was glad to be reassured. But he also told me intimate details of Doris's behaviour, and I didn't altogether like that. It wasn't that these things vulgarized her in my mind; on the contrary, it was beginning to dawn on me that it was people like Doris and Tom Diamond who really knew what passion meant. It was not on her account I was troubled but on his. I was embarrassed for him as a friend, to think that at his age and with his experience he could not distinguish between the things one says and the things one doesn't say. As I write, I blush for my own ingenuousness. It wasn't until years after that it struck me that he distinguished perfectly; that he played on my ingenuousness as he played on Doris's inexperience, for his own amusement, and that he used that standard method of seduction to seduce me as well as her. What did he want of me? Did he expect I should go and tell Tom Diamond? There was a slight suggestion of it in the ominous conversation that followed.

'I shouldn't repeat that to anyone else,' I said a bit gruffly.

'I wasn't criticizing her, Dick,' he replied in a reproachful tone.

'Others mightn't think so,' I said, still embarrassed by the memory of his disturbing confidences.

'You mean Tom?' he asked wonderingly.

'He certainly wouldn't consider it a compliment.'

'And might stick a knife in me?'

'No,' I said sharply. 'Doris would do that.'

It was a strange conversation, superficially friendly on both sides, certainly innocent enough on mine, but with

mysterious undertones which kept on sounding in my head
for weeks. I didn't know whether I was imagining them or
not. Sometimes the provincial astuteness came uppermost
in me, and I felt that this was a totally impossible marriage
which was bound to result in disaster; sometimes the
romantic came on top, and I realized that I was a mere
raw provincial boy and envied Doris the world of real
experience which I might never even touch the frontiers.

4

The wedding was fixed for a Saturday in September, and
the whole Beirne family was in a state of convulsions about
it. Holmes came over the week before to make the final
arrangements. He seemed to be in high spirits, but the
evening before he left he asked me to dinner with the
family at the hotel, and when I arrived I found him in an
unusually despondent mood. I didn't pay much heed to that,
because he grew despondent very easily, particularly when
business was bad, and then soared out of it instantaneously
at the first diversion, like a kid. When he and I were outside
in the hall for a few minutes, he took me by the arm.

'You've been a very good friend to Doris and me,' he
said gravely. 'If anything happens to me, I hope you'll
help her.'

'What is it?' I asked. 'Bankruptcy or just t.b.?'

'It's not a joke, Dick,' he said with sombre reproach.

'Ah,' I said, 'everybody goes through these hysterics a
week before the show. You're not the first.'

Next evening, Doris and I saw him off from Glanmire
Station, and he leaned drearily out of the carriage window,
scarcely raising his voice. Doris was alarmed but too well-
trained to give expression to her fears till the pair of us
were climbing the tunnel steps in the evening light. Then
she leaned her arms on the railings and looked down at the
red-brick station at the foot of its cliff, surrounded by empty
yards, and with the masts of ships beyond it.

'You don't think Martin looked funny, Dick?' she said
in an anxious little voice.

'He probably feels funny,' I said gently. 'Don't you?'

'I do,' she said as usual taking up the joke as though it were part of the conversation. 'But not that way. He frightened me, Dick.'

'He's probably frightened himself,' I replied.

Early next morning a knock came to our door. Mother heard it and answered it. Then she came upstairs to me.

'A Mr. Diamond, I think his name is,' she said with a look of alarm.

I pulled on a dressing gown and ran downstairs. It was still dark. Diamond was sitting smoking in the front room by gaslight when I came in. Of course, he had to begin with apologies for disturbing Mother — as if it mattered!

'I wonder if you'd mind coming up to Beirne's,' he said. 'It's about Holmes. Mr. Bernie had better tell you.'

'Drunk?' I asked.

'No,' he replied,' dead. He blew his brains out in the hotel at Dunleary.'

I could see he was keeping his even tone only with the greatest difficulty. I dressed and went with him in a daze. The dawn was breaking. A group of trees and an old white-washed farmhouse stood out quite clearly on the crest of Gardiner's Hill. The unreal light emphasized the unreal errand. I could have broken down and wept. Doris's father opened the door. Doris herself was sitting over the fire, tearless. Against her wishes we agreed that Diamond and I should go to Dunleary together. She clung to Diamond's coat, saying in a low voice, 'No, Tom, please! please! you must let me come too.'

'I can't, Doris,' he said with something like anguish. 'I can't go unless you stay here. You must understand that.'

I wondered later if he hadn't even then some glim-mering of the truth, because shortly after we reached Dunleary, Holmes's wife arrived off the boat. She was a good-looking, hard-faced, capable woman, and her only emotion seemed to be one of disgust. We got on remarkably well, considering. Considering, I mean, that poor devil in the morgue with half his fat head blown away, and the life of Doris and Tom Diamond's life blown to blazes with it.

Still, I was glad when the two of us were able to go for a walk on the pier. The mail boat went out with all her lights on; the stars came out over the sea, and I realized that adventure had come to me at last, though, as I have said before, in a form I wasn't expecting.

(1953)

A Case of Conscience

Mr. Marlow, the milkman, delivered milk to the Convent School in Essex Street in London. He was a man who didn't believe in religion, and sometimes it gave him quite a turn to see the medieval costume of the nuns. 'Mumbo jumbo,' was how he described it to his wife. 'You take those women and stick them into ordinary clothes and nobody would send his kids there. But call them 'Sister' and cut their hair and put veils on them and they can charge what they blooming well like. You can get away with anything, provided you dress the part. Like lawyers. They don't know any more than you or I do.'

He made an exception of the lay sister who came there two years after he had started delivering. She was young and pretty and she had a nice smile.

'You're not from these parts?' he asked.

'No, I'm from Ireland,' she said.

'Oh! Come a long way from base, haven't you!' he exclaimed.

'I feel a terrible stranger still,' she said.

'Oh, you'll get used to it,' he said.

'I suppose so,' she replied. 'God is everywhere, Mr. Marlow. Isn't that right?'

It took Mr. Marlow aback. Nobody had ever talked to him in that tone before. The parson had said words to that effect when he was a small boy, but the parson had sounded neither convinced nor convincing. This pretty girl in her outlandish costume seemed to think it was true.

'Don't ask me, miss,' he muttered. 'I never made His acquaintance.'

This seemed to take her by surprise as much as her remark had taken him, but she gave him a gentle, timid smile.

'Ah, but you will, Mr. Marlow, you will,' she said. 'God is waiting for all of us.'

It gave him another turn, but it left him with a lingering interest in the girl. She wasn't like anyone else he had met. 'She's a bit simple,' he told his wife.

But she hadn't been there more than six months when he began to notice the change in her. She seemed to lose her high spirits, and though she smiled as brightly as ever when he rang the bell, there was a sadness behind the smile.

'What's wrong?' he asked one morning.

'Nothing, Mr. Marlow,' she said falsely. 'Why?'

'You're not happy,' he said.

'We can't ask for happiness in this life,' she said, clouding over.

'You used to be happy enough,' he said.

'Ah, I suppose I made a mistake,' she said. 'I should never have left home.'

'Somebody picking on you?' he asked shrewdly.

'Of course, I'm not clever.'

'You're not supposed to be clever, are you?' he asked. 'You do your work, don't you?'

'I make mistakes.'

'Everybody makes mistakes. It's how people correct them that matters. This is an unnatural life. All them women living in one house — it isn't right. You're a good-looking girl. You should have a husband and family of your own.'

'I could have,' she said. 'I never wanted them compared with what I thought I wanted.'

'What did you want?' he asked.

'I wanted to have the chapel near me, and to be able to pray and think. Now I can see they don't even want me in the chapel. They say I should be at work.'

'Oh, it's all class,' he growled. 'They despise you because you're Irish and working class, but you can't let them walk over you. You've got to stand up for yourself, girl. Next time one of them criticizes you, you say, "Very well; you come and do my work yourself." '

'I suppose I should,' she said mournfully.

But Mr. Marlow suspected she would do nothing of the sort. He suspected that she would go and tell God about it and ask Him for help, and Mr. Marlow didn't believe in telling God about it even if there had been such a person.

His wife was becoming suspicious.

'You take a great interest in her,' she said.

'She's unusual,' Mr. Marlow admitted.

'But there must be something wrong with her,' Mrs. Marlow said.

'Of course there's something wrong. There's something wrong with everyone, if you want to find it out. That's from your point of view. But there's something worse wrong with them. She believes all this stuff about God being there in the chapel, and so on, and they don't, not really. And they'll take it out on her, you mark my words.'

It was all very mystifying to Mr. Marlow. He did not believe in all that nonsense about God any more than he felt the English sisters did, but whenever he thought of it he found his heart warming to the Irish nun until he even began to make excuses for her and argue with himself that for her, perhaps, there was something in the chapel. He found it even more difficult to explain himself to the Irish nun. Her state was now going definitely from bad to worse. She was simply terrified if one of the choir nuns came into the kitchen while Mr. Marlow was delivering the milk. One morning a choir nun came in as Mr. Marlow appeared, and she began to scold her in her well-bred way.

'Sister Agatha, did you forget you had left the dusting pan in the hall? Someone would trip over that, you know.'

'Strikes me Sister Agatha ought to join the nuns' trade union,' Mr. Marlow snapped before he realized what he was saying.

The choir nun drew herself up and surveyed him coldly. Mr. Marlow put his pitcher down and surveyed her back. Then she turned and left the kitchen, banging the door behind her. Sister Agatha was crying.

'Don't you be a little fool, girl!' he said fiercely. 'That's the way to talk to them, and they know it.'

'Oh!' she said. 'She'll never forgive me now.'

'Who cares whether she forgives you or not? Will you forgive her — that's the question you should ask. Ill-bred woman! Correcting you in front of a third party. Don't you stand for that from her!'

He went on his rounds in a state of fury that was rare with him, aware too that he was behaving foolishly. He knew that he had thrown down a challenge to the choir nun and that it was one he would probably have to answer for. His wife realized it as well.

'Oh, Dan!' she said. 'Did you have to get tied up in something that doesn't concern you?'

'I don't care,' he said angrily, feeling more than ever in the wrong. 'If I can't stand up for my principles at this hour of my life. I'll get another job.'

'But they're not even your principles, Dan.'

'In one way they're not, but in another way they are. They're turning that poor child into a skivvy — the worst sort of skivvy.'

But it was worse than he thought. When he saw Sister Agatha again she was terrified to speak to him. When she did speak it was in a guilty whisper.

'Go away!' she said. 'I don't want to talk to you any more.'

'Why not? I didn't do you any harm, did I?'

'They said it was a disgrace, the way I talked to you. Carryings-on, they called it.'

'Did I do any carrying on with you?'

'No, but they don't understand.'

'I'll damn soon make them understand,' he said in a

loud and angry voice. 'You'll have to get out of this place.'

'I can't.'

'You'll have to. They're out to destroy you, and they'll do it, what's more.'

'But where can I go?'

'Go back to Cork.'

'How could I? Everybody would laugh at me.'

'They will not. You write and tell your mother and father the way you're being treated.'

'I can't, sure. The sisters would know.'

'Very well, give me their address and I will. And tomorrow you're going to walk out of this place.'

'But how can I?' she asked tearfully. 'These are all the clothes I have. And my hair!'

'What about your hair?'

' 'Tis cut.'

'We'll think out a way. Leave that to me. And tomorrow, mind, be ready when I come!'

'Oh, I'd never be able to do it.'

'You'd better,' he said. 'If you don't, they'll send you somewhere else, and then you'll see.'

The following morning he brought in the milk as usual and gave her a look.

'Well,' he asked, 'are you all set?'

'How can I?' she asked, but he knew she was desperate.

'You wait!' he said.

A few minutes later he came in with an empty milk churn and took off the lid.

'Hop in!' he said.

'Into that?' she cried, aghast.

'Hop in, I said, before anyone comes. Come on — I'll lift you. Upsy-daisy.'

Before she knew what she was doing she was in the milk churn and felt herself being rolled through the door and out the yard. Then Mr. Marlow raised her triumphantly onto the truck and started the engine. He drove slowly and carefully to his own door, swung the milk churn to the ground and pushed it through the door. Then he helped her out of the churn. She looked strange in her nun's costume, and his wife gave a little cry.

'Oh, Dan, I hope they won't follow her here.'

'Nobody knows where she is,' he said. 'If they come, don't answer the door. I have to finish my rounds.'

She stayed with them for a few days until Mrs. Marlow had equipped her with some clothes. They saw her off at Euston station, and she sobbed as she thanked them.

'I know you don't believe in God, Mr. Marlow, but He won't forget you for this. He'll be with you when you need Him most.'

Mrs. Marlow said it showed nice feeling, but her husband wasn't really at his ease as they went home on the bus together. He had never had anything against the Irish, but he did hope their God was not going to annoy him further. He had already got him into trouble enough.

(1970)

The Call

Paddy Verchoyle was a man with a hand in half a dozen businesses, most of which brought him in a satisfactory return and would get better with time. Paddy was that sort of man. A bit of a craftsman himself, he didn't like to have anything to do with inferior goods, and would kick up hell with the manufacturer if there was anything wrong with what he sold. He could have been richer, but he might very well have been poorer, and it wasn't poorer he was getting. He had married a nice gentle girl whose brother was an accountant, and after his mother-in-law's death he had suggested himself that Declan should come and live with them. Like most of Paddy's deals, this one had turned out well. Declan seemed to have no inclination to get married. Though Kate raked Dublin for a suitable wife for him, each prettier than the last, Declan seemed to prefer the company of his nephew and niece.

Though Paddy approved of Declan he thought him a queer fish, and no wonder. At home he seemed sociable enough, though a bit touchy, and was very fond of a drink, but every few months he would take a couple of days' leave and go off to a Cistercian monastery in the mountains, and most mornings he was up first and slipped round the corner to hear Mass. Now, Paddy was a good-living man, and he made no secret of it, but this sometimes struck him as going to the fair. Sometimes he twitted Declan about it, but Declan, a tall, thin man, only grinned sadly and said slyly, 'I suppose it keeps me out of harm's way, Paddy.' Which, as Paddy damn well knew, was only casuistry. Sometimes he grew curious about the guest master of the monastery, of whom Declan talked a good deal, and wondered if he hadn't an undue influence, but to answer that question he would have had to accompany Declan on one of his retreats, and he knew he wouldn't be able to stand all that chanting. It made him melancholy even to think of it. When he had a day off he preferred to dig himself into his workshop at the end of the garden and make something.

In the monastery Declan made another friend, who made Paddy think even more of his brother-in-law's strangeness. This fellow, Mick Ring, had the religion too, apparently, but of a quite different kind. He was a small man with an eager, over-boisterous manner — a senior civil servant, who was connected with a number of charities, though he didn't speak too well of the charities. Ring was very popular with the children, though Paddy noticed that he never really played with them. Instead, he put on a performance, but this was intended as much for their mother as themselves. Even the performance he put on for Kate personally, though consistent and flattering, didn't seem right to Paddy. He had a feeling that if he were dealing with Ring in the way of business he would keep his eyes skinned. It was only when he was talking religion or politics that he seemed to Paddy to be altogether sincere, and then it was with the sincerity of a fanatic. On either of these subjects he might prove an ugly character to get into an argument with, and Paddy didn't like arguments that turned out that way. As he had so often said to Kate, what was an argument for except to enjoy yourself.

Kate didn't care much for arguments, one way or another, but she had begun to give up hope of Declan's marrying. Her great friend Nora Hynes, who was a raving beauty, had fallen in love with him and told Kate that she'd marry him at the drop of a hat, but when Kate hinted at this to Declan, he only gave his sad smile and said, 'Nora is a very enthusiastic girl, Kate,' which was true enough, though not to the point. And instead of going walking with Nora, Declan went on long hikes through the hills with Ring, and they ended up in a restaurant in Enniskerry and drank whiskey and ate bacon and eggs.

Then one night, Ring came round, fuller of bounce than ever, and when they were all seated he leaned forward in his chair, his hands joined and a wide grin on his face.

'I'll give ye six guesses what I did today,' he said.

'Tell us, Mick,' Declan said, humouring him.

'I handed in my resignation. God, you should have seen old George Thompson's face when I told him.'

'For goodness sake!' said Declan. 'What did you do that for?'

'That is the occasion for the next six questions,' said Ring. 'But I won't keep ye in pain. I resigned because I'm going to join the Cistercians.'

It was a bombshell, and he knew it. Paddy grinned amiably, not knowing quite what to say, but he watched his wife and brother-in-law closely. Kate was the first to recover.

'Oh, Mick!' she said gently. 'Isn't that wonderful?'

But Paddy saw that it was Declan who was really thunderstruck. His mouth worked for a few moments as though he were trying to frame words that would not emerge, and his face was dead white. Finally he rose and reached to the mantelpiece for his pipe.

'You're not taking anyone?' he asked with his gentle smile.

'It's not a matter for committee action,' Ring said with a slight touch of resentment that even Paddy found unwarranted. But Declan didn't seem to take it in bad spirits.

'It might come under the heading of good example,' he replied.

For the next couple of weeks he was like a man in a dream. He had never been very obtrusive about the house, but now it was almost as though he weren't there at all. In the mornings he got up and went to Mass, then had his breakfast and went to work. After supper he got up and went out walking somewhere about the city and returned late, closing the door gently behind him and tiptoeing upstairs.

'Don't be too surprised if Declan does the same thing as Mick Ring.' Paddy said darkly to his wife.

'Oh, dear, Paddy, I hope he doesn't,' Kate said with a worried air. 'I suppose I shouldn't say it, if it's the best thing for him, but Mother always did want him to get married.'

'Well, I'd be very much surprised if he got married now,' replied Paddy.

It must be admitted in his favour that when Declan did break the news three weeks later, Paddy gave no indication that he had been expecting it, Kate of course just broke into tears, and Declan had to comfort her. Then, with considerable humour he described how his employers had taken the news. They too had been taken aback. Paddy had suspected for some time that they had been considering giving Declan a partnership, and now his resignation opened an abyss at their feet. Could it possibly be that someone really thought as little as that of a promising career?

'We'll keep your job open for you, Declan,' the senior partner had said, trying to delude himself into the belief that Declan was not himself or was suffering a disappointment in love. Declan's reply, too, had been characteristic.

'You'll be doing me a great favour if you don't, Jerry,' he had replied. 'It might be too much of a temptation.' And the senior partner hadn't even seen the joke.

'Oh, if that's the way you feel about it, Declan,' he had said. Of course, he made no difficulty about notice, and now Declan was able to tell Ring that he was going with him.

Paddy took the day off from the office to drive them. He was as glad he did, because he wouldn't have been able to concentrate anyway. Kate broke down completely, and the two kids, seeing the signs of tears on her face, bawled as well. Declan and himself were both in the stage of bearing up when they drove off to collect Ring, who came out, carrying his suitcase as though he were going away for the weekend. It was Declan who asked apologetically, 'Paddy, could we take the road over the hills?' Paddy, with a lump in his throat replied, 'Surely, Declan,' and they drove off through Rathfarnham. Paddy knew that Declan wanted to take his leave of places he had liked in the mountains, so he drove straight to Glendalough, where they had a drink and wandered for a few minutes round the early medieval monastery. Declan, looking at the round tower and the wall of mountain behind it, said tentatively, 'You'd hardly say there was much credit due to Saint Kevin and the rest of them, would you?'

Ring looked at him in surprise. 'That's because you never spent a winter here,' he said. 'Even so,' Declan said with his mournful smile, 'you'd have something to see when the sun came out.'

'Begod, you would not,' Ring said stoutly. 'Half the people round here are mad — with melancholia. No city man can ever size up a place.'

Declan only smiled faintly. They had a drink in Glendalough and then drove on to another favourite haunt of his, Kilkenny, where first he showed them the old churches and then took them to a pub kept by a friend who bottled his own whiskey, and kept a collection of antiques.

'I suppose you'd say this was a better place than Glendalough, Mick?' he asked.

'A man could have a damn good life in a town like this,' said Ring.

'*Better* than Kerry?' Declan asked, almost with malice.

'No,' Ring said, his eyes beginning to sparkle. 'Because here you'd have gentry and shopkeepers and working-class people. In Kerry you have a chance of discovering that there's only people.'

'I don't see what you have against Dublin so,' said Declan.

'I never said I had anything against Dublin,' said Ring, 'but if you want to know, in Dublin it's nearly impossible to see anything. You never saw anything.'

'I didn't?'

'No, you were too damn concerned with your old books and your old job. You should have come to the hostel and seen the way a man can be driven to Hell by three pounds he borrowed from an old woman in Mabbot Street at seventy-five per cent per annum. And mind you, when you borrow money at that rate it's no use going to a lawyer. I didn't go to a lawyer.'

'What did you do?'

'I went down to the old woman herself. She said, "I'll put my son on you," and I said, "I'll put my big brother on your son, and he'll know what it means to meet a man that's not scared of a knuckle-duster." She was a nice old lady as a matter of fact,' Ring continued philosophically. 'Before I left she gave me tea and told me she wished she had a son like me.'

'But tell me, Mick,' said Paddy, who loved a good argument and didn't see at all where this one was tending, 'if Kerry is all that fine, why are the boys and girls getting out of it as fast as they can?'

'Because they're too simple, Paddy,' replied Ring. 'They don't know the value of what they have.'

'I don't agree, Mick,' Paddy said sadly. Paddy regarded himself as a good Catholic but a Catholic with a business head on him, and this was a matter he had thought a great deal about. 'They leave it because the priests won't let them enjoy themselves. A boy and girl — damn it, what else is life for?'

'And that's only more of the romancing,' Ring said violently, 'That's like saying they have to have television. A countryman has no use for a woman only to make his breakfast and keep his bed warm.'

Declan suddenly began to get irritated. It wasn't often he got irritated, and Paddy had never seen him angry, but he felt that at this moment Declan was as cross as he'd ever been.

'And what does a Kerryman want if he doesn't want women?' he asked.

'He wants neighbours,' cried Ring.

'Mick, a man wants more than neighbours,' said Declan.

'What does he want according to you?'

'He wants someone to devote his life to,' said Declan.

'Television!' snapped Ring.

'Now, Mick, it's not television,' Declan said with his sad smile.

'Och, what the hell else is it?' Ring asked explosively. 'What woman is worth devoting your life to? Did you ever meet one?'

Then Declan really surprised his brother-in-law.

'I did. I met several.'

'Never mind the several. Did you meet one?'

'Yes, Nora Hynes.'

There was shocked silence for a moment. Each of them knew that it was one of those occasions when intimacy goes a little too far, and nothing can ever retrieve the situation. Paddy felt that this was a case for Kate. He gave a broad, uncomfortable grin.

'Then why the blazes didn't you marry her?'

'I'm not too sure she'd have had me.'

'Oh, begod, she would,' said Paddy stoutly.

'Then she'd be making a great mistake,' Declan said.

'And that's only more of the damn television,' Ring said with sudden violence. 'Give me another drink, I need it when I hear people talking like that.'

'Ah, why do you go on saying things like that, Mick?' Declan asked reproachfully, 'Every man is entitled to his views.'

'He is not,' said Ring with his eyes popping. 'That's what's wrong with the whole world today, people thinking they're entitled to give their views on anything, whether they understand it or not. That's not a sensible view, man. That's something you saw on the movies somewhere. To a countryman all that sort of thing is no more than hunger or thirst or the want of a home or a pain in the gut.'

'That might be what keeps him a countryman, Mick,' Declan said with as close an approach to indignation as Paddy had ever seen. He intervened, not because he wanted to get into an argument with Ring, but because he feared what might happen if himself and Declan got really serious. A nice situation he would be in, bringing two novices to a Cistercian monastery, and having them arrested on the way for drunkenness and disorderly conduct.

'Now, Mick, I think you're taking it to the fair,' he said. 'I know what you mean, and there's a lot of truth in it, but you're taking it to the fair.'

'It's all fairy tales. The trouble with townies like you and Declan is that you have so much time on your hands for thinking up nonsense.'

'Nor it's not nonsense either, Mick,' said Paddy. 'Not altogether. It depends on what you want from life. What a man like me wants is principally company.'

'What a man wants is neighbourliness,' snapped Ring. 'Someone to give him the cup of tea when he's dying.'

'What a man wants is inspiration,' Declan said slowly and clearly, and immediately the other two knew he was drunk. It was a rare enough occurrence, for Declan was a steady, quiet, determined drinker with a great knowledge of his own capacity.

He steadied up in the car, and they had a look at Cashel and then a meal in Thurles. They were close to their destination now, and suddenly they all began drinking hard, assuring themselves that each drink was the last. But because it really could be the last they let themselves be tempted further. The situation was on top of them now, and they couldn't evade it in any other way. Paddy put it into a nutshell.

'Well, boys,' he said, 'this time tomorrow ye'll have it all behind ye, but I have to go on with the old job just the same. To tell the truth, I often wonder why. Sometimes when I'm shaving in the morning, I look at myself in the bathroom mirror and I say to myself, "Paddy Verchoyle, that's about the ten thousandth time you're after doing that. And why the hell do you have to do it?" First, it's the mother, then it's the wife, and then it's the kids, one thing after another. And yet, you wouldn't like leaving it.'

'Oh, it's a wrench all right,' Declan said. 'I think what I'll miss most is the kids.'

'Oh, begod, they'll miss you a damn sight more,' said

Paddy with a laugh. 'A bob a week a man is big money. I suppose I'll have to contribute that.'

'And I'll regret old Mike Hanrahan that used to wait for me outside the office on Friday nights for his half-dollar,' Ring said with moody humour. 'Mike is so old and dotty he's even forgotten my name, but he knows that if he turns up at five on Friday there'll be a bone for him.'

'I'll see that he gets his bone, Mick,' Paddy said quietly, and they knew he would. A great man for little responsibilities was Paddy. But he suddenly realised that he had now a bigger responsibility than that.

When he got the two men out to the car they were very drunk. He knew it wasn't so much the drink as the excitement, but how was he going to explain that late at night to a priest? The rest of the drive on the mountain road completed his panic. He got safely into the front yard. There was only a faint light in the chapel on his left, and one in the building before him. 'Come on!' he shouted, shaking the sleepers, 'tell me where I'm to go,' but they only grunted. For a few moments he wondered whether it wouldn't be better to bring them back to a hotel for the night, but he was filled with a wild longing to be back with Kate and the kids before morning. He mounted the steps to the lighted building and rang the bell. Then he heard feet slip-slopping on the floors inside and an old priest opened the door.

'It's Father Cormac I'm looking for, Father,' Paddy explained.

'I'm the very man,' said the old priest. 'Come in. What can I do for you?'

'Well,' Paddy said, laughing in an embarrassed way, 'I have two novices here for you.'

'Two novices?' the old priest said, coming out on the steps. 'Is it Mick and Declan? Where are they?'

'Well, the way it is, Father,' said Paddy, 'they're not in a state to come in.'

'I see,' said Father Cormac in a tone that indicated he didn't, and then he immediately added another 'I see' that indicated he did. 'Brother Michael!' he called and a young monk came out the hall to them with a wide grin and a straggly beard. 'It seems there are a couple of new recruits here I'll want a hand with. We'll put them in bed in the guesthouse for the present. I don't think Father Kevin would appreciate them with the other novices.'

Declan allowed himself to be steered into the front room of the guesthouse and recovered sufficiently to say, 'Father Cormac, I don't know how to apologize . . .' before he collapsed into a chair. 'Declan was always a perfect gentleman,' Cormac said dryly. Ring didn't say anything at all. He was out. 'I think maybe we'll keep them here tomorrow as well, Michael,' said Father Cormac.

'Father,' Paddy said desperately, 'I feel very much ashamed of this.'

'Ah, well,' Cormac said professionally, 'the Lord works even through Irish whiskey. I used to be very fond of it myself. As a matter of fact, I still am,' he added. 'Look, couldn't we make up a bed for you?'

But this was too much for Paddy.

'Not making you a saucy answer, Father,' he said, 'I want to wake up in my wife's bed tomorrow.'

'Yes,' said the priest, 'I understand that has great attractions. I was only wondering could you drive.'

'After what I went through today I could drive there blindfold,' said Paddy.

And he did. He was glad of the experience, though he hadn't understood it. Maybe those are the experiences we are best pleased to have had. He understood it even less after a few months when Declan came out. To Paddy he seemed just the same but more of a man. That night he asked Kate if she would ask Nora Hayes whether she would still accept a proposal from him, and Kate very sensibly packed him off to ask for himself. Ring was made of tougher stuff, and he stuck it for more than a year before he too came out and married a widow with a public house.

Paddy still tells the story at length, but he hasn't reached any conclusion about it. This may be the reason he still tells it. Somewhere during that day, he feels, something happened that changed everything. It was not the drink; it was not the last glimpse of spots that had been loved, but somewhere along the way each man had glanced back for a moment on the lighted room of life, and something he saw there had pierced him to the heart.

(1971)

Ghosts

For twenty-odd years we've always had Oorawn Sullivans
for servants; why I don't know, unless it was the only
hope of getting something off the bill. The Sullivan's bill
went back long before my time. When one of them got
married we took her younger sister, and when she died of
consumption we took Kitty. The first week we had Kitty I
found her with all the tea things down the lavatory basin,
pulling the chain. She told me townspeople had great
conveniences.

Then one Thursday last summer, Mary, the eldest girl,
came in to do her bit of shopping. I always had a smack for
Mary for the way she reared her family. I heard her whispering something across the counter to Nan about a bottle of
whiskey and cocked my ears. Oorawn is the Irish for a
spring, but it isn't only water that flows there. All the
poteen they drink in our part of the country rises in
Oorawn. When they have a wedding or a wake they come in
for a bottle or two of the legal stuff and take care that
plenty see them with it. A couple of days after they bring
it back under cover and get credit for it. They call it 'the
holy medal.'

'What do ye want the medal for, Mary?' said I, taking a

rise out of her. 'Is it one of the girls getting married on you?'

'Wisha, the Lord love you, Mr. Clancy!' says she. ' 'Tisn't that at all, only a cousin that's coming home from America on Friday. He mightn't be able to drink the other stuff.'

'Which cousin is that, Mary?' said Nan. 'I never knew you had cousins in America.'

'Wisha, Mrs. Clancy, love,' said Mary, ' 'tis a cousin called Jer that we hardly knew we had ourselves,' and off she went into the usual rigmarole about her grandfather's brother that married a woman of the Lacys from Drumacre; not one of the Red Lacys mind you, but cousins of theirs. I could just about follow her, she might have been talking double Dutch for all Nan understood.

'And how is he going to get up to Oorawn?' she asked.

'Oye, he can probably get a lift,' said Mary, 'or he might get the bus as far as Trabawn Cross.'

'And walk all the way up the valley with his bags!' said Nan. 'Ah, Tim will meet him at the station and drive him up.'

Nan is the kindest soul in the world with my time and car. Still, I suppose she could hardly do less, and Kitty with us. So next evening I left her in charge of the shop and drove up to the station. There was the usual small handful on the train, but the devil an American boy could I see. When they cleared there was only a family of four left by the luggage wagon; father, mother, daughter and son, to judge by appearances.

'Is it anyone you were expecting, Tim?' said Hurley, the stationmaster.

'Only a Yankee cousin of the Oorawns that's coming home,' said I.

' 'Twouldn't be one of them?' said Hurley, pointing to the family.

'I wouldn't say so,' said I, 'but I suppose I'd better make sure.'

I went up to the elder man, a fine, tall, handsome-looking fellow about the one age with myself.

'Your name wouldn't be Sullivan, by any chance?' said I.

'That's right,' he said, reaching out his hand to me. 'Are you one of my Oorawn cousins?'

'No,' said I, trusting in God to give me words in the predicament I was in, 'only a friend with a car. Mick Hurley and myself will take out the bags for ye.'

And while we carried out the bags, I was thinking harder than ever I thought in my life. The American family wasn't my class at all. And as for Oorawn, you might as well drop them on a raft in mid-Atlantic. This was a case for Nan, and damn good right she had to handle it, seeing 'twas she that brought it on us with her interfering in other people's business.

'I'll have to call at the shop first,' I said as I got in. 'Anyway, I daresay after that journey ye wouldn't say no to a cup of tea.'

The one thing about being to a good school is that, like Nan, you can make a fist of anything, even Americans. I took her place in the shop and she went upstairs with them. She came down about ten minutes after, looking a bit dazed.

'Do you know who they are?' said she, frightened and at the same time delighted. 'Sullivan Shoes.'

'I never heard of Sullivan or his shoes,' said I, 'but I wish he was in mine this minute.'

'Go up and talk to them while I get the tea,' said she. 'I told them 'twas Kitty's day off. They're on their way to Paris. We'll have to stop them going to Oorawn.'

I saw Kitty coming down the stairs as I was going up, and she was like a ghost. She must have caught a glimpse of her American cousins and was thinking about the cabin and the pint of whiskey. With the main responsibility now off my shoulders I didn't mind. They were a nice family; the father was quiet, the mother was bright; Bob, the young fellow, was writing a book on something — he took after the mother, but Rose, the girl, was a real beauty. Every damned thing you told her, she took seriously. She wanted to know had we any fairies! I told her we had no fairies since the poteen was put down but the ghosts were something shocking.

'You mean you have ghosts in this house?' she said.

'Dozens of them,' said I, seeing that we were lacking in a lot of the conveniences a girl like that would be accustomed to and we might as well take credit for what she couldn't see, 'The mother, God rest her, knew some of them so well that she used to quarrel with them like Christians.'

'Didn't I tell you what Grandfather used to say about the ghosts on the farm at home?' said her father, taking a rise out of her too.

I nearly laughed when he talked about 'the farm' but I thought it was better to leave that to Nan. All the same I was glad when she came in with the tea. I took a cup and went down to mind the shop, and by the time I came back she was after persuading them to stop at the Grand Hotel. I ran the bags over, and then we set out for Oorawn. The car was pretty full with Rose sitting on Bob's knee. Their father sat in front with me where he could see a bit of the country. On a fine evening the sea road is grand. The sea was like a lake, and the mountains at the other side had a red light on them like plums.

'Is there only this road from Oorawn to Cobh?' he asked me.

'There's only this road from Oorawn to Hell,' said I. 'Why?'

'I was thinking,' said he, 'this must be the road my grandfather travelled on his way to America. He used to describe himself sitting on their little tin trunk at the back of an open cart. My grandmother was having her first baby, and she was frightened. He sang for her the whole way to keep her courage up.'

'There was many a homesick tear shed along this road,' I said, because, damn it, the man touched me the way he spoke.

'Count the ruined cottages, and you'll see your grandmother wasn't alone.'

Then the road turned off up the valley and over the moors, a bad place to be on a winter's day. When we reached the Sullivans what did we see only Bridgie, rising up like an apparition from behind a bush with her skirts held up behind, and away she flew like the wind to the house. I was wishing then I hadn't Nan with me. It was bad enough, a lonely cottage in the hills that was expecting one American labouring boy from Butte, getting a blooming family of millionaires or near it. Signs on it, that was the last we saw of Bridgie.

I will say for Mary Sullivan that she made a great effort not to look as put out as she was. I smelt when I went in that she had just been baking for him.

'Wisha, and are you Jer?' she cried, wiping her hands in her apron before she'd touch him. 'Law, I'm hearing about you always. And your family and all! Ye must be dying for a cup of tea!'

'We've just had tea, Mary,' said Nan, being tactful. 'I don't want to put your cousins out, but Tim and myself have an appointment in town.'

'Why then, indeed,' said I, planting my ass on a chair near the fire, 'the appointment can wait, because out of this house I don't stir till Mary Sullivan gives me tea. Have you griddle cake, Mary?'

'I have, aru,' said she. 'Do you like griddle cake?'

Nan gave me a look like a poultice, but the woman didn't know what she was talking about. If the Sullivans' cousins had left that cabin without a meal, the disgrace of it would have driven Mary to her grave.

'I hope we're not putting you out too much, Mrs. Clancy,' said Sullivan, 'but I'd like it too. It isn't every day a man comes back to his grandfather's house.'

'Your grandfathers house?' cried Mary. 'Ah, my darling, this isn't your grandfather's. Your grandfather's is about three fields away. 'Tis only an old ruin now.'

'Whatever it is,' he said. 'I'd like to see it.'

'Will I show it to you?' she said, at her wits' ends to please him.

'After we have the tea, girl, after we have the tea,' said I. 'What a hurry you're in to get rid of us!'

'Hurry?' she said, laughing. 'The divil a hurry then, only the state we're in. Mrs. Sullivan,' she said, holding out her two hands to the American woman, 'we're a holy show.'

'Ah, Mary,' said I, 'if you took my advice five years ago

and bought a vacuum cleaner, you needn't be afraid to
hide your face today.'

'Do you hear him?' cried Mary. 'A vacuum! Lord save
us! You'll have to drink your tea out of a mug.'

'Have you ne'er a basin?' said I.

'Why?' said she. 'Would you prefer a basin? Or is it making fun of me you are?'

The two younger girls were standing in front of Rose
with their fingers in their mouths, looking at her as if she
were a shop window.

'That's right,' I said. 'Have a good look at your cousin,
and stick to the books and maybe ye'd be like her some
day.'

'Wisha, how in God's name would they, Mr. Clancy?'
said Mary, really upset at last. 'And don't be putting foolish
notions into the children's heads ... Your daughter is a
picture, Jer,' she said with the tears of delight standing in
her eyes, and then she took Rose's two hands and held
them. 'You are, treasure,' she said, 'I could be looking at
you all day and not get tired.'

'Why then, indeed, Miss Sullivan,' I said to Mary 'as
we're getting so polite with our misters and misses, you're
not too bad-looking yourself.'

'Och, go away, you ould divil, you,' said she, giving me
a push. Nan was mortified. She felt she'd never get a day's
good of Kitty after that push.

'There never was a Sullivan yet without good looks,
Mary,' said Sullivan, 'and you have your share.'

'Wisha, God forgive you, Jer Sullivan!' she said, blushing
up, but I could see the way the spirits rose in her.

We had the tea, and the griddle cake, and the boiled
eggs and then we had the whiskey. — the first bottle of
proper whiskey opened in Oorawn for generations, as I told
them — and then Sullivan got up.

'Now, Mary,' he said, 'if you'll forgive me, I'd like to see
the old place before it gets too dark.'

I noticed he brought his glass. He went on ahead with
Mary; his wife and daughter with Nan, Bob with me, and
the kids bringing up the rear, too bewitched to talk. Mary

was apologising for the dirt of the fields.

The sun was going down when we reached the ruin of the little cabin. It was all overgrown, and a big hawthorn growing on the hearth. Sullivan's face was a study.

'Grandfather used to say that the first Sullivan to come back should lay a wreath on the grave of the landlord that evicted us,' he said in a quiet voice.

'A wreath, is it?' cried Mary, not understanding his form of fun. 'I know what sort of a wreath I'd lay on it.'

'Now,' he said gently, a little embarrassed by us all, 'I'd like to stay here for a few minutes by myself, if you won't think it rude of me.'

'Don't stay too long,' said his wife, 'It's turned quite chilly.'

We left him behind us, and made our way back over the fields.

'He's a very gentlemanly sort of man,' said Mary Sullivan to me. 'Oh, law, wasn't it awful the way ye caught Bridgie?'

I saw the girl thought it was the same thing that was detaining her cousin, but I didn't try to enlighten her. I knew what he wanted with in the old ruin by himself. He was hoping for ghosts; ghosts of his grandfather's people that might be hanging round the old cabin so that they could see him there and know he had brough no disgrace on the name. I was touched by it the way I was touched by what he said about his grandfather. There was something genuine about the man that I couldn't help liking. I had an idea that the Sullivans would have no reason to regret his coming.

'Well,' I said, when he came back with his empty glass (I was afraid that someone would start asking him questions and he wouldn't like it), 'we may as well be making tracks.'

As we were driving back down the hill I was pointing out the various landmarks to him. Behind us, Nan was explaining to his wife that Oorawn was exceptional and that all the 'peasants' weren't as backward as the Sullivans. Some of them had fine cottages with beautiful gardens. You could see the Americans were a bit disappointed because there wasn't a garden.

Then as we reached the coastroad Nan tapped me on the shoulder and said: 'We'll call at Hopkins' as we are passing, Tim.'

'We will not,' I said.

'We must, Tim,' she said, getting as sweet as honey to cover up my bad temper. 'Mrs. Hopkins promised me a few slips.'

As long as Nan is in the shop she never yet has learned anything about country people. How the blazes would she and she calling them 'peasants'? I knew well the game she was up to. She wanted to show the Sullivans that we had good society, and herself and myself were the hub of it. But I had thought even she would know who the Hopkins were and why we couldn't bring the Sullivans there. She didn't. She nagged and nagged till I lost my temper.

'Very well,' I said, 'go to Hopkins and be damned to you!'

And I turned in by the gate with the urns on top of the pillars. The Major was out under the portico with his dirty old cap over his eyes, and his face lit up when he saw me. The Major's wife won't let him take a drink unless 'tis with visitors, and he knew I could lower it for him.

'Just in time for a little drink, Clancy,' he said. 'And is that your charming wife?'

'These are some American friends called Sullivan,' said I, 'that want to see your house, and I came with them to make sure you didn't try to sell them anything.'

'You talk about selling things!' he said, delighted with me. 'You damned old ruffian! In the good old days I'd have been on the magistrate's bench and seen you up in the County Gaol. Don't believe a word this old rascal says to you, Mrs. Sullivan,' he says, pawing the American woman's hand.

It seemed supper was late, and Mrs Hopkins asked us to have it with them. It went against my grain, but I knew it was what Nan wanted. The Major's wife was one of the Fays of Frankfort. In her young days it used to be naval officers, but since the daughter grew up she went in more for social welfare. The Americans were delighted with the big staircase and the plaster panel on the first landing with a big picture in the middle of it. Then Bella came down after changing, a big, tall, broody-looking girl. You never saw anyone light up like that American boy did. We had our supper in the front room overlooking the bay, and they were delighted again with the fireplace and the paneling, and then Bella took Bob and Rose off to see the house. They came back in great excitement, and their mother and father had to be shown it.

'You don't want to see the Bossi mantelpiece, Clancy?' says the Major, going off into a roar as he filled my glass.

'If 'tis one of those fireplaces you can't put your boots on, I don't,' said I.

'Or the historic plaster ceiling in the saloon, Clancy?' he says. 'I'm sure you'd love the historic plaster ceiling. Wonderful for shooting at with champagne corks. Pop!'

'Don't forget to show them your ghost!' said I. 'Was it some priest ye hanged or someone ye put out of his house?'

'Look at him!' said the major. 'You can see the sort of chap he is, sitting there drinking my whiskey and hating me.'

Nan gave me a look meaning that she didn't know where her wits were when she married me, but I was past caring. The younger ones went out to the garden, and after a while the others joined them. Nan was collecting her slips. The major was taking advantage of me beyond my capacity. I knew what he'd say after when his wife studied the decanter. that 'twas my doing.

They all came back for a drink and Sullivan was talking to Mrs Hopkins about the backwardness of 'the peasants' and she was telling him about her club for peasant reform. He mentioned the subject of bath-rooms, and I could see he had Bridgie on his mind. The Major couldn't get it out of his head that I was trying to sell something to the Americans and using his house as a blind. He kept looking at me and roaring. And, God forgive me, there was I roaring too, calculating how many gallons of petrol it would take to send his historic old house blazing to Heaven. I was excited and when I have a few drinks in I'm very wicked.

By the time we left, the Sullivans were arranging to take Bella out on their way back through London. I tore back the road with the rocks rising up at me like theatre scenery, thinking of the couple that travelled the same road on their tin trunk so long ago. Sullivan had the same thought in his mind.

'That was a delightful end to a remarkable day,' he said.

'It was,' I said. 'Almost as remarkable as the day.'

'You probably can't appreciate what it meant to me,' he said.

'You might be surprised,' I said.

'All my life,' he said, 'I wanted to stand in the spot where the old couple set off on their journey, and now I feel something inside me is satisfied.'

'And you laid a wreath on the grave of the man who evicted them as well,' said I. 'Don't forget that.'

The funny thing was, it was his wife that knew what I meant.

'What's that?' she said, leaning forward to me. 'You mean the Hopkins were the landlords who evicted them?'

'They were,' said I. 'And cruel bad landlords, too.'

I knew 'twas wicked of me, but the man had roused something in me. What right had any of them to look down on the Sullivans? They were country people as I was, and it was people like them that had gone crying down every road in Ireland to the sea. But they were delighted, delighted! Mrs. Sullivan and Nan and Bob and Rose, they couldn't get over the coincidence of it. You'd think 'twas an entertainment I put on for their benefit. But Sullivan wasn't delighted, and well I knew he wouldn't be. The rest were nice, but they were outside it. They could go looking for ghosts, but he had ghosts there inside himself and I knew in my heart that till the day he died he would never get over the feeling that his money had put him astray and he had turned his back on them.

(1972)

The Grip of the Geraghtys

1

Timmy McGovern was a born boon companion, though, as
his friend Tony Dowse said, very excitable. He was a big
Rabelaisian man with a handsome, laughing face and a
lock of dark hair that streamed over his right eye. He was
the local representative of a Dublin hardware firm, and a
great success at his job because there were few salesmen as
welcome in the little West Cork towns where you can live
for a year without meeting anyone to talk to. He knew all
the lonesome little shopkeepers and officials, talked
Rabelaisian or Voltairean to them as the occasion required;
and they were sorry to see him go and would have felt it
a slight on him not to give him an order, all the more
because he didn't really care whether they did or not.

He was married and lived with his wife and two children
in a neat little house on College Road. She was one of the
Geraghtys of Glenameena; a neat, bird-like little woman
who looked very small beside her husband. Timmy looked
big whatever side you took him from. His face was big and
his body was big, so big that his feet would hardly support

it, and he had to walk with small, mincing steps to keep his balance. When you saw his scale best was when someone drove him home from the pub late at night and he walked into the neat little front room, all flushed and with his dark hair mussed, bubbling over with talk. Then the little front room with the two leather chairs and the two china dogs that balanced them, and the Paul Henry print over the tiled fireplace, seemed to contract and shrink, and everything in it tried to get out of Timmy's way though it only got in it worse; and he stumbled over the rug, knocked down a side table and caught his hip on the arm of a chair — not with the drink only but with the terrible size he seemed to have grown sitting at his ease in a bar.

Timmy was most at ease in a bar, though again, as Tony Dowse said, he was excitable. It was the fault of his generosity of spirit. You met Timmy for the first time, and he told you stories and flattered you with his attention, and when you separated you felt you had made a friend for life. But five minutes later Timmy would meet your worst enemy, and flatter *him* with his attention, and tell him funny stories against you, and next time you met him Timmy would act cagey because he was wondering how much you might have heard till you wondered was he a friend at all. He was, as Tony Dowse knew, only he gave himself too readily to everyone and the good intention got lost. Tony didn't really give himself to anyone; he had tried it fifteen years before with a woman and given it up after a few months as a bad job.

It seemed that Timmy couldn't give up. After their years of friendship Tony knew the pattern as well as he knew some poem he'd learned in third book. Timmy would meet some girl who was a bit out of the ordinary, and within five minutes he would be performing like a peacock, talking Rabelaisian to rid her of her inhibitions and Voltairean to rid her of her scruples, singing folk songs to rouse her passions and doing Irish step-dancing to make her laugh. Next evening when Tony and himself went for their walk round College Road which terminated at the Western Star, Timmy would be talking darkly and secretively about the horrors of his married life.

'You were always the wise one, Tony,' he would say admiringly. 'You knew when you had enough and you quit.'

'I did not quit, Timmy,' Tony would say, lifting his head in a long, refined wail. 'The circumstances were entirely different.'

'Of course they were different,' Timmy would say excitedly. 'Circumstances are always different, but the feeling is the same. A man needs intellectual companionship.'

'Oh, now, you could go farther and fare worse,' said Tony, who had a sort of sympathy for Elsie McGovern.

'I know, I know. I'm not complaining about Elsie. She was always a good wife according to her lights, and I'm grateful for it, but there was never any real understanding between us. Elsie is a peasant and a peasant doesn't understand general ideas.'

'That's where you're wrong,' Tony would say, flapping his big soft hands in protest. 'Every woman understands general ideas till she has a man where she wants him. Then the general ideas go out the window. It's only human nature.'

'No, Tony,' Timmy said fiercely. 'It is not human nature. You're suggesting now that there's no such thing as an intellectual woman at all.'

'All I'm suggesting is that they're not intellectual to their husbands. To me they're all just women.'

Tony knew the pattern, only it sometimes struck him that it might be getting worse as Timmy got older. The Twomey girl was the worst example to date. To begin with she was twenty years younger than Timmy, and on top of that she didn't seem to have any inhibitions or scruples at all. She even managed to spend a week in West Cork with him with nobody the wiser. West Cork was another of the things Tony Dowse had got over a long time ago. He had done a walk there one summer with Timmy and decided that the natives were all savages and that the publichouses were too far dispersed, but Timmy had never got over it. He still talked about the long white winding roads, though Tony remembered that after a mile Timmy's feet started to give him trouble, and of the wonderful peasants, though only a week or two before he had been denouncing his poor decent wife as one. He was a man without a stitch of logic in him. And here he was now, hinting darkly that even Cork wasn't big enough for him. A married man with two children, blathering away about the beauties of London and New York.

'I made a great mistake, Tony,' Timmy said in his eager way. 'There's a certain age when you have to make up your mind about things, once and for all. You were clever, of course. You made up your mind a long time ago.'

'I did *not* make up my mind!' Tony wailed. 'Don't go on with that sort of flattery. There was no making up my mind at all. It was made up for me.'

'Mine is being made up for me,' Timmy said darkly. 'The trouble is that even Dublin isn't big enough.'

'If you're thinking about what I'm thinking of, no place is big enough,' Tony said, wrinkling his nose in distaste.

'London is, Tony,' Timmy said firmly. 'That's the mistake we make in this country. It's too small for us. We're an emotional race, Tony, and we need a place we can expand in, like London or Paris or New York.'

'Only a couple of weeks ago it was West Cork,' Tony groaned. 'You're never consistent, Timmy.'

'But that's a different thing, Tony,' Timmy explained excitedly. 'It's Nature, but it's not civilisation. This place has neither nature nor civilisation. At least in a big city you can have civilisation.'

'Meaning you can live with anyone you like,' said Tony. 'You're an awful romantic man, Timmy McGovern. You're always getting yourself into impossible situations.'

'Ah, but this is different, Tony.'

'So was the business of the nurse — what was her name?'

'Oh, it's not alike,' Timmy said irritably. That was the worst of Tony Dowse as a boon companion. He was a born field-worker, a man who remembered everything and compared everything and never once made the great breakthrough that would enable him to recognise a unique discovery. There had, in fact, been something like a scandal about the nurse, a great riding woman who had taken Timmy to the Horse Show where she had wanted him to buy a horse for her because it looked so lonely, and afterwards quarrelled with him because he had taken the dealer aside and said she was tight and had no money anyway.

'No, I know it's not alike,' Tony drawled sadly. 'All women are different at first, but they end up just the same. I keep on telling you but you never listen to me. What's the trouble this time?'

'Oh, nothing, nothing,' said Timmy in a way that showed there was something seriously wrong. 'Only her sister came across some letters I wrote her.'

'Is that the girl that goes with Chris Nolan in the Income Tax office?'

'That's what I mean by saying Cork is too small,' Timmy said, wincing.

'Any place would be too small that had that fellow in it,' Tony said with a curl of the lip. 'Did she show them to her father?'

'That's what I don't know, Tony. I wish I did.'

'Because you know he could make trouble.'

'Why would he make trouble?' Timmy asked angrily. 'The girl is old enough to know her own mind.'

Tony shut up suddenly. He had been on the point of breaking into one of his usual generalisations and saying 'All women are of an age to know their own minds' but stopped because he realised that Timmy wasn't. Quite suddenly he felt sorry for the girl, a thing that hadn't happened him in twenty years. He knew Timmy's style of letter-writing when he was in an excitable state, and realised that all the stuff about the long white winding roads and the wonderful peasants was the material that had composed Timmy's excitable unsyntactical letters to young May Twomey. He went home, thinking gloomily how long ago he had dreamed himself that somewhere there might be a nice girl who felt the way he did about Communism and the immortality of the soul. He hadn't met one, to his knowledge, but maybe May Twomey was dreaming of a man who felt about things the way she did and who would talk to her sensibly in the intervals of mussing her up.

Timmy went home, even gloomier, because of what he had admitted to his conscious mind and wondering what sort of old devil May's father might turn out to be. May herself said he was a great card and would be delighted to know they were living together — a thing he had never had the chance of doing himself — but Timmy sometimes thought that in her radiant optimism she tended to make mistakes about the nature of fathers. He hadn't passed on her views to Tony because he knew Tony would only say sourly 'All fathers are alike.' Everything was alike to Tony. As Timmy had once said to him, his epitaph should be 'It's all the same.'

Next morning Timmy found he didn't want to go to work. It was a thing that had happened to him before, and it always filled him with wonder — how peaceful his little home on the College Road with its two nice children, two nice chairs and two nice china dogs could seem and how cruel and turbulent the world outside. When he did venture out towards eleven o'clock he did not take his usual route into town by the Western Road. Instead he walked down past the Protestant Cathedral, intending to cross the river into the South Mall, but as he turned the corner he saw a man coming up past St. Marie of the Isles' Schools whose build and gait seemed suspiciously familiar. On the spur of the moment he went into the cathedral. He had never been in the Protestant Cathedral before and it impressed him. It looked just like any other church. There was no one around, but it occurred to him that if anyone arrived he would be in the position of a casual tourist, and that might mean he would have to offer explanations, so he dropped on his knees and pretended to be praying. At least he began by pretending, as a good Voltairean should, but the familiar attitude produced a totally unfamiliar response, and befoe he knew where he was, he was praying like mad to the Protestant God that nothing serious would happen.

In a curious way it comforted him and he went along to his office, amused by his unexpected piety and thinking what a good story it would make when he met Tony. He dictated a few letters to his secretary, and when she had gone sat thinking about the nature of prayer.

Unfortunately, he hadn't got very far with it when there was a knock at the door, and there stood May's sister, Joan. He had never met her, but he knew her at once by the bold, determined Twomey look in her eyes. He smiled; even if he was to be hanged Timmy could not have resisted smiling at the hangman, and the effect would have been much the same.

'I'm delighted to meet you, Miss Twomey,' he said.

' 'Tis scarcely mutual,' she said in the cutting tone he had noticed once or twice in May when someone had annoyed her. 'I believe you have some letters from my sister.'

'Letters?' he asked, as though he was hard of hearing.

'Yes. Letters from her to you.'

'I don't know what you mean,' Timmy said, getting on his dignity.

'Oh, yes, you do,' she said. 'You see, I have letters from you to her. And what's more, Mr. McGovern,' she added, tossing her head, 'I may as well warn you that I intend to use them.'

'I'm sorry you feel like this about it, Miss Twomey,' he said nervously.

'And how the hell do you think I should feel about it?' she asked, and this time she actually put her hands on her hips like a market-woman, a gesture Timmy had never before associated with a well-brought-up girl. 'I think you must be out of your mind,' she added judicially. 'A married man with two children, writing letters like that to a schoolgirl!'

'I can explain that, Miss Twomey,' he said, his eyes clouding. 'I don't think you'd be quite so hard if you knew the sort of life I lead. I'm not complaining about my wife, of course, but there was never any understanding between us. When I met May I knew she was the only girl in the world for me. I love May, you know,' he went on with a faint, sad smile. 'I'd die for her this minute.'

'Thanks, Mr. McGovern,' Joan Twomey said saucily,

'but at the moment what she needs is someone who'll live for her, which is the reason I'm here. I came to get her letters, and to warn you that the next time you meet her or write to her I'm going straight up to your parish priest with the whole lot of them, and I think you know what the result of that will be.'

Timmy knew. At least, for the moment he thought he knew. Given a bit of time, he might have realised that the result needn't be as serious as all that, but the girl wasn't giving him time, and the prospect of explaining himself to the parish priest in his own home was more than he liked to contemplate. That is the worst of out-and-out idealism; it tends to exaggerate the obstacles.

So Timmy gave in, and handed over May's letters. Only for the time being, of course, just to give himself time to think. It was only ten minutes later, when he had time to think, that it dawned on him that handing over her love letters to her sister just like that might be something he would find hard to justify to a romantic girl like May. A half an hour later when the fact had really sunk in it struck him that it was something he might never be allowed to explain. Romantic girls were like that. They expected you to be butter to them and iron to the rest of the world. But the trouble was that unless a man was iron to romantic women, as Tony Dowse was, he could never be anything but butter to anybody.

He didn't eat any lunch and went to bed. He told Elsie that he wasn't feeling well, which was true. By night-time she was alarmed and wanted to call up Joe Hobson, Timmy's doctor, but Timmy didn't yet want him, because he knew that Joe would already have heard talk and would have made up his mind about the illness and what he believed would be wrong, because Timmy felt that his fever and pains had nothing particular to do with May Twomey. Obviously it was something he had been sickening for. That was the worst of living in a small place like Cork. Even your own doctor tended to examine you on the basis of gossip.

So Elsie sent for Tony Dowse instead, and Tony arrived

with a bottle of whiskey, and the two old friends went over the thing again. Timmy didn't need to hedge with Tony, who knew all about the business already, and didn't take it as lightly as Hobson would.

'Ah, you overdo it, Timmy,' he said, showing his teeth in his sad sheepdog smile.

'I know I overdo it, Tony,' Timmy said impatiently. 'I'm overdoing it these twenty years. But it's no use telling yourself you overdo it when you're built that way.'

'Not much, no,' Tony agreed mournfully 'We set ourselves on certain tracks and we have to go on. You're right there. It's not going to be easy to change. You should say it to Joe.'

'But what will Joe say?' asked Timmy. 'He'll only tell me I must be a man. It's easy to be a man if you never look at the side of the road a woman walks on, the way he does. And I can't talk to anyone else. He'd be hurt.'

'He would,' agreed Tony. 'He's very sensitive about things like that. Ah, well, we'll hope for the best.'

But Timmy couldn't hope for the best. He knew damn well the pains were only getting worse and that he couldn't sleep, and all Joe Hobson said when at last he had to be called in was that Timmy needed a holiday in France. All Hobson could suggest whenever he was at a loss was champagne and a little holiday in France. Bachelor remedies, both, and quite unsuitable for Timmy's lowered condition.

The funny thing, as Timmy discovered, was that the worse he got, the more resigned he became, and the more grateful for the quiet service Elsie gave him, getting the kids out to the neighbours and sitting downstairs with a paper till he signalled for something. He realised it all again, how beautiful his little home was and how devoted his family, and he only regretted that he couldn't do more for them. He could now see quite clearly what would happen when he died. The insurance was insufficient; the little house would bring in only a couple of thousand that would not keep them for more than a few years, and then it would be up to the Geraghtys — a hard, hard lot!

And then, when he had convinced himself that he was

really dying, the great scheme flashed upon his mind. He applied for a new life insurance policy for three times the amount of the present one. If he was really dying he would get the straight word, not the careful evasions of Joe Hobson and his wife. If he wasn't he would get the straight word too.

The summons to the insurance company's doctor on the South Mall shook him, but he got up, bathed and took a taxi into town. He had a long time to wait for the doctor, who was a silly old man and looked where he should not have looked if he was a gentleman, and then refused to tell Timmy the verdict. 'You'll hear from the insurance company in due course, Mr. McGovern,' he said firmly and Timmy went home to bed again in despair. He knew now what the answer was.

The answer from the insurance company came three days later and Timmy opened it with trembling hands. After that, he got up, dressed himself and went into town. It was a Saturday morning, and the boys were gathered in Casey's pub in Patrick Street, so Timmy told them the whole story of the insurance policy, beginning with the pain in the chest and ending with the insurance company's letter, accepting him as a good risk, and only Tony Dowse failed to laugh because he knew where the story should really begin and he couldn't help being sorry for a romantic girl who perhaps still wondered whether there wasn't a man who would think the way she did about Communism and the immortality of the soul.

2

Then Elsie fell ill, and everybody but herself knew it wouldn't be for long. A night nurse came as well as her sister, Kate, from Glenameena, who looked after the children. Kate was taller than Elsie, a good-looking woman of thirty five or so. She had always tried to boss Elsie, and still did, though Elsie, for all her muddled weakness, had the stubbornness of her kind. Kate had warned Elsie not to marry Timmy, and Elsie had married him just the same. Now they disagreed about how the children should be brought up, and Elsie still continued to disregard her advice. In fact, they disagreed almost about everything, and Elsie knew she was very poorly indeed when she consented to Kate's coming at all. She said Kate was a born trouble-maker.

It wasn't so much that Kate was a trouble-maker. She was a clever woman who loved power, and of course, she hadn't been in the house a week before she found out about Timmy and the nurse. The nurse, Josie Dwyer, was a pretty, cheerful, conscientious girl with great inclinations towards the intellectual life, and she had never met anyone so profound as Timmy before. As for Timmy, he was certain he had never met before such a mixture of gaiety and gravity. She had agreed to marry him after Elsie died, and had even let him make love to her, not for the fun of it, but because she felt the purity of their intentions justified it. The children liked her too.

But Elsie had her own doubts which had nothing to do with Kate's. She had discovered in conversation that Nurse Dwyer's last patient had died, a thing Elsie couldn't conceive of under proper medical attention. She complained to Kate that she was sleeping too heavily and woke each morning with a bad headache.

'I don't think she can have much experience,' she said. 'I'm not as well at all as I was before she came.'

Elsie was a stubborn woman. Without telling Kate she held her sleeping pill in the corner of her mouth till the nurse's back was turned and then slipped it out and under the pillow. Later, Nurse Dwyer came back and looked at her before lying down herself. Elsie waited for her to give some indication of dozing off before she took the pill. For some reason she wasn't sleeping easily without it.

Later, the door opened quietly and without opening her eyes she knew it was Timmy. She would have welcomed the chance of a chat with him but she couldn't have it without revealing the trick she had played on the nurse, so she kept her eyes shut. Even that way she could feel him looking at her from the end of the bed.

'How is she?' he whispered anxiously.

'What do you expect?' replied Nurse Dwyer in the same tone.

'Isn't she making a great fight for it?' he asked.

'She might hang on like that for another couple of months.' whispered the nurse in a professional tone that sent a shudder through Elsie. It was like hearing youself sentenced to death in a dream: the voices had taken a remote and mysterious quality like voices in a dream.

'She's sleeping well, though,' said Timmy.

'That's only the morphia,' said the nurse. 'I only wish I could give her sister a dose.'

'Kate!' whispered Timmy. 'What did she do to you?'

'She's watching us the whole time. You'd want to be careful.'

And then Elsie opened her eyes and stared at them with bitter accusation. Now it was Timmy who felt he was in a dream, and he gave an awkward laugh.

'Elsie,' he said. 'I didn't know you were awake.'

'Call Kate for me,' Elsie said shivering.

'Now, you don't want to wake Kate up at this hour,' he said pleadingly.

'Call Kate for me!' she cried, her voice sharp with hysteria. There was the sound of footsteps upstairs and they knew Kate had heard.

'Ah, she codded us nicely,' Nurse Dwyer said crossly and rose to put on her dressing gown. As she tied the girdle Kate came in and paused dramatically.

'What is it?' she asked.

'What did I say about that sleeping thing?' Elsie asked shrilly. 'They were trying to poison me.'

'We were not trying to poison you,' Nurse Dwyer said disgustedly. 'You'll wake the children if you go on like that.'

'Oh, I'll wake more than the children. I'll show ye up. Saying I might hang on for a couple of months. Ye thought ye were rid of me.'

'Kate, it was all a misunderstanding,' Timmy said gravely, trying to master the situation. 'I called in on my way to bed to see how Elsie was. I didn't know she was awake, and I talked to Nurse Dwyer. I might have done the same with you.'

'Hardly the same, Timmy,' Kate said with a cynical smile. 'You never spent a weekend in Glengarriffe with me.'

'What did I tell you?' Nurse Dwyer commented with a shrug. 'I knew she was spying.'

'Oh, it didn't need much spying,' Kate replied without rancour. Indeed, she felt none. Her rancour was reserved for occasions when she felt inferior, and now she was mistress of the situation. 'I think you'd better leave Elsie to me,' she added, holding the door open for them. 'My room is empty — if you need a second room.'

Next morning while Kate was making herself a cup of tea in the kitchen, Timmy came in, his fat face puffed with sleeplessness.

'I have something to say to you, Kate,' he said in an excited voice.

'Well?' she asked.

'I didn't tell you the whole truth last night, Kate.'

'I hardly thought you did, Timmy.'

'Neither you nor anyone else knows the way things were between Elsie and me,' he said sternly. 'Elsie was always a good wife, but there was no understanding between us. When I met Josie Dwyer I knew she was the only woman in the world for me. I'd die for that girl, Kate.'

'She can't stay here another day,' Kate said promptly.

'She doesn't intend to,' said Timmy.

'I wouldn't allow it,' Kate said peremptorily. 'I'm not saying there was anything wrong with the stuff the nurse gave Elsie, but people will talk.'

'There was nothing wrong with the stuff, Kate, and you know it,' shouted Timmy. 'But she wouldn't stay here anyway, after what's happened. I'm driving her back to her digs now.'

After driving Josie home, Timmy called on Tony and they spent the afternoon in a pub, discussing the situation. Tony was full of alarm. It was beyond belief the number of young women who could be taken in that way by Timmy and risk scandal and misery for him, but Tony was beginning to doubt if any of them would ever get any benefit from it.

'You're getting worse, Timmy,' he said at last, shaking his head sadly.

'I'm getting desperate,' said Timmy.

'You're getting worse,' said Tony. 'You're hitting wild.'

'But I have to hit wild, Tony. This is my last chance. It's Josie or suicide.'

'Yes, and last year it was May or suicide, and the year before that there was the other nurse — the one that wanted to buy the lonely horse — but you're taking bigger and bigger risks.'

'But there's no risk in this, Tony,' Timmy said in anguish. 'I was wrong about May Twomey. I admit that. It wouldn't have done. But now, though I'm sorry for poor Elsie, the future is clear.'

'The future is never clear,' said Tony mournfully. 'If the police start enquiring into Elsie's death, it'll take more than a few soft words to put suspicion off you. Take my advice, and whatever you do, don't see that girl again until Elsie is dead and buried.'

Timmy saw what he meant, and agreed that he always gave good advice, but even Tony didn't know what hell the house was between a dying woman suspecting she was being poisoned, Kate with her good-humoured scorn and the terrified children, creeping up and downstairs. Inside a week Timmy had spent another night with Josie. Tony knew he had it bad.

A few days before she died Elsie called the children.

'I'm going on a long journey,' she began.

'I wouldn't speak to them like that, dear,' said Kate brightly. 'Mummy isn't well,' she told the children. 'She means she may have to go for a little holiday.'

'Woman, can't I even speak to my own children and I dying?' Elsie asked angrily, and then went on to tell them what sort their Daddy was and what sort of woman he would bring into the house when she was gone. She warned them to remember her, and to remember that if they were in any trouble they were to go to their Aunt or their Uncle. Kate stood by, with tears in her eyes, thinking how much nicer she could have put it all.

At the funeral people avoided Timmy, all but a few old cronies like Tony who got him away quickly and quietly back to the house. Kate was already there with her bags packed. Timmy took fright at once. He showed the others into the little sitting room and talked to her in the hall.

'You're not going, Kate?' he asked, and she smiled at his simplicity.

'I don't think my father would like me to stay on any longer than I could help,' she said.

'I thought you might do it for the children's sake,' he said. 'At least until I can make other arrangements.'

'Only until them?' she asked sweetly.

'You know what I said and I mean it,' Timmy said, at the end of his rope. 'I'm not apologising to you or anyone else for that.'

'Very well,' she said shortly. 'But you'd better make them soon.'

A few nights later Timmy was sitting with the whiskey long after Kate had gone to bed and heard a loud knock on the door. He decided it was probably Tony, and wondered why the blazes he didn't tap on the window as he usually did. But when he went out to the door he found no one there. The street was empty. He stood and listened to see if he could detect any sound of laughter from a group of corner boys, and then closed the door behind him with a puzzled air. Kate's door opened and she looked at him down the well of the stairs.

'Was that someone knocking?' she asked in surprise.

'No, Kate,' he said with a reassuring smile. 'Only some kids playing on the street, that's all.'

She looked at him doubtfully and turned on her heel. He could see she wasn't convinced. As he went upstairs he distinctly heard the knock again, but this time it was quiet as though whoever it was was tiring of the joke. Apparently Kate did not hear it, and Timmy affected not to do so either. All the same it made him depressed.

He was discussing it in the pub with Tony a week later, and Tony wrinkled up his nose in distaste. He mightn't be a Voltairean of Timmy's kind, but all the same he had a deep respect for reason. He said there was no such thing as a ghost.

'I know damn well there's no such thing,' Timmy said excitedly. 'All I'm asking is how do you explain it.'

'I'm not trying to explain it, Timmy,' Tony said wearily. 'Call it hysteria if you like!'

'Hysteria?' echoed Timmy indignantly. 'I was sitting at home the other night while Kate was at the pictures, and I distinctly heard the key in the front door and the feet going up the stairs. It was ten minutes after before Kate came in from the pictures.'

'And how did she get out again?' Tony asked cynically.

'You think it was Kate?'

'Why didn't you go out yourself and ask her?'

'Because I was petrified,' Timmy said. 'That's why I didn't go out. I went upstairs after and there was nobody there. I tell you, Tony, there are things you can't explain.'

'There are things you can't explain for the time being, Timmy,' Tony said patiently. 'There's nothing you can't explain in the long run. The noise was probably next door. These modern houses — you wouldn't know whose wife you were fighting with. You're a terrible man, Timmy, and you're getting worse. First it was women you couldn't live without; now it's ghosts. If you ask me, the women are only ghosts, and the ghosts are women.'

In the middle of the night Timmy was wakened by shrieks from the children's room. He rushed in and found the two kids in hysterics.

'What is it now?' he asked.

'Mummy was here, daddy, mummy was here!' they whimpered.

'Ah, ye were only dreaming,' he said, pretending to laugh. 'Mummy wasn't here. Mummy's gone away.'

'But she's back, daddy,' sobbed the little girl. 'She was here! Tommy saw her too.'

Kate came in with a suspicious air.

'What is it now?' she asked shortly.

'They think they saw their mother,' Timmy said despairingly. 'I don't know what to say. I'm distracted.'

'Ah, they were dreaming,' she snapped scornfully. 'You're getting as bad as they are. Go to bed and leave them to me.'

Tim went out. He heard Kate talking to the children in a motherly tone. As she passed his door he was lying on the bed smoking.

'Kate!' he called.

'What is it?' she asked.

'What am I going to do?'

'I told you already what my uncle Dan did.'

'What was that?'

'He had Mass said in the house.'

'But didn't it lower the value of the house?' he asked nervously.

'Why would it lower the value of the house? If he didn't do it, it would have no value at all. Take my advice, Timmy McGovern, and see Father MacCarthy in the morning. If you don't, I won't spend another night here. That's my last word.'

Next morning Timmy felt as though he had been very drunk the night before. At night it was very hard to believe in Voltaire, but in the morning light it was harder still not to. All the same he shaved, dressed and went to the presbytery to see Father McCarthy. He and the parish priest were old acquaintances. It was even said that once when Timmy went to Confession to him the parish priest could be heard laughing all over the church. Now, he did not feel so much like laughing.

'You'll think I'm mad when you hear what I came about,' he said.

'That would depend on how much I was going to get out of it,' Father McCarthy said shrewdly. 'It wouldn't be a marriage by any chance?'

'Not a marriage,' said Timmy. 'A ghost!'

'That seems to me a clear case for the married state,' the priest said gravely. 'Jokes aside, though, will you have a little drop?'

'Who told you I went in for that sort of thing?' Timmy asked, braving it out. 'You have spies everywhere. Of course, I don't believe in that sort of thing, but women find it upsetting.'

'They do, they do,' said Father McCarthy, measuring him out a full glass. 'You mean your sister-in-law, I suppose? I met her at the funeral. She must be getting on a bit now.'

'Thirty five,' said Timmy.

'As old as that!' said Father McCarthy. 'So you have a ghost? It happens, of course, it happens. But what does this one do?'

At that hour of the day with the sun shining outside in the priest's garden it was the most embarrassing story ever told by a true Voltairean, and Timmy couldn't help imagining the ugly curl that would come on Tony's long upper lip if he heard it, but the priest only grew more interested as he went on.

'Well, we may have to have Mass said there eventually,' he said with a sigh. 'In the meantime, I'll look over the house myself. If three o'clock would do you, I could call then.'

At three, when Timmy answered the priest's knock he found him examining the knocker.

'Oh, nothing wrong, nothing wrong,' he said, smiling brightly at Timmy. 'Only to make sure that it couldn't happen accidentally.'

Then he closed the door behind him with a bang; opened it again, and closed it gently, looking at the hinges. He seemed particularly interested in the carpet which led down the stairs to the door, lifted it in several places and slipped his hand underneath. Upstairs, he looked out of all the bedroom windows, opened them and studied the wall at either side.

'I think we'll give it a week and see how 'twill develop, Timmy,' he said. ' 'Twouldn't surprise me if you heard no more of it. I'll have a word with your sister-in-law before I go, just to put her mind at rest.'

'Miss Geraghty, I'd like a word with you,' he said

amiably as he was going out. He led her into the little
front room and closed the door behind him. 'You know, I
wouldn't like that man to be driven too far,' he said,
cocking his head at her. 'His nerves aren't all that good.'

She stood back with folded arms and faced him with a
complacent smile.

'That was why I insisted on his seeing you, Father,' she
said earnestly.

'You did right, Miss Geraghty,' he said. 'Timmy is a man
I'm very fond of, and I wouldn't like to see him upset. I
don't think he will be upset from now on. By the way, I
suppose you wouldn't know who put the fresh oil on the
knocker?'

'Was there fresh oil on the knocker, Father?' she asked in
astonishment. 'I never noticed it.'

'You will if you look,' he said. 'Mind you, it's only a
drop but it tells a lot. As I say, I don't think we'll have
any more trouble with this ghost. I hope not at any rate.
If we do we may have to take serious steps, and I know you
wouldn't like that, Miss Geraghty.'

But the priest had interfered too late. Timmy's nerve
was broken, and when he and Kate got married a couple of
months later (no sooner, indeed, than was advisable,
according to gossip) Tony felt his nerve was broken as
well. All the time he had had the wild hope that there
might be some reality behind the shadows that Timmy
pursued, but now he knew that they too were only figments
of the imagination.

'Women and ghosts!' he said mournfully over his lonely
drink in the pub. 'Isn't that a man's life for you?'